CURSED
DEMON

CREATURES OF THE OTHERWORLD
BROGAN THOMAS

Brogan Thomas
BOOKS

6th April 2021

CURSED DEMON

CREATURES OF THE OTHERWORLD

BROGAN THOMAS

For more information, address: info@broganthomas.com

Edited by S. Maia Grossman
Cover design by Melony Paradise of Paradise Cover Design

Ebook ASIN: B08G2PNQ59
Paperback ISBN: 978-1-8381469-2-4
Hardcover ISBN: 978-1-8381469-3-1

First edition March 2021

10 9 8 7 6 5 4 3 2 1

www.broganthomas.com

For my hubby

CHAPTER ONE

A leaf flutters down and he dramatically jumps to the side, his hooves scrabbling for purchase on the stone track. My heart misses a beat and for a fraction of a second my body tenses. *Keep him straight, keep him forward, chin high, breathe. Relax.* I repeat the mantra in my head over and over.

It's not helping.

Only one of us can freak out at a time, and it's never my bloody turn.

My vampire dressage trainer, Nuno, has sent us to ride around the estate to cool off after this morning's lesson. Nuno wants us to bond. Bond, ha, tell that to the snorting beast I am sitting on. Every little thing he can find is a grand excuse to spook. I'm trying my best to keep my posture elegant, pliable, to move with him and not to tense up, but I can already feel my shoulders creeping towards my ears. I let out a shaky breath and again force myself to relax.

The name on his paperwork is so fancy, it amuses me that he has the unfortunate stable name of Pudding. "Pudding," what a laugh. If you combined the energy of a fancy sports car with a hair-trigger bomb, you still wouldn't get the scary power of this horse. He feels like he is going to explode.

All. The. Time.

I love riding. But Pudding, my new gelding, is...urm...a challenge. We aren't clicking the way I thought we would. I know it's my fault as I want to ride Bob, my hairy Irish cob. I trust him and he trusts me, and we perform dressage like we are doing magic together. But I've been firmly encouraged to ride a 'proper' dressage horse, and both sides of Pudding's breeding are impeccable. He is made for dressage. I guess he just isn't made for me.

The beast underneath me shakes his head—my urge to get off is enormous. But then, Pudding would be worse with me on the ground—undoubtedly he'd stomp all over me. It doesn't feel it at the moment, but from experience, I know I'm still safer to be riding him. I roll my eyes. Bloody horse.

The day is beautiful. Morning sunlight filters through the trees above us, painting glowing stripes on the track—golden lines that Pudding keeps attempting to leap over. Yay, I'm having such a good time. *Not.*

Keep him straight, keep him forward, chin high, breathe. Relax.

The birds sing, and his hooves crunch rhythmically. I gently stroke his mahogany neck with my left hand, and he snorts out a breath.

For the first time, his head and neck start to relax. We both begin to relax. I puff out a sigh, and just as a smile touches my lips, a duck hidden behind the hedge to our left takes flight with a dramatic snap of wings and an echoing quack.

The whole hedge wobbles.

My eyes widen in horror and before the quack has even dissipated, Pudding springs into action, and we go from what feels like 0–60 miles per hour in a split second.

Oh hell.

No amount of pulling on the reins is going to stop Pudding's panicked flight. Instead, I bridge the reins in my hands so they don't get yanked from my grip, and I grab a handful of mane for good measure.

Oh bloody hell.

"Ooh, ooh, steady, steady," I say in a soft, lilting tone.

His hooves thunder beneath us, and the world is a blur of colours as it flies past at a breathtaking rate. My eyes water as the once-gentle wind batters my face. "It was a duck, silly boy, it's okay, it's okay. Steady boy, steeeaaadddy. I would never let anything hurt you, steady." Years of practice keeps the fear out of my voice.

It doesn't stop me from internally shrieking, *I'm going to die*, but Pudding doesn't have to know that.

Pudding's left ear flicks back, and his strides slow.

Oh thank God.

"Good boy, steady now, walk, whoa." His mad dash slows to a canter, a trot, then finally a bouncy walk. The energetic movement makes my boobs bounce, and my chest aches. Ow.

I fight the urge to slump in relief as I unlock my cramped left hand from its death-grip on the reins to stroke his now-sweaty neck. "Good boy, steady, walk." God, my entire body is trembling with the adrenaline that is coursing through me. I feel sick, and my mouth is dry.

But ha, I'm alive. *I'm alive.* I want to jump off and kiss the ground. Take that, universe. I'm alive. I giggle with relief. "I'm a master rider—" As soon as the cocky words leave my mouth, without provocation Pudding leaps and spins.

Oh crap.

The saddle is no longer underneath me. Catapulted, I find myself airborne. In what feels like slow motion, the ground meets my face. I crash to the floor with an *oof*.

Oh bloody hell.

Wheezing, I roll up onto my hands and knees and lift my throbbing head to watch Pudding's retreating bottom as he gallops away in what I hope is the direction of the stables. His hooves thunder into the distance, dee dum—dee dum— dee dum, without me.

The urge to curl up into a ball and sob is huge.

"No, no. Oh, no, noooo," I whisper in disbelief. I scrape my gloved fingertips across the stone ground in frustration. Louder and with abject horror I shout, "Pudding, come back. Please come back. Pudding!" What if something happens to him? What if he gets tangled in his reins? "Oh my God, please don't get trapped in your reins," I cry.

I undo the chin strap and pull my riding hat off and rub my forehead with frustration. "No, no, no, no...this isn't happening. It's not bloody happening." The thought of him hurting himself, hurting his posh dressage-horse legs with his mad dash back to his friends at the stables, makes me dizzy with fear for him.

I rapidly blink to fight back my tears.

Instead, I force myself to get up. My legs wobble underneath me. Ouch—I think I've bruised my ribs. I press my hand to the sore spot and my hand also throbs in pain. My right palm underneath my glove is bleeding, although miraculously my handmade soft leather glove remains intact. I pull both gloves off and carefully tuck them into the waistband of my jodhpurs. I can't say the same for my favourite riding hat—it's scuffed and dented, and it will have to be replaced. It did its job. I give it an appreciative pat. I landed on my face; I could have easily been sporting that dent in my head instead of in the hat.

I plop it back onto my head.

I roll my shoulders and huff out a frustrated breath. The rest of me feels...okay...as okay as being chucked ten feet into the air and slammed down onto a stone track can be okay.

"Yeah, Emma, you're a master rider," I grumble. I wince as I pick a piece of gravel out of my bleeding palm. I turn and hobble in the direction Pudding fled. My ribs ache with the movement and my head pounds.

Gah, I am so stupid—I can't believe I left my mobile in my bedroom. What the heck am I going to do?

A glance about, and I realise that our mad dash has taken us far away from the usual hacking route and into an area of the estate that I haven't ventured to explore before.

I shouldn't be here.

In the world I live in, magic is commonplace, with all manner of supernatural people: shifters, demons, witches, vampires, and an abundance of fae. But there's a divide among the races—creature versus creature, with humans like me struggling to survive. It is all about the strong against the weak. It is all about power.

I kick a small stone. Humans like me do as we are told. To stay alive, we follow the rules. Barely tolerated, we are an afterthought to the powerful creatures around us. It has always been that way, since the beginning of time. I'm human and weak, but I'm also an anomaly: no one knows what my human breeding is mixed with. Combined with how I look...I roll my eyes. Everyone covets beauty. In this dangerous patriarchal world, with the tricks that I can do I'm a prize. Enough of a prize to gain the attention of a first-level demon and a measure of protection. *All* I need to do is follow his rules.

Bloody hell, I shouldn't be here.

I swallow. My mouth and throat are dry. I hunch, and I keep walking. Hopefully no one will find out I ventured into a restricted area.

The trees stir with the breeze, revealing a bright-white building. It shows up in my peripheral vision to the left.

I look towards where Pudding has disappeared and then look left at the mystery building. Huh.

A niggly voice inside my brain tells me, *Go look. Get help.*

It is a terrible idea.

I drum the tips of my fingers on my thigh. I look at the building and then back at the track. Pudding will be back at the stables now, and I have at least a thirty-minute walk to get back to him. If I can find a phone and ring Sam at the yard, hopefully she can keep a lookout and grab him before anything further happens to him.

I nod; it is a good idea.

With my mind made up, I turn, grit my teeth, and barge my way through the trees. I drop my head so the dense branches scrape against my dented riding hat and not my face. My riding boots slip on the loose earth, and I almost fall as I scramble down a soft soil embankment and head towards the building. With each step towards my goal, my heart beats a little faster. It's now hammering in my ears. My breath puffs out of my mouth a little more with every stride I take.

I should not be doing this.

Why am I doing this? Pudding, that's why. God, my horses will be the death of me. I shake my head and keep walking.

The white building is large and squat-looking, with no windows. As I have some creature DNA, I can sense magic. So as I cautiously hobble toward the building, I can feel the magic surrounding it. The perimeter ward buzzes. I feel it thrumming in my bones—the witch-made magic is usually enough to stop anyone not keyed to it from entering.

A ward is a magic force field. Wards tend to be golden in colour and shaped like a dome. They can give you a nasty shock or kill you, depending on the ward's purpose. They are designed to keep people out or keep people in.

This ward is a real piece of work; it crackles menacingly and flashes different colours as I get closer. The whole building screams *keep out, or else*—it's a killer ward.

With that helpful thought, I can't help the smug smile that pulls at my lips. At least I can do this.

I walk through the ward.

CHAPTER TWO

The magic slides off me like I don't exist. I might be mostly human, but my unknown father has given me some neat tricks. Magic has zero effect on me.

The unlocked front door soundlessly opens when I pull it. I stick my head inside and take a peek.

All is quiet.

I have an excellent excuse for why I'm here. But a feeling of dread fills me. Like a good demon's pet, I am well trained. Yet I am breaking another rule. I gulp.

I step into the dark corridor and let go of the heavy door. It automatically closes behind me with a *whoosh*. I jump forward to avoid the door almost smacking me on the bum.

The ceiling lights click on automatically with a hum. The harsh, bright light makes the now-grey corridor look worse, if that's even possible. Everything is grey: the walls, the floor— I tilt my head up—yep, and the ceiling. This place is grim, and I can't help the full-body shiver that racks me.

I stand in a square pocket of light. My nostrils flare, and like a proper nutter, I sniff loudly. I can't make out any scent. Not that my nose is any good—it's not like I'm a shifter or a vampire. Those creatures have an excellent sense of smell. But like a weirdo, I do it anyway. I can smell horse. I snort out a laugh.

What a dickhead.

I shake my head in self-deprecation. I'm glad I'm alone so no one can see me make a fool of myself.

"Hello." I cough to clear my dry throat. "Hellooo, is anyone here? Hello? I fell off my horse, and I need to ring Sam at the stables. Hello?" My voice echoes back to me and my ears strain to hear a reply. Nope, nothing.

I shuffle down the corridor. Like something from a horror film, the lights come on with a buzz in front of me, and with a click, they turn off behind. It leaves me with a single square of light so I can never see what's in front of me or what's behind. Without windows, this building is like a grey tomb.

"Gosh, this place is so creepy." I shiver again. Halfway down, I find an office and bingo, a phone. *Yes.* I make my call.

"Hi, Emma...yeah. I've got the snorting, sweaty monster. What do you want me to do with him?"

My legs sag with relief, and I slump against the office wall.

"Oh, thank God. Oh, Sam, it was horrible seeing him gallop off like that. The stirrups flapping and the reins dangling. I felt so helpless. Is he okay?"

"I found him running up and down the fence line of the mares' field, snorting and screaming for their attention. Yeah, the daft bugger is fine. I'm glad you rang; I was about to do a security alert and send the guards out to search for you. I was so worried. Where are you? Why didn't you answer your phone?"

"I left my phone in my room—I didn't think I'd need it." I nibble on my lip and ignore her question about where I am. The less she knows, the better. "Would you please hose him down and check his legs? I should be back before you've finished if I hurry."

"Yeah, yeah, I'll pamper the shit out of him, not that he deserves it. Are you okay?"

"I need a new riding hat, perhaps new ribs," I mumble, then say with a contrite huff, "I'm fine, I'm fine. It was my fault, not Pudding's. I feel like a right idiot."

"I don't know why you feel like an idiot. It's not your fault that silly old vampire told you to hack the monster of a horse out for a cool-down. That man has a sadistic streak a mile long.

I knew it was a mistake for you to ride out on your own. Look, I will sort this beast out for you *if* you promise to go have a hot bath. Hopefully the warm water will help with the bruising. You don't think you've broken your ribs, do you? Ribs are the worst. I promise, Em, Pudding is fine. Please take care of yourself, and just this once let *me* help you." I assure Sam that my ribs are just bruised, and we end the conversation with my reluctant agreement to have a long soak in the bath.

I have a feeling I won't be able to stop myself from checking on Pudding later. Not that I don't trust my friend, but I know I won't be able to relax if I don't see him with my own eyes. At the moment all I can see when I close my eyes is Pudding tear-arsing away.

I shake my head with disgust. I should have at least kept hold of the reins.

I head back down the corridor to the exit. As I hobble, I force my glum mood away. It happened, and Pudding is safe. I feel like we've both had a lucky escape today. It could have been a lot worse.

I hear a strange noise; I grind to an abrupt stop. I tilt my head to the side, hold my breath, and listen.

I can hear a...a dog...I think. Yeah, I can hear a dog crying in pain. I don't even contemplate my next action. My feet instinctively follow the sounds of distress. My love of animals overrides any common sense that I might possess.

I hurry down the grey-on-grey corridor. The hum of the creepy lights follows in my wake, each square of light clicking on and off as I progress. My ears strain as I follow the cries. Goosebumps rise on my arms.

I stop when I come to an ominous-looking solid-steel door.

I think this is where the sound originated. A standard gold ward wavers in front of the doorway. I swallow and nibble on my lip; I hold my breath and listen. Yes...this is the room. I've found the source of the cries.

What are you doing, Emma? Making a phone call is one thing; poking around in locked, warded rooms is quite another. Of all the mistakes I have made, this may be my worst one yet. I gulp. I should not be doing this.

This is the point of no return. I shuffle forward, then thrust my hand into the ward; it parts around my fingers. I grip the doorknob. "Please don't be locked...please be open," I whisper as I twist. The door clicks, and with a hard shove, I swing the door open.

The light from the corridor spills into the room. Cautiously —I do have some semblance of self-preservation—I keep my toes on the other side of the golden ward so it's between me and whatever is in the room. Slowly, my eyes adjust to the dim interior.

"Oh." My heart breaks at the sight of the puppy. The fluffy, cream-coloured puppy with red tips on its fur is huddled in a ball in the far corner. I rub my chest, and my eyes fill with tears. "Poor baby." Without thinking, I hustle into the room. "Oh puppy, please don't cry." The tiny puppy—no, I'm wrong, the creature's wild energy tickles at my senses—the tiny *wolf shifter* lifts its head, and my gaze meets big, soulful green eyes. Green eyes filled with pain. The shifter continues to cry as it crawls across the concrete floor on its belly towards me. My heart misses a beat and a lump forms in my throat. The cries and the fear rolling off the shifter pull at something deep inside of me. Without thought or worry that the pup is going to chew my face off, I cover the distance between us and drop to my knees. I scoop the shifter pup into my arms. I ignore the pain in my ribs as they scream in protest. This puppy needs me.

A quick undercarriage glance, and I realise the shifter is a *girl*.

Oh, no. Oh bloody hell.

I swallow the building lump of now-fear in my throat. Female shifters are as rare as rocking-horse poop. Oh heck, I've stumbled into an impossible situation. *Wars* are fought over female shifters.

The pup buries her head in my neck, digging her front paws into my collarbone as she scrambles to get closer. Each breath she takes and the subsequent cry she makes tugs at my soul. Her puppy breath tickles the hairs on the back of my neck. A frightened tear runs down my cheek, and I rub my face against the shifter's soft fur to hide it.

"It's okay, it's okay. I've got you, it's okay. I am going to help you get home, you're safe now. I'm going to do my best to get you home," I whisper, swallowing the lumpy clump of fear that is now stuck in my throat. I rock her in my arms.

Both of us tremble.

I rock her and stroke her soft fur. Finally, after a few minutes, her whole body sags, and she stops that awful crying.

I feel her trust.

Total trust. In. Me.

I grit my teeth as a quiet rage slithers through me. Fire sparks in my chest. It's my automatic response to bullying, to injustice, and a quintessential need in me to help the underdog. She can't stay here.

She can't stay here, not in this room, and not on the demon's estate. I'm...I'm a pampered pet, but others...they are not so lucky. I have to do the right thing.

This shifter needs *me*. I clutch her soft, furry body to my chest, and determination thrums through me. The need to keep her safe is almost overwhelming.

If I don't get her out of here, something bad will surely happen. Leaving her isn't an option.

That kind of black mark on my soul? It is not something I'm willing to live with.

"It's much easier to fight your way out of trouble than to fight a guilty conscience," I mumble to her. I hug her to my chest and smile sadly. Another tear rolls down the side of my nose. I *was* the girl who always played by the rules, not because I'm perfect, but because I learned to *play* perfect. A neutral, calm, elegant facade. It has kept me relatively safe.

God, I'm going to be in serious trouble for doing this, but sometimes you have to do what you think is right. Even if you are punished for it in the end.

And I will be punished.

Yep, I am breaking all the rules today.

CHAPTER THREE

Again, my freaky thing with magic works to my advantage. As we hurry out of the building, the ward slides over us. So far, so good. I have found that the trick seems to work for anything or anyone that is touching me.

I hurry towards what I hope is the west boundary of the estate. My sense of direction is appalling, and it is even worse after my roller-coaster ride on Pudding. My brain feels like Pudding stuffed it into a washing machine on spin. With each step, the shifter gets heavier and heavier in my arms. Any time I even think about putting her down, hoping she will follow me, she cries. My arms feel like they are going to drop off, and my ribs...God, my poor ribs...*Suck it up, Emma.*

I hobble along. My heels feel painfully red-raw, undoubtedly bleeding as my handmade riding boots rub them. These boots are not made for walking; they especially are not made for tromping through trees and scrambling over walls.

We slink passed another ward, the last one—which surrounds the whole eight-hundred-acre estate—and we end up down the road at a local grocery store.

The shop is sandwiched between a kebab shop and a Chinese takeaway. My legs almost buckle with relief when I realise the shop is open.

I peer about and puff out my cheeks. All it would take is for someone who works for the estate to notice us and everything I've done so far, everything I've risked, would be lost.

I have never done anything so stupid or so brave.

As luck or fate would have it, we bump into a shifter. The pup sniffs the air and wiggles in my arms, also sensing the shifter.

The guy gives me a flirtatious smile. "Fuck, you're hot. You lost your horse, blondie? You can come and ride this—I will even let you whip me." He cups his groin and thrusts his hips at me. My mouth drops open, and my nose wrinkles with disgust.

Ewww, what an idiot.

This right here is why I prefer my horses over people—at least their shit comes out the right end.

I resign myself to fate and the fact that this horny shifter is all the help we currently have. No one else is around and needs must. I can only hope and pray that he doesn't do anything stupid. Like, attempt to kidnap me or the pup. "Can you help us?" I say in an urgent tone. "I need to get in contact with *her* pack." I widen my eyes meaningfully and nod down at the wiggling bundle of fur.

It's as if I've said the magic words.

The shifter snaps to attention. His focus switches from me and the rude stuff undoubtedly going on in his head to the female shifter in my arms. His nostrils flare, and his eyes comically widen. He promptly backs away from us with his palms in the air.

"Oh, fucking hell. Oh, fucking hell," he says, shock and panic lacing his tone.

Oh no, oh God, he looks as if he is going to make a break for it. I step forward in a vain attempt to stop him. Instead of running, he digs into his jacket pocket and fumbles for his phone. He holds a finger up for me to wait. "Sir, that missing pack you are hunting...I think I've found one of the kids."

* * *

After we've both guzzled down some water, I find a safe place in the shop to wait while the nervous shifter stands guard. I sit on the floor in a dusty corner with my back propped up against a buzzing fridge. In this position, I can see the door, and through a handy gap in the shelves I have an excellent view of the street.

Now that I have stopped moving, my entire body feels like one enormous bruise. My feet are throbbing and my long boots are digging into the back of my knees. I daren't take them off, so my poor feet and ankles will probably swell like balloons.

The shifter pup crawls across me and curls up on my lap. I unconsciously stroke her fur as I fret about what is going to happen to me when I get home. The anticipation. God, there is a peculiar agony to waiting, when you know something terrible is going to happen at the end.

The demon sees everything.

I regularly glance at the shop's clock. Time seems to have sped up.

I need to get out of here.

The longer I'm away from the estate, the worse things are going to be. But I can't seem to force myself to leave, not until I can see with my own eyes that she is safe.

"They are here," says the gruff voice of the shifter as three black Land Rover-style cars pull up to the kerb. I struggle back to my feet and scoop up the pup. My riding hat and gloves, I leave on the floor. I will grab them in a moment.

I watch with nervous interest and a smatter of relief, happy knowing that I can finally hand over my furball to somebody who knows what they're doing. The car doors open, and what I can only describe as a squadron of men spill out onto the pavement.

Unease skitters through me, and the small hairs on my arms rise.

Wearing black fatigues, loaded down with shifter-killing silver weapons that catch the sun and glint in its light, the men who exit the cars aren't standard shifters. No, the fatigue-clad men who exit those vehicles are in an altogether different class. A predator class of their very own. My relief turns from nervous trepidation to abject horror.

They are bloody hellhounds.

"Oh my God, you didn't tell me they were hellhounds," I say to the shifter with a squeak.

Hellhounds are powerful shifters with rare fire magic, the shifter council's elite fighting force. I've never seen a hellhound before. I don't really want to see a hellhound again. My pulse picks up, and my fear wafts off me in waves. It's something that I can't control...heck, any sane person would freak the fuck out. Hellhounds. What my now-pounding heart can attest to is that hellhounds are *scary*.

What the hell—pun intended—have I gotten myself into?

Ten pairs of eyes lock onto my position. The hellhounds fan out. Frightened butterflies crash against each other in my belly, and my heart pounds so hard it feels like it's going to explode out of my chest.

Oh bloody hell.

I have the urge to slap myself silly. I've made a colossal mistake—I know it instinctively. Alarm bells are going off like clappers in my head. I groan. Why did I think I could just drop off the shifter pup and skip back to my life?

I didn't think. I am an idiot.

I got so caught up with fear over what the *demon* will do to me, I forgot about other dangers. For my stupidity, I blame my fall from Pudding and the blow to my head.

Keep your eyes down. Try your best to be invisible. Only speak when you need to. Hand the pup over, and at the first opportunity, run.

In the big bad world of creatures, you have the powerful, and then you have the prey. Ha, I know which category I firmly fall into. These hulking monsters that prowl towards me, that tower up above me like army-clad trees, are at the very top of the power scale. They're on a godlike level.

I'd rather sit on Pudding while he bolts down a motorway than stand here with ten hellhounds advancing. Hunting.

Hunting. Me.

Oh my God. I stand trembling in the shop doorway and keep my eyes respectfully lowered. Out of the corner of my eye, I watch as the hellhounds continue to approach. The shifter that called them is bouncing from foot to foot. I wouldn't be surprised if at any moment now, he didn't drop to the floor and prostrate himself in submission.

Come to think of it, *that* sounds like a good idea. Throwing myself on the floor while wailing, "Please don't kill me." Yeah, begging for mercy might be the way to go.

My heart pounds faster and faster. Yet I force myself to stop trembling and keep still, so still. I'm afraid to even breathe too loudly.

I need to get a grip on myself. I slam my eyes closed, like a coward. I welcome the comfort of blackness to the view of the encroaching hellhounds. I hug the little shifter to me in a vain attempt at unrepentant self-reassurance. She stirs in my arms. I open my eyes and glance down. Her bright green eyes blink up at me. Her little tongue comes out, and she licks underneath my chin. "Eww, puppy spit. Thanks for that," I say with a small smile. I return the sentiment with a quick kiss to the top of her head. "You're worth the hassle of this living nightmare, pup." *I think.*

The biggest, meanest hellhound shoulders himself through the others, and they part for him like a wave. I forget to keep my head down and instead I slowly trail my eyes over his massive form as he prowls toward us. The scowl he wears makes him look *petrifying*.

God, but he is handsome—handsome in the way deadly creatures are. I take a deep breath and try to ignore how my body quakes in fear. His wild, masculine beauty only serves to make him appear more lethal. His aggressive hellhound energy hits me with the force of a double-decker bus. I'm surprised I don't see it crackling in the air between us.

This creature is downright terrifying.

"What the fuck did you do to her?"

My surprised gaze flicks up to his. Familiar but livid green eyes meet my own. His glower is like the slash of a knife. I tamp down the urge to check if I'm bleeding. Those eyes— there is no doubt in my mind that he is related to my pup. I've found her pack. Stupidly, I give him a tentative smile.

"Are you dense? I asked you a question. What the fuck did you do to her?" he barks again. I drop the smile and gulp. His face, his face is angelic, proud. He is almost too much to look at. Too beautiful, too breathtaking, too ominous...

Whoa, I'm so confused.

This is not a normal reaction to a gigantic monster of a man who is so angry he's almost frothing at the mouth. Has he got some freaky hellhound attraction magic that I'm not aware of? I am supposed to be immune.

I shouldn't feel anything but fear when I stare into his green eyes. I force myself to look away rather than ogle. I know better than to make eye contact with this man.

Why the hell did I look him in the eye in the first place?

I drop my eyes to his chin.

"She smells of horse. Is that intentional? To mask her scent?" one hellhound says in the background.

"What. Did. You. Do," he growls. I jump and glance down at the pup in my arms, not understanding his question. "What have you done? How can she be in wolf form? She is a nine-year-old child."

Oh, wow. My eyes widen. *Oh, I see.* I know that born shifters do the whole shifting thing in their twenties. I can see with my own eyes that she is tiny. I want to smack myself on the forehead for not putting those two things together. Poor pup.

All I can do is shrug—well, I try to shrug, but my rigidity makes the motion look strange. I have no idea what happened to her.

I want to hunch into myself, but I force myself to keep rigid and stand straight. His scary presence seems to require good posture. I might be mostly human, but I have my pride. I might feel like prey, but I don't have to act like it.

"I'm sorry...I don't know...I found her like this and came straightaway to get her help. I don't know anything else. I'm glad she is safe, but I need to get home." My voice drifts away into mumbles. *Gah, nice one, Emma. Very assertive.*

The hellhound crosses his arms. He taps his massive hand against his forearm in a rhythmic motion and narrows his eyes when it becomes apparent to him I have nothing further to add.

I swallow again. Pure fear is clawing at my throat.

I need to get home.

Ha, I talk a good game, but now I'm hunching for all my worth in an attempt to hide my shaking. With shifty eyes, I quickly search the hellhounds, looking for...looking for...there. *Him.* One hellhound is quietly watching the proceedings like a rock in a rolling storm, seemingly unaffected by the masculine rage of his peers.

I kiss the top of her head. "Goodbye, pup. Be brave, be safe, and be happy," I whisper. She whimpers as I shuffle meekly towards the hound I have chosen and hand her over to him. He has kind grey eyes; they stand out against his dark skin and hair. He takes her gently in his massive arms. I brave a final stroke of her fur. Then I skitter away.

"Where did you find her? Where is the rest of my pack?" asks the scary hellhound as he follows me with his eyes. He looks me up and down, taking my measure, and his lip curls with disgust. Oh yeah, he finds me lacking.

I self-consciously adjust my top and the waistband of my jodhpurs. Since puberty, I have never had a man look at me with anything other than interest or poorly concealed lust. Not very nice, but unfortunately it's the world that we live in. This guy looks at me as if he wouldn't think twice about pulling my head off and using it in a game of football.

I'm a thing to him, not a person. A thing that is in his way. I take in a shaky breath, lift my chin, and meet his eyes head-on.

I am not a *thing*.

"I didn't see anyone else. I hope you find your pack. I really do. I am sorry, but I can't be of any further help. I really have to go." My voice is quiet, but I'm proud to say I keep it even, strong, resistant.

I can't explain where I found her—I can't give any details that would implicate the demon. Not out of loyalty, but self-preservation. You don't snitch on the people that are your prime protection. *You don't break their rules, either,* the helpful voice in my head pipes up. *Mhm, thanks for that.* Heck, I have to get out of here. I back away as Mr Angry Hellhound advances.

He steps into my personal space, dwarfing my five-foot-six frame. The humongous man must be almost seven feet tall, and his body is every bit as pleasing as his face. Massive shoulders, each arm bigger than the span of my waist. Body corded with slabs of powerful muscle. Narrow hips.

This hellhound is made to be feared.

I throw away my moment of false pride and bravery with a wobbly smile and an awkward double-thumbs-up.

I gave the scary hellhound double-thumbs.

Oh, God, what the heck am I doing? I fold my arms behind my back. Next I will be doing jazz hands. The hellhound growls and the look he throws me is one of pure, acrimonious rancour. I can feel his angry energy as it buzzes over my skin.

28

He wants me dead.

Bloody hell, he is going to eat me. Like a packet of pork scratchings, there is no way I won't be tasty. Crunchy.

I gulp.

Why can't he say thank you, like a normal person? I didn't steal his kid. I barely refrain from opening my mouth and pointing that fact out to him.

"You refuse to answer me?" he asks, his voice quiet— deadly. I know that I've crossed some invisible line with him.

The two of us are staring each other down. I catalogue each thick bulge of muscle, not for its beauty but as proof of all the ways that he can hurt me. Stiffening, I straighten my spine and brace myself for the consequences. Which will probably be painful.

I hear a grunt, a thump, and the scrabble of claws on the pavement. Then a bundle of cream-and-red fur barrels around the hellhounds. My pup dives between the scary hellhound's legs and throws herself in front of me.

"For fuck's sake, Owen."

Adorably, she growls and snaps her teeth.

"Sorry, John, she bit me," the grey-eyed hellhound says, poorly hiding his small smile, which is directed at my pup and her adorable antics.

She turns her head and gives me a look as if to say, "Go on then, run."

I spin and run into the shop. Like an idiot, I waste precious seconds grabbing my hat and gloves—I don't want to be accused of being a litterbug. I was eyeing the back exit before, and that door is now calling my name. I need to get home.

There is a sound behind me.

Before I can turn, I feel a sharp blow to the back of my head, and then darkness.

CHAPTER FOUR

Blood pools in my mouth. It dribbles from my cracked, swollen lips and drips lazily down my chin. John—the hellhound—paces the outside of his hand-drawn, archaic circle...a circle he thinks he has trapped me in. He snarls. I roll my head back against the pillar, grinding the back of my head into the brickwork. Wearily, I keep my eyes on his prowling form.

I don't want to be here.

If I hadn't helped the female wolf shifter, I would be home in bed. But I did, and I'm not. I huff out a painful breath.

I don't want to be here...here in a hellhound's torture chamber. Everything hurts, my body is a mess, and I know, deep inside, that...that I'm done for.

I've been internally fighting myself, fighting my fear, fighting my own body, which is begging for me to close my eyes and let the blackness take me away.

My name is Emma, Emma, Emma. I repeat my name over and over again. It's my anchor.

I want to go home.

I want to go home. Please, God, why are you punishing me? I'm not magical like other creatures.

I'm not strong or unique. I'm just me, half human with a mix of some unimportant creature. Nothing special. I lick my lips. My tongue feels oddly big in my mouth.

My lack of uniqueness didn't stop me from helping the female shifter, John's *sister*. It didn't stop me from doing the right thing, and doing so sent me on a direct path to this hell.

John wants information. Information that I haven't got.

Every decision in life has good and bad consequences. That saying? No good deed goes unpunished? Yeah, that should be my motto. Crap, perhaps I should have that tattooed on my arm to remind myself to think things through before I act. That is...if I ever leave this fucked-up situation alive.

My breath rattles in my chest. John narrows his eyes at the sound. "Fuck you," I mouth without any venom. My rude words are a poor attempt at bravery. A vocal shield. A cracked, broken shield. I try to hide behind it as the thick fog of terror rolls inside me. The cracks are spreading, and soon nothing of me is going to be left to protect. His disapproving expression only deepens at my silly word. He folds his arms, content to just watch me, a look of mild repulsion on his face. Yeah, the feeling is mutual, buddy.

I hate the pretty bastard.

Gosh, I really messed up this time, and now I'm reaping what I've sown.

No.

No, I have to be honest with myself. I knew. I knew things would go to shit when I helped that little pup.

I couldn't have imagined this, though, a *hellhound*. God, I thought my demon master would have been the one doing the punishing.

Not her *brother*.

I thought...I thought the shifters would be grateful...ha, I'm so naïve. Stupid. Stupid. Stupid girl. I am a kind-hearted fool.

Doing the right thing, what would be the harm? A bit of risk to get my blood pumping?

Well, my blood is certainly pumping now, all over the bloody floor.

The daft thing is...I can't blame John entirely. The hellhound has shown himself to be a primordial beast with primitive black-and-white views. If I had a family...a pack and someone had taken them, hurt them, wouldn't I do everything in my power to get them home safe?

For a person I loved...I would burn down the world.

The entire world could burn, and I would pull them from the wreckage. That makes me a bad person, doesn't it?

I also can't help asking myself the question, would I make the same mistake John has, of not recognising innocence over guilt?

Ha, that's some serious Stockholm syndrome shit right there, Emma. I have way too much empathy.

Yeah, bloody pesky empathy.

I absorb joy and stress like a sponge. My nana—my mum's mother, was an earth witch. She had an incredible off the charts ability to communicate with the world around her.

Unfortunately, I inherited nothing witchy, as my weird immunity to magic isn't a witch trait. I like to think my empathy and love of animals comes from her.

My nana died when I was four, so my memories of her are fuzzy. When I think of her...I can remember flashes of warmth and love. My nana would have wanted me to do the right thing. Yeah, what would be the harm.

My chains clink. I wish I could rub my face. My wrists throb, a dull pain compared to the rest of my injuries. Can you call something an injury when it's inflicted by someone else? I don't know; my mind is slowly shutting down, just like my body.

When I first woke up chained to the pillar in a basement, I freaked out. Luckily I was alone, so the hellhound didn't get a front-row seat to my frightened thrashing. After that, I kept my dignity for those first few hours. Only my bleeding wrists told the story of my early struggle. Once I'd calmed, I got a better idea of my surroundings and my messed-up situation. Redbrick walls, discoloured at the bottom from damp. The damp was almost the same height around the room. It was like someone had drawn a line. To keep myself from freaking out further and to gain some semblance of control, I counted the bricks. Eight. Eight rows of the darker bricks. Except in the far corner, where I counted nine.

At the top of the wall directly in front of me, a half-circle window draws my gaze away from the hellhound and the strange hand-drawn circle at my feet.

Before, the window cast a perfect half-circle of light onto the dusty, mouldy floor. For hours I watched, chained to that pillar as the curved light moved with the sun. It slowly edged across the floor until it was almost gone. That was when the hellhound returned and subjected me to his ministrations.

"Demon, you will tell me where they are, the others you stole. My mother, my other little sister. You will talk, demon, or otherwise, things are going to get much worse for you." His voice is deep, soft, tipped with barely controlled anger.

Urm, how can things get any worse? The urge to manically laugh at this idiot, calling *me* a demon...*Not a demon, dickhead,* I want to scream at him.

Beg.

Plead.

But my voice no longer works. A person can scream for only so long before their throat gives out.

I live with a demon, a first-level demon. I think *he* would have mentioned if I had any demon DNA. The reason my demon master likes me so much is the mystery of my breeding. I'm like a human equivalent of a lucky dip: you don't quite know what you're going to get.

John's a shifter so why can't he smell my humanity? I guess it doesn't matter anymore.

My tummy screams at me. I pant in pain, but I bite my lip so I don't cry out.

So much pain, an endless ocean of it. With waves that try to engulf me—drown me.

I take a steadying breath and try to force down my nausea. The pungent smell of mould with the undertone of urine stings my nose. I gag, and the sick burns up my throat. Suddenly I projectile-vomit over myself and the floor like a character from *The Exorcist*. John makes a sound of disgust and walks away. I blink in shock.

In the dim light, it's pale green.

Wow, that doesn't look good.

What does pale-green sick mean? Nothing good. His knife before...it must have internally nicked something. At least I emptied my bladder early on, and I don't have to live with the indignity of wetting myself *again*.

Sick, blood, and pee…what a combination to have on my skin. I hope John is enjoying the odour.

Not long now, the helpful voice in my head pipes up. God, everything hurts. The pain is a living thing clawing at my insides.

It would be so easy to let go.

Emma, just close your eyes.

No. I grind my head against the wall. The rough scratching that is almost white noise drowns out my wicked, unhelpful thoughts and the slow pounding of my heart.

My eyes drop. I glance at a dry spot on the floor wistfully. I wish…I wish I could sit down—the concrete looks mighty comfy. But I can't. The chains he has attached to my delicate wrists to hold me aloft will not let me. My legs are now useless noodles, unable to support the weight of the bag of bleeding meat that the hellhound has made of me.

I'm such a fool.

I'm such a fool that even now after everything that has happened, I would *still* have helped the pup escape.

I'm such a fool.

John spins back towards me, and my heart misses a beat as his big body steps over the chalk line and into the circle.

A circle he thinks will keep me from accessing my *demon* powers.

The circle pulses. I don't hear it, but I feel it. It reverberates through me. It echoes deep in my bones. Whatever magic it contains doesn't touch me.

Ha, still not a demon, dickhead.

His body dwarfs my own, and I lift my eyes to his. My throat bobs and the heavy chains rattle as a full-body shiver takes me. I am so cold.

He leans half an inch closer, his bright eyes full of the orange fire that is his fire magic. Those eyes are so terrifying. Yeah, beautiful and terrifying. Even after everything, he is still painfully beautiful. His proud cheekbones and that square jaw...unnaturally handsome, a vicious sort of beauty.

What is wrong with me?

I'm so confused—my attraction to him makes little sense —it's magically enhanced...it must be.

I flinch away as his hand reaches out, and he tucks a piece of my matted blonde hair gently behind my ear. He is so close, breathing deep, so warm...I feel the heat radiating off him and into me. Scalding.

"You dare to wear the disguise of a girl...you even smell human," he whispers intimately into my ear, his low words brushing against my skin like velvet. "Yet you do not fool me, demon." The hellhound cups my face. His fingers gently brush the underside of my jaw and he tilts my face up. His gaze searches mine. He has absurdly long, curly lashes, the colour of fine gold. "Death always comes. Even to something like you, demon, there is always a way." His hand drifts down to my neck, and he rubs his thumb up and down my throat. "You are a fucking curse on the world." I don't think he is aware of the way his thumb brushes back and forth over my jugular, testing my pulse. Until his thumb pauses. He frowns as if he doesn't like the feel of my weak pulse fluttering in his grip. "Tell me about my pack."

I swallow, and his grip tightens.

I freeze. The prey animal in me recognises the danger of this beautiful man and the precipice of the thin ice I stand upon. To have fire magic, to be a hellhound, he has to be an old, powerful shifter. I see the violence and age in his eyes. A thousand years of battle, war, and pain. My heart hurts for him, for the loss of the man he could have been. So many deaths, so much pain. It has turned him into a monster.

In the quiet times like this—between his violent attentions—I usually talk. I tell him everything about my life.

Everything.

Nothing is off limits. Almost every thought I've ever had in my head waffles out of my mouth. I tell him. Our time is so intimate. He knows me better than I know myself. Yet he doesn't believe a word I say. God, I tried my best to convince him. Before my screams robbed me of my voice, that is. Now I have no voice left to talk, I have nothing else to say, to prove. This hellhound has cut me open, and my secrets have poured out. He has ignored every single one, picking through them with disinterest and grinding them beneath his boots.

Who I am doesn't matter.

His presence is intense. Now that I can no longer speak, we communicate with energy alone. It vibrates around us.

When I continue to ignore him, his eyes flame with his fury. "I'll let you heal if you answer my fucking questions," John bellows. He tightens his hold on my throat and slams his fist into the pillar beside my head. My ears throb as his angry voice echoes around the room, and my insides feel like they have liquefied. I slow-blink. A mixture of blood and sick bubbles from my lips.

I try one last time.

I widen my eyes and try to plead with him, plead to the logical side of the man, the rational side trapped inside him, caged in by the monster. John curls his lip and continues to stare at me, his dislike nearly palpable.

John knows magic doesn't work on me. I explained it all to him, yet he mockingly still believes that I'm the mastermind behind his stolen pack. That I'm a demon.

"I will let you heal *if* you answer my questions..."

I close my eyes in defeat. No matter what the monstrous hellhound wants, I can't answer those questions.

How can I answer them when I don't know?

I feel his breath against my cold face—hot breath. My own breath rattles. He lets go of my throat. A click and a rattle, and with deft hands the hellhound releases my wrists from the chains.

With my hands free of the chains, my useless body flops to the floor with a bang. My head hits the unyielding concrete with a *crack*. My already dodgy, fading vision goes black.

Wow, you really do see stars, I think as my vision comes screaming back with multicoloured flashes of light. I think of all the cartoons I watched as a kid that I scoffed at, and I mentally apologise. Stars are a thing.

The hellhound growls with poorly concealed contempt.

I lie where I've crumpled. Compared to everything else, the pain from the blood rushing to my newly released wrists, arms, and shoulders fades into the background. Wow, wishes do come true. Didn't I wish for the comfort of the floor?

I settle in and watch John prowl towards the edge of the circle. Deliberately he smudges the hand-drawn lines with a shiny boot.

What is he up to now?

"No tricks, demon." Yeah, 'cause I'm so sneaky. "Crawl. Leave the circle, heal yourself. Crawl, demon." I give him a look of what I hope is total incredulity at his ridiculous demand. Crawl? Is he taking the piss? Perhaps a few hours ago, but now? What would be the point? Not that I can heal myself here or on the other side of the stupid, useless demon-trapping circle. *Still not a demon*.

Mhm. Do I attempt to crawl...offer the very last of my dignity?

No.

No, the floor is the softest I've ever felt, I'm happy to stay here.

Die here.

In response to my lack of movement—in John's mind, I guess I should scuttle across the floor like a demon cockroach —he strides back towards me, grabs hold of my ragged top, and drags me across the floor, onto the other side of the circle.

I moan in pain. I scream in my head.

"Heal, damn you," John barks. I can feel more blood soaking into my ripped top—the fabric sticks wetly to my skin. He runs his hand through his short, blond hair in frustration. He looks down at me, his legs wide apart, his big muscly arms across his broad chest. He drops his chin. John taps his fingers against his forearm impatiently. He waits.

He waits.

Bloody hell, John, you'll be waiting a long time. The breath rattles in my chest. My heart slows. I can't take a full breath.

I didn't realise that the human body had the ability to feel so much pain. A person could go mad. I thought, wrongly, that after a while, your body would shut down, that the nerves would stop firing and then everything would become one big...well, I imagined it would be like being wrapped in cotton wool. Muffled. Perhaps it's me and my creature DNA that keeps the pain so vivid?

Oh God. Oh God. Oh God, make it stop, please, please make it stop.

"Why aren't you healing?" His fiery eyes have turned green. He prods me with his foot. *Careful, John, you don't want to get your shiny boots dirty,* I think dimly.

I wonder if when the sun rises, I'll be lying in the half-circle of light...I'd like that. Will it touch my face?

I guess I'm done.

"Why aren't you healing?" He drops into a squat and pushes the hair away from my face. He stares intently at me and lets out a low growl. I can't respond—nothing works. After a few seconds, John picks up on my broken state. "You piece of shit. You fucking manipulating piece of shit."

I blink. Each time I open my eyes, the time between gets longer and longer.

If you fall asleep, you will die.

That is okay. I'm ready.

I don't notice that John has left until he returns with a potion vial. He tips the whole thing onto the skin of my throat; it trickles down the back of my neck. He might as well have splashed me with some water.

What a waste of a healing potion.

"Why aren't you healing?" he says again, and his voice has changed. Gone is the harsh whisper, and instead, I almost fool myself into thinking he is concerned.

"Why aren't you fucking healing."

Because.

Magic doesn't work on me.

CHAPTER FIVE

I float inside my head. Will I find peace? Is it over? This whole torture experience has been kind of cathartic. I guess there's nothing like a hellhound torturing you to find out what you're truly made of. A genuine fucked-up horrific experience of self-reflection. It feels as though I have lived a hundred different lifetimes with John—each one violent and bloody. I guess that is what terror and pain do to you— fast-track your soul.

Helping the pup has settled and redeemed something inside of me. For as long as I can remember, a rotten part of me has taunted, cajoled, whispered that when it came down to it, I would be exactly like her.

My mother.

Proud to say I'm nothing like you, Mum.

Ha, it always comes down to your parents in the end, doesn't it? Her lack of affection, lack of closeness, her poorly concealed hate, put a shadow over me. I was five when my mum sold me to a demon so she could jump the queue to become a vampire.

I forgive you, Mum.

"Emma, don't fall asleep." His voice...soothing and *agonised.*

I hate you, Mum.

"Emma, don't you fucking dare."

I love you, Mum.

"She is not healing. We need to get her to a hospital."

I don't regret helping you, pup.

CHAPTER SIX

I wake. Huh, I'm alive. Oh, and now there's the cotton-wool–cloud-like feeling. I blink my eyes open to greet the world through a drug-fuelled haze. Colours sharpen enough for me to make out a face. A demon looms over me, his face still somewhat blurry.

"Arlo," I mouth. His blue-grey eyes that normally sparkle with devious delight are flat. His expression shows nothing, not even anger. I guess I've been unconscious for a while if he has gone from the spitting-mad "I'm gonna rip your throat out" stage to this calm, scary and uber-controlled phase.

I yearn for him to hold me, God, I want him to hold me. Stroke my hair and tell me that everything is going to be okay.

That I'm safe and nothing will ever hurt me again, that he won't allow anything or anyone to hurt me.

The demon does none of those things.

Silly me.

Arlo runs a gentle finger down my cheek. "I had high hopes for you...you were my favourite. Look what you have done to yourself: broken. Broken beyond repair. If I wanted you broken, damaged, I would have done it myself," he says. Frowning, he rubs his thumb over his finger as if he is removing dirt from the digit, dirt from touching me. "You went and involved yourself in *my* affairs, in *my* business. Look at how that has turned out. Look what your kind heart did. You are ruined, and you did this."

I beg with my eyes for forgiveness, unable to say the words. It has no impact. Like it had no impact on John. I tremble and my tummy aches.

Arlo's eyes narrow, and his pouty mouth turns down. He steps away and walks towards a floor-to-ceiling window. My fuzzy gaze quickly takes in the unfamiliar room. It's made of glass—I feel a little like a fish in a tank. I presume we are in a hospital.

I shift a little and dull pain ripples across my torso. Ouch.

I go still. I wait for more pain but luckily, through the cotton-wool feeling imposed by the drugs, the pain remains a dull steady throb.

The demon turns, and my mind jumps a little. Did I miss what he was saying? Fuzzy. Everything is so fuzzy. "I hope you learned your lesson. I need not punish you when you did such an excellent job on your own. Your life has changed— your status in my household has dropped to the very bottom. Now you are a cautionary tale for the others. No one will step out of line for centuries. That is the *only* reason I won't kill you. I will keep you. Though I will never touch you again." He steps back to the bed, a fake, smug smile on his full, puffy lips. "I would have let you die. I don't like broken things." Arlo's eyes run across me, and he curls his lip. "The poor, poor hellhound is distraught—I can see the guilt eating him alive. Poetic really, two broken souls twisted together by fate, forever entwined." He waves his hand to indicate the room. "John Hesketh paid for all this, found a vampire surgeon that has a passion for non-magical intervention. The doctor butchered you to keep you alive."

Arlo chuckles. He leans closer and whispers, "Did John Hesketh play with you in an attempt to rescue his mummy? What secrets did you confess? Mmm? How long did it take? To destroy my pet?" He uses the tip of his nail to lift my chin. "Would you like to know something interesting, Broken Thing? While you received the hellhound's special attention..." he pauses dramatically and leans close, his icy breath fanning my face. Goosebumps break out on my arms. Arlo raises an eyebrow. His eyes sparkle with joy. "...They were already dead. His pack. Before he even met you, they were dead. Dead for over a week."

CHAPTER SEVEN

The world is full of monsters with friendly faces and angels full of scars. — Unknown

My surgeon, Mr Hanlon, is a miracle worker. I call him The Professor in my head. He is a vampire, short and thin with big, bushy grey eyebrows, and although his hair is short, it's wiry and sticks out at the sides. He looks like a mad professor. Quick to smile, he comes across as being quite strict, but he doesn't fool me—the man is a saint.

Most medicine nowadays is magical; medical equipment is a combination of magic and technology. Things that look like simple medical scanners are chock-full of magic. Magic is another useful tool in a doctor's arsenal. If someone breaks an arm, the bone will still have to be reset before the doctor applies a healing potion. Nobody wants to have to re-break bones when someone has used a potion too soon. Magic accelerates healing; it knits everything together and replaces tissue that is missing. Over the years, they have developed lucrative medical magic to cure most diseases and infections. Wounds that used to take weeks if not months to heal can now regenerate in minutes, lifesaving in combat or emergencies.

Healing potions work on beings of every race, even if they have ornate powers of their own. Healing potions work on everybody...except me.

Mr Hanlon says he has never met a person like me before: someone immune to magic, a magical void. Even he doesn't understand my freaky powers.

It thrills him, the challenge I present...well, after he got over his initial shock of me breaking a few of his expensive machines. Magic combined with technology can be temperamental, so add in my immunity and the hospital's fancy tech tended to implode.

The Professor was ecstatic to have performed my magic-free surgery, to dust off his training and theory. I can imagine in my surgery he had the ardent glow of a child left alone in Toys R Us with a credit card, and the words *buy whatever you want* fading in his ears. The opportunity to get his hands in and actually play around with my organs was a rare treat.

The weirdo.

He tells me at every opportunity that I'm his best work.

Of course, some people need alternative health care—mainly the rare, mostly purebred humans who are adamantly against the practice of magic, and people who can't afford treatment, as healing potions can be expensive.

When it comes down to it, it's really only humans, witches, and young shifters who need regular intervention by doctors. The other races have their own innate gifts for everyday healing.

I'm not too proud to say that I'm jealous—I wish I could magically heal.

I have been in the hospital now for over two months. For a small stab wound the damage was extensive, the knife shredded my appendix and some of my small intestine. I've had two major operations and a battle with sepsis. Frustratingly, no matter how many bags of antibiotics they pump into me, I still seem to get small, nasty infections. At one point, I dubbed myself *Pus Girl* as a joke. It was so gross, how much pus my body could produce. Litres of the stuff, gag.

But I'm alive.

To save my life, I have...I have an ileostomy, a stoma. Which is an artificial hole in my abdomen wall, where part of my small intestine has been pulled through, and it collects my faeces in a bag.

My Professor is confident, given enough time and adequate healing on my part, he should be able to put everything back.

The stoma sits on the lower right-hand side of my tummy. It's bright red, and it looks like a small rose. It's alien-like. The texture is like touching the inside of my cheek.

Yes, it is surreal.

Something that should be on the inside of my body is now on the outside.

I name the stoma Bert. I purposely treat Bert like a wayward life-saving pet. I won't go into details, but having a stoma can be messy. So having the mentality that it's *Bert's* fault when things inevitably go wrong has helped tremendously.

Bert is the naughty one, it isn't me. It's not me.

Everything still feels unreal. It is like I'm permanently trapped in a bad dream.

Why did this happen to me?

I guess naming Bert allows me to get over the shock of my *new normal*. Ha, "my new normal." God, I hate that phrase. I don't want this new bloody normal. I liked me just the way I was.

It's a challenge to fight the grief over the changes to my body. I guess I've lost myself a little. I've learned to be stronger in keeping optimistic about my illness, but I've lost some of my fire. I no longer feel as confident. I have a deep-seated need to not be near people. Instead of being that bubbly talk-the-ear-off-a-person, I've turned into somebody awkward.

I'm supposed to be a brave and independent woman. I rub the scars on my wrists, left over from the chains. It's one of the many strange habits and quirks I've developed. My scars randomly ache with the memory of the cold metal on my skin. I rub them to reassure myself that the shackles are no longer there.

Some days, it's like it has reduced me to a lesser person. I'm frightened all the time, and I hate myself for feeling this way.

I've always been a positive person, so I force myself to hold on to that positivity—clinging desperately to it with my fingers and toes. Any time bitterness tries to creep in, I forcibly push the destructive thoughts away.

So many scars. Inside and out.

I have to see them as life-saving. If I don't...well. In my waking moments, I don't allow myself much contemplation. I'm not so fortunate when I sleep.

The nightmares...they plague me. I have to remain brave and mentally keep moving forward. If I stop to think...if I dwell on the bad...I will undoubtedly drown in my sadness and fear.

I've quickly learned that true bravery can be just the act of getting out of bed in the morning while fighting your mind, body, and those destructive inner fears.

Eating is difficult. Food has become my enemy. If I eat the wrong thing, I either throw up or I get a horrendous stomach ache, and Bert goes nuts. It's demeaning. Gosh, I'm moaning. I must stay positive.

Mr Hanlon is doing his rounds. He stands before me and pokes at the tablet in his hands. Having been so poorly, I found it almost impossible to string a semblance of my thoughts together. Now that my head has cleared from the drug-fuelled haze and I'm feeling more like myself, I take the opportunity to ask him some *important* questions.

"No, you won't be riding your horses for quite some time," the Professor answers. He looks at me as if I'm completely nuts. I'm sitting cross-legged in an attempt to stretch the tight muscles in my legs and back without using my poor abs. I wiggle in response to his stern look. "I'm hoping that you will naturally heal so I can do a reversal operation and put everything back in its rightful place." The professor taps the tablet. "The tachycardia and your weight loss are concerns. I have to warn you, Emma, that organs don't like to be played with. I'm sure there will be many challenges ahead of you with your digestive system. The food you can eat—but that is a discussion for another time. I have no doubt you will handle it with your customary grace and courage. Let's get you home first. If your next set of test results are clear, you can go home. Ideally, once you leave the hospital, I strongly suggest *no* horse riding and also that you avoid lifting anything heavy."

"Heavy?" I ask for clarification. *Heavy* to me is a couple of bags of horse feed, perhaps a 25kg bale of shavings.

"Objects no heavier than say...a small kettle of water," Mr Hanlon replies with a helpful smile. My heart dips, and I rub my face and temple with frustration.

Oh bloody hell.

I force myself to nod. "Thank you, Mr Hanlon." I give him an overly bright smile. I nod again and cast my eyes upward in the vain hope that it will help me not to cry.

How am I going to look after the horses?

If I still have my horses, that is. I have not seen Arlo since I woke up. At the time, he purposely didn't explain what my "drop in status in his household" meant. I swallow my nerves and the constant nagging worry.

"Everything good or bad happens for a reason," I mumble.

I am grateful I'm alive. I'm grateful I'm alive. I'm grateful I'm alive.

Oh, but it hurts. I rub my chest with my knuckles. I want to care for my horses. How can I care for them when everything to do with horses is heavy? It is perhaps a silly thing in the big scheme of things. But Bob, my hairy cob, has been the centre of my world for over ten years. I can't imagine not spending time with him, caring for him. These past long weeks of not knowing if Bob and Pudding are safe has been horrendous.

Heck, I struggle even to sit up without flapping around like a fish. Because of my surgeries, my abdominal wall has been cut to pieces and all my muscles have wasted away. I know for a fact that for safety reasons, I cannot do a thing with Pudding—he is such a shithead. But I'm not *me* without my horses. I rub the pain in my chest again.

Mr Hanlon gives me a gentle pat on my shoulder and leaves the room.

Be positive. Be brave. I'm hopefully going home...if I have a home.

Arrah. *Quit it, Emma.*

I think of the potato quote: *"The same boiling water that softens the potato hardens the egg. It's about what you're made of, not the circumstances."*

Ha, "what I'm made of." I roll my eyes.

I'm like Frankenstein's monster.

John's monster.

I stretch my right leg out and roll my shoulders. I wonder if he is proud of his creation. As if my thoughts have conjured him, the hellhound appears outside my glass 'tank.'

John stands in the doorway. He is wearing a black T-shirt and trousers that mould to him. His unsettling green eyes take me in. Smart and clear, they evaluate everything with calm precision.

My eyes widen. I freeze on the bed. Sweat breaks out around my hairline, and my left eye twitches sporadically. Why is he here? To make an apology? "Sorry I stabbed you, Emma." This is so not appropriate. I cautiously move my hand to rub my twitching eye. I then narrow both of my eyes as I stare up at him. I can't wrap my head around the fact that he is *here*.

"We need to talk," he says.

Boom.

As soon as I hear his voice, the room darkens. Bitter-tasting bile rises up my throat. Belatedly, it becomes apparent to me that...*I'm screaming.*

In a panic, I clamp my hands over my mouth. One on top of the other to hold in the sound. My fingers dig into my cheeks. The scream is now muffled, yet it continues to bubble in my throat. A flood of frightened tears runs down my face unchecked. They pool at the top of my fingers and drip slowly down my wrists, the salty tears making a minor cut on my wrist sting.

My God, it is like all my nightmares have come together into human form.

I shake my head. No. No to the horrified disbelief that is rattling around in my brain, that John is *here* in the same building as me, has he come back to hurt me? I don't want to talk to him. I'm a mess, thanks to the man standing before me. He wants to talk? His blasé tone does not inspire any confidence. Just bone-deep fear. Oh God, why is he really here?

John remains in the doorway, his body relaxed. A penitent expression flashes across his face. But it disappears so quickly, I think I must have been mistaken. His eyes are assessing, judging.

Judging *me* as I struggle for control.

I fight the overwhelming, demanding urge to manically fling myself from the bed and run, or at least attempt to hide, with my fingers in my ears in the vain, childish hope that if I can't see him or hear him, he will leave me alone.

Oh my God, if he takes one more step...

NO. My panicked thoughts screech to a halt as I gain control of myself. I am *not* doing that to myself. I'm not.

John is another form of *infection* that I have to fight.

I will not let my primal fears control me. I force myself to stay on the bed, with my elbows I hug my knees to my chest. My breath struggles to escape from between the dam of my hands, and my nostrils flare as I pant. I can't get enough air through my snotty nose.

He patiently waits until I stop freaking out, then continues as if I hadn't interrupted him with my screaming. "I'm worried about your safety...the consequences of your helping my sister." The consequences of what you, John, did. "I have the means and the resources to get you somewhere safe. You're not safe with Arlo." John says the demon's name as if they're old friends, not current enemies. The smooth rolling of his voice twists my insides. Nothing in John's tone indicates any awareness that the demon was behind the kidnapping and subsequent deaths of his pack.

Of course he knows...after months of investigation, the hellhound will know everything.

"He has removed his protection—there is no longer a claim on you. It will only be a matter of time before someone makes their move."

Why the hell does John care?

"Arlo will never let you go. He will dangle you like bait to see what he can catch."

A fishing reference...how apt, considering I've lived in this fishbowl of a room for weeks.

I rock. "Don't pretend you care," I mumble around the fleshy barrier of my hands. John tilts his head.

Now that I have full control of myself, I cautiously drop my hands from my mouth. Licking my lips, I not-so-surreptitiously put the hospital bed between us as I shuffle to the other side of the bed. My abdomen sharply twinges a protest as I quickly stand. I sway on my feet. My blood pressure is still dangerously low, and as I've gotten up too fast, dizziness hits me. I blink rapidly to clear the black dots that dance across my vision. As soon as I feel steady enough, I slowly back away.

My already-stressed heart pounds, causing my neck and jaw to ache. I keep moving backwards away from the hellhound until my bum hits the glass window and I can go no further.

I wipe my hands across my face to clear it of tears and cough to clear my throat.

I take a deep breath.

It's all going to be okay—or it isn't, but that's okay too.

I can't stop my hands as they stray of their own accord to rest protectively in front of Bert. John's eyes track the movement and he frowns.

I swallow and lift my chin, and bravely I say again, "Do not pretend that you care." It comes out wobbly. More strongly, I say, "You just want to use me. I assume you have some big nefarious plan? I will not allow myself to be used, hellhound. Haven't you...haven't you done enough?"

I bite the inside of my mouth and I force myself to continue—I have my own questions. "Your sister," I say through a growing lump in my throat, a nasty lump of fear that is doing its best to rob me of my voice. I need to know— not knowing has driven me crazy in this hospital bed and only this man has the answer. "Is she okay? Did she shift back? Is she safe?"

He flinches. It's only a micro-expression, a tightening of his mouth, a flick of his right eyebrow that he can't quite staunch. "Do not talk about my sister," he growls. "Don't even think about her. Her welfare is not your concern." His gorgeous face twists into a fearsome expression and his now-livid energy sucks the air out of the room.

I shrink back further into myself. If I could, I would dig a hole right through the window at my back and escape. Isn't it normal to ask about my pup?

I point a trembling finger at him. "You are a monster, John Hesketh. I see you."

Oh crap, I've said too much. I nibble on my bottom lip. But because I'm a glutton for punishment and I can't help myself, I square my shoulders, lift my chin, and blurt out, "Arlo told me you paid for my medical treatment. Excuse me if I don't say thank you. You are the reason I'm here. Please leave. Leave me alone. Get out. Please, just get out. I never want to see you again. You've done enough."

"I will send someone to help you. Guard you—"

"No."

"You have no choice," he growls.

No, I never have. "I hate you," I snarl, my pulse pounding heavy in my veins and my entire body shaking with fear.

John's confident demeanour slips a little at my words. I swear that for a second, he almost looks uncertain. But then his eyes flash with that awful orange flame.

"Good," he says with a cruel twist of his lips.

CHAPTER EIGHT

After the whole visit debacle, I recognise the fingerprints of John's interference everywhere. As I put two and two together, I realise quickly that not only has he paid for my treatment, he has also purchased all the toiletries and clothing that have conveniently appeared during my hospital stay.

It is a strange feeling, being vulnerable around someone who's both hurt you and tended to you.

A tiny insistent sliver of compassion, keeps reiterating that the hellhound has lost his pack. *Lost,* what an insignificant word. John didn't *lose* his pack. The demon, my demon master, murdered his family. That tiny shard of compassion insists that John is doing his best to ratify his mistake.

No—God, I smash that shard to pieces. I can't allow myself to be that naïve.

I rub my face and weave my fingers through my hair. I tug until the strands pull painfully against my scalp. I have to force myself to not believe my own hopeful lies that John somehow cares.

He does not.

It's ludicrous of me to think so. He is using me to get at the demon. He has inserted himself into my life like some kind of virus. I was right with the analogy of him being an infection. He is the worst kind of infection.

John is *poison*.

I am not even going to pretend to understand what is going on in that man's head. At least after he demanded my compliance, he thankfully left me alone.

For the millionth time, I stare out of the window that overlooks the hospital carpark. In the world outside this insular room, drizzle soaks the ground. It is the kind of day when the cold seeps into your bones.

My blood results have come back clear. No infection. I am finally free from my pus-girl status—they have finally cleared me to go home.

Home.

I turn my head and take in all the packed stuff on the bed. "How on earth am I going to carry it all...all this stuff?" I mumble. I fold my arms and hug myself. I've heard nothing back from the estate. So I'm unsure of where I'm going.

Is the estate still my home?

I poke at the bags.

The hospital has its own portal, so at least I don't have far to travel. Portals are a witch-created gateway system that uses ley-line magic. The witch magic attaches the doors to other doorways all over the world—you have to know the correct gateway code to go anywhere and you have to have permission—otherwise you're going to get an unpleasant, possibly even fatal greeting by a ward on the other side. Well, *I* wouldn't. But it would be rude and dangerous to pop out of a random gateway.

I can't explain why the gateways work for me and other magic doesn't. I guess the ley line magic is so vast, my magic is like a teardrop in the ocean—it isn't strong enough to interfere.

Only the rich and powerful have access to portals, so perhaps I'm wrong with my assumption that I will use one today. My gaze flicks to the cold, wet day outside. Heck, I might have to walk home.

A knock on the glass behind me has me spinning around. A refined and regal-looking elf is standing in the doorway. Not a nurse. She bows in a formal greeting. "Emma, my name is Eleanor. They have assigned me as one of your personal guards. Will you allow me to escort you home?" She smiles.

Eleanor is beautiful. Her enormous dark-brown eyes and pointed ears show her to be a full-blooded Aes Sídh, a fae warrior elf. Her shiny black hair is long and styled in intricate plaits, as is their custom. The cut of her clothes makes her look simultaneously archaic and futuristic. She is dressed in a loose, black high-necked long-sleeved top and pants. I know hidden underneath, on one of her arms, will be her magical warrior markings—they look like humans' tattoos. Supposedly the markings glow as the warrior does freaky fae magic.

I blink at her like a divvy while my mind takes a second to catch up. *One of my personal guards*. Oh. Okay. Ha, the guards. Of course I ignored that significant detail from John's visit.

Home...I swallow and hunch over a little. I rub my arms in a vain attempt at self-comfort and gnaw on my lip. I'm sure the nurses could assist me to the portal...I could refuse. Couldn't I?

But the sensible part of me gives me a nudge to accept help.

"Do I have a choice?" I ask quietly, still rubbing at my arms.

The fae can't lie. In response to my question, Eleanor doesn't answer. Instead, she offers me a beatific smile, then glides towards the bed to gather my things.

Okay, then.

"Eleanor, it would be an honour to accept your help," I mumble politely. John confuses me, frightens me, but it isn't this lady's fault. Eleanor is doing her job, and there is no need for me to be rude. Plus, she is a scary badass warrior. I don't need anyone else angry with me, especially an Irish Aes Sídh.

Heck, I have no idea what I risk in going home; it might be handy to have a badass warrior by my side, even if she comes from unsavoury circumstances.

"Excellent. Is this everything?" She indicates my pile of bags on the bed.

"Yes. I am sorry...I can't help you carry them...I have... urm—"

Eleanor interrupts my pathetic attempt at an explanation. "I am aware of your limitations." I nod and shoot her an awkward, wobbly smile.

Instead of Eleanor grabbing the bags like I thought she would, the warrior mark on her right arm glows. The light bleeds through her black long-sleeved top, and the bags on the bed twitch and rattle. I'm fascinated. My lips part with disbelief as with an upward hand gesture from Eleanor my bags slowly rise into the air.

Wow, okay, that's a nifty trick.

Not sparing my fishbowl room a backward glance, I meekly follow Eleanor out of the room and down the corridor. The bags bob about in the air behind us as we walk. I warily monitor them—I don't want to interfere with the handy fae magic. It should be okay as long as I avoid getting too close.

Eleanor slowly leads me down the corridor after I refuse the use of a wheelchair. I'm determined to leave this hospital under my own steam. After a while I regret that decision as my body screams at me to rest, but I've done enough sitting around for a lifetime. *Push through it, Emma. One step at a time.* With my dodgy, exhausted vision, the walls of the hallway ripple. I am pleasantly surprised that I'm not bouncing into them. I take walking in a straight line as a win.

When we arrive at the portal gateway on the ground floor of the hospital, we are greeted by a massive hellhound in wolf form. I squeak and take a wobbly step back.

"Emma, may I introduce you to your other guard, Riddick. My employer has informed me that Riddick will remain in wolf form while in your presence."

Both the elf and the hellhound watch me in silence as they wait for my response. My pulse hammers away until it's all I can hear. Not another hellhound, oh God. I wonder if Riddick can smell Bert. The thought makes me hunch over, and my lip twitches. I rub it on my shoulder before my whole face starts.

My new guards stare at me. They're still waiting for a normal response to the introduction.

Come on, Emma.

I blow out a nervous breath and subject them both to my elegant jazz hands.

Jazz hands.

I cringe. *What the heck was that?* I lace my wayward, now-shaking hands across Bert protectively. Ha, to think I used to be refined.

In response to my out-of-control anxiety, Riddick drops his heavy bulk to the floor. On his belly with his head on his paws, he whines.

My mouth pops open in shock as I eye the giant wolf prostrated before me. He has a thick cream-and-red coat and the brightest green eyes. Wow, he could be related to my pup, as he looks like a colossal male version of her. I dismiss the thought as silly. I've not seen many shifters in animal form, so I've no idea if the red colouring is standard or not.

Riddick's massive tongue rolls out of his mouth. He gives me what I can only describe as a doggie smile. I can't help my answering grin—I'm a sucker for animals. Even though I know there is a giant, scary man underneath all that fur, I can't help but appreciate his kindness—he is going out of his way to set me at ease.

"I'm…" I cough to clear my throat, "…I'm sorry. You must forgive me, I'm not myself at the moment. Pleased to meet you, Riddick." My hands twist in front of me. "Urm, may I ask how long you are both assigned to guard me?" I blink at Eleanor.

Eleanor is frowning at me. She must think my behaviour is nuts. Because it is—is Arlo right, am I broken? No, I am not...I am just dented. "This assignment is a permanent position."

"Permanent." What the heck?

"Permanent? Oh, I'm sure I'll be okay with your help just today." I titter. Oh crap, I don't know how I've qualified to have a warrior elf *and* a hellhound as guards. The more pertinent question would be, what on earth have they done to gain *me* as a permanent assignment?

Colour me surprised when Eleanor inputs the gate code for the main house at the estate. I don't know how John has gotten away with having his people on the demon's estate. Being a demon, Arlo is incredibly territorial.

I keep my rogue hands pinned to my side as my fingers twitch with the need to stroke the hellhound's soft fur. I'm nuts. Who in their right mind wants to stroke a hellhound?

The gateway flashes, and without any fanfare, we step through.

CHAPTER NINE

When we step out of the portal, Doris, the estate's housekeeper, greets us in the hallway. "Miss Emma, you are back, and you have brought friends." Her voice is laden with distaste. With a sniff, she tucks her dark hair behind her ear while looking me up and down. A sly look enters her watery blue eyes. "We have moved you. The Master's new favourite is now in your old suite of rooms..."

In response, I beam a smile at her.

I'm sure Doris expects me to be rolling around the floor in floods of tears wailing, "Why me, why me. I love him." When I don't, she narrows her eyes and barks out, "Follow me."

We all traipse behind her as she leads us to the back of the house. When we get to my new accommodations, I am a tad uncomfortable—when the demon said I was now at the bottom of his household, boy, he wasn't kidding. Embarrassed, I wonder what my guards will make of this.

I shuffle my feet. God, I want to go back to the hospital, to my light and airy fishbowl.

This room is shit.

Gone is my airy suite of rooms and in their place is a Harry Potter–worthy cupboard under the stairs. The door doesn't open fully as it hits the bed—the room is big enough for the single bed, and that's it. It's an empty storeroom with no window, so there isn't any natural light, only a single, dangling light bulb.

In a house where there are dozens of empty bedrooms, this is indeed a statement. But it's okay, it's totally fine. I can work with it.

"Cosy," I say with a smile.

"I got some of your essentials," Doris says, indicating with a nod the small cardboard box and single pathetic black bin-bag dumped in the middle of the thin, sagging mattress.

"Huh, how nice. It appears I have my own Homer hole," I say with amusement as I pay homage to my favourite animated TV program. I grin at the sagging mattress. "Thank you, Doris, this is perfect, and thank you, it was very kind of you to rescue my things." Doris *humphs* crossly. She folds her arms underneath her boobs and glares.

Ha, what can I say? I'm an irritating people-pleaser. Sorry, Doris, I'm still not at the point of throwing myself to the floor and wailing.

I can't help the grin that tugs at my lips. If I had the energy to do a happy dance, I would. It's a relief, such a relief, to no longer hold the title of the demon's pet. I guess I shouldn't be thrilled that Arlo has relegated me to some lowly position and that I have to sleep in a storeroom, but until this moment, I didn't realise how much I wanted out of my opulent cage. I never saw being his favourite as a grand prize. I can't help a full-body shudder. Wow, what a lucky escape.

Everything happens for a reason.

"The bathroom is upstairs...on the *third* floor," Doris continues snidely. Riddick growls at her, and she jumps a little. I grin at him. "Did I say the third floor? I meant third door...it's up the corridor." Doris gives me an embarrassed nod, hands the key to the room over to Eleanor, and quickly scampers away. I pat Riddick on the head—*good boy*—as I shake my head in bemusement at her retreating form. I've lived in this house for over seventeen years; it's like she has forgotten I know every inch of the place.

I clap, then smile at my two guards. Conversationally I say, "Did I tell you I have horses?"

* * *

When we arrive at the stables—which are directly behind the main house, so it isn't too far for me to walk—the first thing I notice is the silence. The rain has stopped and the sun is shining through the heavy grey clouds. Instinctively I know something is wrong...it's just too damn quiet. As soon as I spot the empty, cleaned-out stables, my legs buckle. A big furry body stops me from falling to the ground. Riddick props me up.

All the horses. Gone. The horses are *gone*.

Gone, gone, gone echoes around in my head. They have cleaned the building out. It's empty. Overwhelming panic fills me and for a few minutes, I can't think. Useless. I'm utterly powerless. "Bob...I have to find him," I whisper brokenly through a solid lump in my throat. My heart is slamming, my gut is twisting, and I can't stop shaking. My vision goes hazy. "I have to find my best friend, I can't lose him. Pudding, I didn't have time to check on him, I fell and I didn't have time to see if he was okay. Oh, God." Eleanor's eyes meet mine, and they shine with concern.

Check the field.

I rush towards the fields. The wooden post-and-rail horse paddocks are empty. The surrounding silence is deafening.

For several minutes I stand staring in utter disbelief. What do I do? I rub my temples.

What do I do? No. No. No. Bob...my Bob.

My horses are gone, Bob and Pudding are gone.

This, this finishes off what is left of my soul. I don't want to be here anymore. This world is too much. Everything is too much. My mouth contorts in grief, and I cover my eyes with my hands.

Riddick huffs out a breath and gently nudges me. Without thinking, I drop one of my hands and dig my fingers into his fur to ground me. The giant hellhound offers me comfort.

"What are you sniffling about?" comes a familiar voice. I drop my hand from my face and lift my head to meet the blue eyes of a vampire girl. She narrows her eyes, assessing me with her hands on her narrow hips. She looks almost homeless, wearing dirty jogging bottoms and a red strappy top, her brown hair scraped up into a messy bun at the top of her head. It has clumps of hay sticking out of it.

"Sam," I mumble, "the horses are gone..." I wave my hand, pointing out the obvious.

"Yeah, they were all sold within a few weeks. You *really* pissed that demon turd off. I'm sorry, Em...Pudding, that spooky shithead, was sold for crazy money. He is so talented, there was a bidding war over him. He has gone to Germany. I couldn't afford to buy him..." I nod sadly, hurt that I never got to say goodbye. "...Not after I bought your hairy cob." I blink at her.

"You bought...Bob?" I whisper in disbelief.

"Of course I did. You owe me fourteen and a half thousand pounds. Who knew Bob was worth so much? Contrary to popular belief, vampires aren't made of money, you know." She smiles at Eleanor. "I'm only eighty. Horses took over my human life, and the passion followed me into my undead one. Creatures like me will never be rich if we have horses. The fuckers cost a pretty penny—"

"Thankyouthankyouthankyou." I rush towards her, instantly snapping out of my melancholy.

"You're welcome. Just don't hug me." She holds out her hands to keep me away. "I don't want bashing with that poo bag. God, Em, I thought you'd been in the hospital. They let you out looking like that? You look like shit." She puts her hand at the side of her mouth and says to Eleanor, "Pun intended." Eleanor looks horrified and Riddick growls. I giggle and smile so big, my cheeks hurt. Only a genuine friend would take the mick out of someone that has a stoma. I love this girl.

"I love you, Sam, and I've missed you. Would you mind if we went to see my horse?"

"I can't believe it's taken you so long to ask. He's in a *shitty* stable." She grins and wiggles her eyebrows at the word *shitty*. "So don't get mad, I had to hide him somewhere. I bought him a Shetland pony as a companion. I know how much you like them." I roll my eyes. Sam knows the little ponies are a nightmare to deal with, scary waist-high monsters. I bet poor Bob has been terrorised. I'm convinced that the Devil himself created Shetlands and then went out of his way to make them extra feisty.

Sam grabs me and gives me a fierce hug. "Don't you dare pull that *shit* again. I have been worried sick. Sick. What were you thinking?" She gives me a little shake. "You bloody idiot. I'm so glad that you're okay. Whatever you need, I'm here for you—don't forget that. I charge for tough love, though, and sniffling all over me will cost extra."

We all follow Sam as she leads the way. I'm so tired, I feel sick. I lean more and more against the hellhound.

There is a whinny, and Bob's head appears over the ramshackle stable door. "Bob," I shout, and he whinnies again. I rush to open the stable door. It sticks halfway and Sam has to tug it open for me. My hands shake as I step inside the stable. With wide tear-filled eyes, I take in my boy. He looks great.

"Bob, I thought for one horrible moment that I lost you. God, I have missed you so much." Bob avoids my reaching hand with a head toss. He flares his nostrils at me and narrows his eyes. He gives me an angry look, as if he has just realised something. He wrinkles his nose. Then, almost knocking me over, he swings away from me to face the back corner of the stable.

"Bob?" I say, feeling a little hurt as he presents his hairy bum to me. He peeks over his shoulder and then turns his face back to the corner with a horsey huff. "Bob...are you...urm...cross with me?" I whisper. His ears flick back as he listens to my voice. "I didn't leave you on purpose. I'm so sorry, I have missed you so much. I promise I will do my best to never be away from you for so long again. I'm so sorry, Bob-cob...forgive me?" Bob huffs out a sigh. I step to his side and scratch his blue-grey dappled bottom. He wiggles it, deliberately moving my hand to a different prime scratching spot. Once he has deemed my bum-itching time adequate, with a grumble he turns back around.

Bob's warm brown eyes take me in. He stretches his neck and blows warm breath at me. He slowly moves so his heavy head rests on my shoulder. I ignore the nagging voice in my head to be careful. I run my hands gently across his soft muzzle and rub the base of his ears. Bob huffs hay breath at me and his eyes close in contentment. "God, I have missed you. I have missed you so much." With a sob, I move forward, throw my arms around his neck, and bury my face in his long silver mane. I breathe him in. "Now I feel like I've come home," I whisper.

CHAPTER TEN

I scamper down the corridor to the bathroom with my hands full of my wash things and pyjamas. I try my best to avoid looking at myself in the bathroom mirror. If zombies existed, I would be seriously concerned, since if a guild hunter copped a look at me lately they'd so take me out. And not in a good way.

When I catch my reflection, I shudder. My skin is so pale... there isn't any pink in my lips or even underneath my nails. With my pale blonde hair and dull blue eyes beyond the obvious poorly zombiism, all I see is the ghost of a girl.

After a quick shower, a vigorous tooth-brush, and a Bert-bag change, I'm ready for bed.

"Is it okay to leave the door open?" I ask Riddick, as I rock from foot to foot in my pyjamas and twist my fingers in front of me. I feel silly, asking like a child to keep the door to my room open and the hallway light on. With no windows, the storage room is dark, and I've been living in a glass fishbowl for months. It shouldn't have been a surprise to me, but I didn't expect this room to feel so claustrophobic. The size of it and the lack of light is disconcerting. There's no way I will sleep in here without the door being open—there's no air.

Riddick replies with a small sigh, and ever so slowly he nods his head.

For what must be the millionth time in my life, I wish magic would work on me. From what I can gather, Eleanor communicates with Riddick through a magical mind-link. So cool. I wish I could talk to him.

I take his head-nod as permission and beam a smile at him. "Thanks, Riddick."

I tug the door, and it scrapes against the bed frame and bounces back. I narrow my eyes and ram the door with my left shoulder, being mindful of Bert. Oof. I still can't get it fully past the bed, but with another forceful shove, I wedge the door against the bed so it's stuck wide open. I take a step back to survey my handiwork and rub my now-aching arm. I smile with relief: it's much better. The chandeliers in the hallway flood the storeroom with soft light.

Take that, Doris. I don't mind the lack of privacy.

The bed creaks and groans as I get in. "Woops," I squeal and flap my arms about in panic as my body unwillingly rolls into the centre of the bed. Oops. I let out a snort Bob would be proud of and giggle. Oh my God, I forgot completely about the Homer hole until I lay down. The dip in the mattress makes it impossible to sleep anywhere else. I might need a rope ladder to get out in the morning. I cover my mouth with my hand and continue to giggle, then huff and wiggle as a spring digs itself into my back.

Huh, when I thought about my first night back, I imagined so many nightmare situations. An uncomfortable bed wasn't anywhere on the list of penalties for returning to the estate—the scene of my crime—after I stole the little shifter out from under the demon's nose. I thought they would relegate me to the same creepy building, the same prison I stole her from. Or perhaps I'd be kept in some deep, dark dungeon, never to be seen or heard from again.

I nibble my bottom lip.

Yet here I am with a personal guard keeping me safe. It feels almost too good to be true.

The duvet cover is soft, and the pillows are squishy. I run my fingers across Bert's seal to make sure he is nice and tight. Finally, after more wiggling, I settle on my side, my hands tucked underneath the pillow.

I peek down at Riddick. The huge hellhound is lying in the corridor directly in front of the room's threshold. I don't know what he thinks about my antics getting into bed. I grin; he must think I'm a right idiot.

The bright hallway light dances on his fur and highlights his beautiful glossy red coat, making him look extra fluffy. Underneath the pillow, my fingers twitch with the urge to stroke him. *Hellhound weirdo*, I chastise myself. His full attention is directed down the hallway as he keeps watch.

It's in quiet moments like this I think of my pup, especially as I'm looking at the hellhound. No one will talk about her—it's as if she never existed. I don't know where she is or if she is safe. The shifters are incredibly closed-lipped; you can't ask about a female shifter, it isn't safe and the one man who knows would get violent with me if I asked him again, if the look in his eyes is any indication. Even though I don't want to, I have to push her to the back of my mind. If I'm meant to help her or see her again in the future, our paths will cross. Otherwise, I have to have faith...faith that she's okay and that the shifters are looking after her. Heck, I can't even protect myself...this is crap. "Please be safe, pup," I whisper under my breath into the universe. "Please be safe."

When Riddick continues to feel my eyes on him, he sighs and turns his head to regard me. His solemn green gaze takes me in.

"'Night, Riddick. Thank you for keeping me safe." He doesn't acknowledge my whispered words, but he doesn't have to. His shifter magical energy creeps towards me. It floods the room with gentle, comforting waves.

I sigh, and my body relaxes.

He makes me feel safe. Being metaphysically enfolded in his warm energy is a different type of intimacy, a feeling of peace and protection that to anyone else would be unnoticed, underrated. I have never felt it before. I close my eyes and let it wrap around me. It might be my imagination, but I'll take it. It warms my soul. I don't understand why, but I'm grateful.

Warm and safe, I sleep.

* * *

There is a deep rumbling growl. My eyes fly open. My throat is burning and the remnants of a scream die on my lips. Immediately, I throw my hands up and cover my mouth.

Oh no. I shake as the tentacles of my nightmare slither away from me. I was screaming. *Oh no.*

I attempt to sit up, but the dip in the bed makes any movement difficult. I hear another growl and my eyes fly to the door. Riddick's gigantic form is blocking the doorway.

He is growling at someone in the hallway.

My heart slams in my chest with fear and I give a panicked wiggle, and Bert and my abs twinge in protest as I finally flop and roll enough to get sufficient momentum to scramble out of the bed. My feet hit the floor with a thud and one tiny step finds me out in the hall.

There is a disgruntled crowd of people in the hallway—most of them in nightwear—facing off against Riddick. At the head of the group is Doris.

Oh, heck, it looks like I've woken the entire house. My burning, sore throat tells its own tale. I kind of hoped that once I'd left the hospital, I would have left the terrible memories behind. Unfortunately, it looks like that isn't the case. I understand why everyone looks upset. I clutch my arms to my chest and rub them. No one wants to be woken up in the middle of the night by bloodcurdling screams.

I try to step around Riddick's bulk, but he swings to the side to block me, his soft red-and-cream fur brushing my legs.

As soon as Doris sees me, her eyes narrow and her finger comes up. "You," she says furiously, jabbing her finger in my direction. "You will remove yourselves immediately from my house." Not your house Doris, our territorial demon master might have some objection to that comment.

I fidget and tuck a piece of sweaty hair behind my ear. "I'm so sorry, did I wake you? I must have had a bad dream. Please forgive me. I didn't mean to frighten anybody," I say, mortified. When all I get in response are dirty looks and poorly veiled anger, my eyes fill with tears.

I know most of these people...while they aren't my family, we have lived together for years. I have never once treated them without kindness and respect. Yet they now look at me like I am a stranger. My heart hurts.

I don't belong. I don't belong anywhere.

For a split second, Riddick takes his eyes away from the hallway crowd to check me over. His bright green eyes meet mine, and he looks haunted. Oh, no, I think I've traumatised the poor hellhound.

"I'm so sorry," I tell him.

"You will be," snarls Doris. She claps her hands. "Everyone else back to bed. I will handle this...this thing." The half-dozen bodies disappear back down the hall...leaving Doris, two guards, Riddick, and me.

I rock from foot to foot as Doris steps aggressively towards me, her pointy finger heading towards my face. I flinch. Riddick's low growl rumbles around us and miraculously it has her remembering herself, and she quickly retreats.

I know if he wasn't here, she would have hurt me.

Her face pinched with fury, Doris pulls her purple dressing gown tighter around herself and crosses her arms underneath her bust. Her eyes flash with the need for retribution.

Oh bloody hell, she is so mad.

"There is an empty room available in the barracks out the back," she spits. "It is vacant during the evenings, as the guards are on the night shift with everyone asleep during the day. That means your attention-seeking screams will have zero effect. You have no care for others, Miss Emma. Your behaviour tonight was appalling, and it proves just how selfish you are. You'd better keep quiet during the day—woe betide you if you disturb anyone else." Her pointing, jabbing finger is back and I cringe at her words. "Your dog guard will not protect you if you do." The guards shuffle and one takes a step back.

The *dog* in question flashes his teeth. I step in front of Riddick in case he bites her. Last time I checked, people don't control what they dream. But I keep my mouth tightly closed and drop my gaze to the floor, attempting to look properly chastised. Which isn't hard to do—I feel horrible. Riddick might not be here next time to keep me safe, and I have to live here. I don't want to make this woman my enemy.

God, I am so embarrassed. I already look a mess, and now everyone knows I am a mess on the inside too. *Broken.*

"Grab your things." Wow, we aren't even waiting for the morning. I look at Riddick, my eyes wide with panic. Oh no, what am I going to do? I dare not tell her I'm not allowed to carry anything. Surely she will think I'm making it up to be difficult.

"I will gather Emma's things," Eleanor says as she glides up the corridor. I breathe out a sigh of relief.

"Thank you, Eleanor, I'm sorry for the trouble." Gosh, not a full night has passed and I've already been evicted from the main house.

Doris huffs and stomps away. Crikey. I shiver. I think if she could, Doris would have marched me out of the main house by the ear or with her foot kicking my bottom with every step. Whew, I am so glad she didn't dare cross the growly Riddick. I never thought I would be grateful for John's intervention, but at this moment I'm grateful for my guards.

"Come on then," Doris snarls from the end of the hallway. I jump and quickly go to follow her, but I am stopped mid-step by a giant furry body. I blink at Riddick in confusion, and in response he drops his head and licks my bare toes.

"Ew," I grumble, wrinkling my nose as I glance down at my now-slobbered-on, wet feet. "Did you have to lick them?" I pat his head. "Good point, though. Let me grab my shoes."

CHAPTER ELEVEN

The demon wants to talk to me—he has called me to a meeting. I don't want to talk to him. Just when I think I've obtained some semblance of freedom, the demon calls me back.

Freedom? Ha. I roll my eyes heavenward at the thought. I've jumped from the demon's frying pan into the hellhound's fire. There's no freedom for me.

No, I'm the pinball in the creature machine—I have a demon flipper on the left and a hellhound flipper on the right. As the ball, I have no hope of going in my own direction and have to instead just allow myself to be bashed about. Fun times.

I dress casually in hospital chic, which comprises comfy leggings and an oversized, slouchy jumper. The softness around the scars on my tummy area is key. My pale blonde hair is a sheet that falls down my back to my waist—it's the only part of me that looks good. When I dressed this morning, my pale face looked gaunt, my cheekbones stood out sharply, and I had bags under my eyes. I had hoped that the sky-blue jumper would bring out the colour of my eyes and make me look less washed out, but it didn't.

Before I step into the room, I anxiously run my fingers around the circular seal on Bert's bag, which is hidden underneath my clothes. It has become a nervous habit: tracing it with my fingertips, double-checking, always checking to make sure the adhesive of the small opaque bag is intact and that it remains tight to my skin. I shoot my elf guard a nervous smile.

Eleanor is accompanying me—when I suggested she didn't have to come, she gave me a badass eyebrow-raise, which I interpreted as, "Are you kidding, I'm your guard."

Silently she nods at the closed door and my head wobbles in response. "Nope, I am not ready," I whisper. "Can't we stay out here?" Eleanor ignores me as she knocks on the door and then opens it. I take a deep breath and step into one of my favourite rooms in the house, the library.

Opulent yet inviting, the library is the only room in the demon's house that hasn't been modernised. I take another deep breath in, and the earthy, sweet-vanilla, musky smell of books fills my senses.

Floor-to-ceiling open oak bookshelves line the walls—shelves full of wonders. Apart from the stables, this is the room where I spend most of my time. The demon is aware of that. I hope he isn't trying to ruin the space for me. I quietly sigh. Probably.

Arlo sits in a throne-like chair. The piece of furniture is bigger and more ornate than the other chairs in the room. It is an unsubtle psychological ploy aimed at manipulating anyone who isn't aware that the demon is the most important person present.

The demon is dressed impeccably in a charcoal custom suit. Most of the time his black hair which is long on top, short on the sides, flops boyishly into his blue-grey eyes. Today his dark hair is gelled back away from his face, highlighting his high cheekbones, delicate nose, and prominent, puffy lips.

Three men that I've never encountered before are sitting around him in a semicircle.

I stop in the centre of the room. "Master, you wanted to see me?" I lower my head and eyes respectfully in a formal greeting.

Out of the corner of my eye, I see Eleanor position herself to my right and slightly ahead of me. She also formally nods and takes up a protective stance.

I have to fight to maintain a serene expression. Gosh, I want to fidget. I've burning questions inside me. But I clamp my lips closed and keep everything I'm feeling off my face. I wear a blank mask. My spine is snapped straight with shoulder blades together and chin held high. I am attempting to be a picture of pure elegance, so I hide my hands behind my back, where no one can see them trembling.

The demon taps his puffy lips once, twice, and moves to sit on the edge of his chair. The energy that surrounds him thrums with excitement. His devious eyes sparkle.

Uh-oh. This will not be a pleasant meeting. Arlo is too excited. Bad things happen when the demon is in a playful mood.

Why does the demon want me here?

I take in the three visitors with trepidation. From their energy, the other men are prominent in status. To be in this room, they would have to be.

Unusually, the men are all from different races: a vampire, an elf, and a shifter. If I said that out loud, it would sound like the start of a bad joke.

The vampire draws my gaze first, and my eyes fall to his nails—eww, his nails. His freaky dirty long nails, which are more like claws as they dig into the padding of the chair. He is ancient-looking, not old in a human way, but old for a vampire. He has lost that vampire vitality that they all seem to have and he looks faded...like a well-preserved mummy, a skull with hair on. He has long brown hair, secured with a bow at the nape of his neck. Yes, a black bow. That isn't the only thing strange about his attire...his black shirtsleeves are lace.

Yes, he looks like a crazy old vampire.

The elf has enormous grey eyes and long blond hair plaited in a style similar to Eleanor's. That's the only comparison I can make between them, as the elf isn't a warrior and he is wearing a suit. His regal bearing might indicate royalty. I tilt my head as I wonder which court.

The shifter is wearing more modern clothing, jeans and a long-sleeved white top that hugs his muscly torso. He sprawls across his chair, his legs wide apart in a classic alpha pose. As I take him in, he hunches forward, leaning on his elbows. His hands dangle between his legs. He hasn't taken his eyes off me since I entered the room, and when he notices my attention, he flexes his biceps. I barely refrain from rolling my eyes. Bloody shifters. I think perhaps he's a cat shifter, as he has a golden mane of hair that reminds me of a lion's. The man's energy is powerful, and before I met the hellhound, I would probably have been terrified of him. But his power level isn't even on the same scale. He can stare all he wants; he doesn't frighten me.

Huh. None of them do.

My eyes snap back to Arlo. With fervour, he has started introductions. "Gentlemen, may I introduce Emma. Unfortunately, since an encounter with a hellhound..." the cadence of his voice, which is customarily marked by a refined English accent, is extra posh today..."she is broken," he adds with a dismissive wave in my direction.

"Broken? Why would we want one of your broken pets?" the elf spits out. I flinch. He sniffs, looking over at me with barely veiled disgust.

"I like broken," Crazy Vampire pipes up, clapping his hands.

The elf continues, ignoring the vampire, "What is she? I can see she could be beautiful, but why would any of us want her?" He stands, adjusts his suit jacket, and glides in my direction. He halts in front of me.

Eleanor deliberately shifts her weight. After a quick glance at my guard, the elf smirks. He doesn't touch me. But he does lean closer, so close our breath mingles. The elf stares deep into my eyes and I confidently stare back.

I am not bloody broken. I am strong and I am brave.

"Yes, she is beautiful. She looks better now with the angry flush on her cheeks. Her eyes are so unusual—multicoloured, exquisite."

My eyes are perhaps another gift from my unknown father. They are different shades of blue, ranging from light sky to dark violet. They change colour. Some days the colour can have multiple hues, depending on my clothing and also my mood.

With a final smirk at Eleanor, the elf glides back to his chair. Once he has taken his seat, the men start a discussion about me. A debate. It's as if I'm not in the room, as if I'm of no consequence.

I fight the urge to fidget, this time with anger. *Keep straight, keep eyes forward, chin high, breathe. Relax.* I repeat my riding mantra in my head. It's kind of apt for this situation. I don't move, and I don't acknowledge them. I have no control. Not yet. But I will. I'm a cool, calm void.

I don't know what has motivated the demon to chair this farce of a *meeting*. But I will not give him any ammunition to use against me.

"Emma is immortal," the demon dramatically declares. With that bold comment, he silences the men. Four sets of eyes take me in. Three now look halfway intrigued. "Yes, immortal. But she can be damaged, and she does not self-heal. I recently found out that her ornate magic allows her to fight the ageing process. My extensive tests have shown that now that Emma is twenty-two-years old, she will stay like this"—he waves at me—"forever."

Ha, that is news to me. *Immortal?* I frown and make a whatever-you-say face. Luckily I catch myself before they notice and school my face back into its blank mask.

Immortal. Why is he lying?

"What is she?"

"What was she bred with?"

"Emma's breeding is a conundrum, such an exciting mystery. She has many talents. She is an accomplished *horse* rider..." he smirks at me.

My nostrils flare. The demon mustn't be aware that Sam bought my horse for me and that Bob is safe. What a dickhead.

"...Dancer, and she speaks several languages. I believe over a dozen." I barely refrain from rolling my eyes—it's two at a push; I can speak French, badly. "Her magical talent is that she is immune to magic. Magic has no impact on her. Absolutely none. Imagine what you can do with that kind of power...she can walk through wards, and magical attacks do not touch her. It is as if the magic tries to avoid contact. She is remarkable, unique."

Eleanor shifts her weight beside me. I glance in her direction, and she returns a contemplative look. I roll my eyes and tuck a wisp of hair behind my ear.

"I could use her as a magical shield?" asks the elf. His grey eyes light up with interest.

"Of course."

"Would those traits pass on to her children?" asks the shifter.

The demon nods. "Perhaps."

"Can I give her more scars?" the vampire disturbingly chirps up. The other men ignore him.

"Now, that is interesting. I would like to see her without clothing," says the shifter. Eleanor tenses and steps further in front of me. "Girl, take off your clothes," he barks.

I lift an eyebrow. *Urm, no, you perve.* I ignore him.

Arlo tilts his head and a small smile tugs at his lips. "Emma, take off your clothes. We're all intrigued by the damage the hellhound made." He pouts with his puffy lips, his eyes gleaming with glee.

My lips part in shock. *What?*

"I like scars," the crazy vampire says with a strange giggle.

I blink at Arlo as if he has lost his ever-loving mind.

"Now, Emma."

Now? Right now, all I want to do is sink into the ground. Fine beads of sweat form on the back of my neck and I feel my cheeks heat with humiliation. The demon smirks at me.

No, no, no, this is a nightmare. I want to cry and I have to chomp viciously at my lip to stop it from wobbling, and my mouth fills with the taste of blood. My eyes desperately fly to Eleanor. Her face is blank and I know instinctively she's unable to do anything to help me. Currently, there's no risk to my body, and I guess there's nothing in her terms and conditions of employment to bodyguard my mind.

I wish Riddick was here.

This whole situation isn't normal—the demon would have never done this before. Now his eyes dance with a sick delight. This is his way of *punishing* me. And it's working.

My entire body trembles. I don't know if I can do this. I don't want these strangers to see me. Bert is private. More private than my skin and bone.

I briefly close my eyes. I can't let them win. I can't. I won't.

I am brave enough, bold enough. If I can survive the hellhound, I can do this. Let them see...let them look. I don't care what they think. People only hurt you if you let them. I will take what they dish out with my head held high.

I'm enough.

My fingertips brush the edge of my jumper...

The door behind me opens. Without looking, I feel the energy in the room shift.

I *feel* him.

Tingles rush up and down my spine, and I tense. His angry energy smashes around the room, an immense wave of crashing power. I brave a peek over my shoulder.

"Why wasn't I invited to this sale?" John asks menacingly.

CHAPTER TWELVE

John prowls into the room, his face a mask of violence as he takes in the seated males. His broad shoulders and rippling torso are highlighted by his tight black fatigues and the sun shining through the windows. My heart misses a beat.

"Gentlemen, this meeting is over," he snarls.

Oh, thank God.

My clamped-up fingers let go of my jumper, and shivers of relief and apprehension work up my spine.

Huh, relief?

I don't understand why the hellhound's presence makes me feel *relieved*. With everyone's eyes on him, I break my rigid, controlled stance and tug at my hair in exasperation.

He didn't hurt me intentionally. I remember the flash of horror in his eyes when he found out I couldn't heal...and he has taken care of me since then. I groan.

God, I'm an idiot. Am I really trying to stupidly convince myself that this is a timely rescue? Do I expect him to protect me? Defend me? Ha.

I let go of my hair as I shake my head. Am I enamoured by the hellhound?

I'd like to at least say my apprehension is from sheer terror...but there is a sick part of me that inappropriately reacts to the low, sultry timbre of his voice.

Oh bloody hell. I blow out a breath. *Come on, Emma, you are being ridiculous.* It is one thing to be attracted to bad boys—something I usually don't suffer from. It's another thing to be attracted to bad men. John Hesketh is a really, really bad man.

At this moment, I need to be honest with myself. No one—no one has made me feel as self-aware as John.

It is like I am cursed.

I swallow and rub my chest. What does that say about me? I know—crap, I know that isn't healthy and I don't understand it. It's wrong. The direction of my thoughts where the hellhound is concerned is wrong on so many levels. What a dickhead I am. It is gross, how gorgeous he is. I look heavenward for patience.

John glares at the shifter. "I'm too old a wolf to be fucked by a kitten." He nods at the exit. "Out." Without further ado, the elf and cat shifter quickly exit the room.

Pure indignation crosses the still-seated vampire's face. "Why?" he whines. "I want to play with the girl. Aren't we going to see her scars?"

"Out!" John roars.

I hunch in response and squeeze my legs together. I have a sudden urge to go to the bathroom.

The vampire giggles. As he rises from his chair, he snarls, "Arlo, you've disappointed me. I always expect lots of fun in your presence. Get rid of the killjoy hellhound and next time, I will arrange the entertainment." As he saunters out of the room, he adjusts his lace sleeves. On the way past my shaking form, he gives me a devious smile. "See you soon, pretty broken girl." The door clicks shut.

The silence in the room is deafening as the hellhound and the demon take each other's measure.

"Let's not lie to one another—we are beyond that now. You and I are evil men." As John speaks, he runs his thumb across his lower lip. It's unsettlingly sexy.

Quit it, Emma.

Lording it on his fancy chair, Arlo lifts his chin in response to John's words and pouts prettily. "John, John, John, you come into my territory, into my *home* without invitation."

He leans forward. "You dare to embarrass me in front of my guests? You dare to threaten me? Me? Shifter, you've gone too far." Between one breath and the next, the demon drops his pretty facade. His eyes slowly bleed black.

I shiver. I hate it when he does that. Like rain, the blackness drips down until it covers his eyes entirely with endless darkness. He flashes huge fangs, and his black eyes glitter. Tilting his head, he leans back in his throne-like chair, and ever so slowly, Arlo claps his hands. "Bravo on your impudence."

In response, John's whole face lights up with a smile. A creepy, familiar, predator smile. "You owe me, demon. Perhaps you are stronger? Perhaps I am…" His eyes glow orange.

Oh crap, bloody hell, this isn't good. My heart hammers in my chest, and as no one is watching me, I take a wobbly step back towards the door. I think I need a nap.

John holds out his hand, and a bright-blue flame appears on his palm. The flame hypnotically dances. I tilt my head to the side, and my mouth pops open. *Oh. That is the famous hellhound magic.* Huh. I wonder if Riddick can do that.

My eyes flick around the room at all the flammable books. I rub the back of my neck. Oh heck, only *that* hellhound would have *this* showdown in the library. Oi hellhound, put the flame away.

I take another shuffling step back towards the door. Each tiny step back is, I hope, unnoticeable with the ongoing drama in the room.

"Your pathetic flame will not work on me, hellhound," Arlo scoffs. "I'm Demon. We are born within the flames. They nourish us. Please, John, lend me your strength." He opens his arms and curls his fingers in invitation. John raises an eyebrow. "Come, boy, you are out of your league."

With the misdirection of the flame, neither the demon nor I notice the knife in John's other hand. That is, until he throws it with impossible force. It flies across the room. The weapon spins end over end through the air, and with a meaty *thunk*, it buries itself in Arlo's shoulder, pinning him like a pretty butterfly to his fancy chair. I blink.

The demon makes a startled noise, and before he can grab the handle, another knife flies, hitting his other shoulder, *thunk*. John's colossal form prowls forward. I take another few steps back. His head snaps towards me. "Stay," he says in a deadly whisper.

My feet freeze. "Okay, no problem. I will stay right here, on this spot," I mumble, pointing to my feet, and then I throw him a thumbs-up. Beside me, Eleanor lets out an exasperated sigh. Unconcerned with me and without further acknowledgement, John continues his almost leisurely prowl towards the pinned demon.

Arlo laughs. "You've been playing warrior for too long, boy. I'm older than time itself, older than this world. Which incompetent idiot told you that these demon blades would influence me? Mhm. Sadly, you have been misinformed. The symbols carved into these blades are useless. I will still be wreaking havoc when this planet is dust. You are useless, pathetic. Spending all your time protecting this world, yet you couldn't protect your pack." Arlo laughs mockingly. "Taking them was shamefully easy. You think these knives can hold me?" In answer, John slams another blade into the demon's left wrist, then another into his right. Another knife in the thigh, then another, until the demon can't move an inch. With each new blade, the demon laughs malevolently.

My whole body shudders. In my desperation, my eyes search out Eleanor for reassurance. The elf is no longer by my side. Instead, she is crouching over the sizeable oriental rug in the centre of the room. With a flurry, Eleanor flips the rug several times, revealing a circle.

A familiar circle.

My legs buckle, and I plop to the floor on my bum. My stomach screams in pain, but all I can do is stare at the circle in horror.

Oh my God.

Desperately I search for something else to look at rather than the ominous circle. I turn my head and instantly regret it as I watch in shock and growing horror as John grips the back of the demon's chair and drags it and its pinned passenger across the library floor. The loaded chair's legs scrape thick gouges into the once-beautiful parquet, and in the demon's wake, dark-green blood drips and smears onto the wooden floor.

Arlo's laughter dies when he sees his destination.

The circle.

He starts to struggle in earnest. He looks so angry, so vengeful, but behind those emotions, I see fear and panic. I hug my knees to my chest. As he struggles, clumps of gelled hair fall into his eyes. With his eyes full of hair and darkness, Arlo has never looked more human. A sob chokes out of me, and my hand flies to my mouth.

My unashamed tears fall.

He's all I've known since I was five years old. The demon ruled my life, but he never truly hurt me. He has always treated me with an odd fairness. All I had to do was follow his rules. Rules that I broke...did I set all this into motion?

Arlo showed me no love, but...but now do I have to watch while the hellhound destroys him? Oh God, I don't know if I can.

John lifts the chair and Arlo over the lines of the circle, I assume to make sure he doesn't damage them. The chair hits the floor with a wobble and as soon as it settles, the circle flashes a bright-white blinding light. I slam my eyes closed. The bright light seers the back of my eyelids. I blink to clear my vision. The symbols on the floor glow and hum.

I can sense the circle's power from where I am sitting, and it makes the hairs on my arms stand up. I run my tongue over my teeth...my teeth ache.

My eyes fly to Arlo and I watch in horror as his face morphs...it *bubbles*. I can see the bones moving as his face rearranges itself into something nightmarish. Gone is the ostentatious pout. He looks more like the pictures in the old books that depict demons. Gone is the pretty face that I have known for seventeen years, and in its place is something *other*.

"I will make restitution. You can have the girl," the demon screams. More of his blood splatters to the floor. Me? He is offering me?

"She is worthless. You were going to sell her. What would I want with the girl?"

"That was a bit of fun at her expense. I saw your guilt... you want her for yourself." The shape of his mouth has changed, so Arlo's voice is rough, guttural.

Are they talking about me?

"Guilt? What you saw was what I wanted you to see. There is no guilt, demon. Just this." John shakes his head and smiles mercilessly.

I rub my chest, God, I'm so stupid.

Arlo glares. "Haven't you worked out what she is? Yes...yes, of course you have—you knew straight away, didn't you. Come on, John—your pack, it wasn't personal; it was business. I had no intention of hurting them. Things happened beyond my control." The hellhound slams another knife into the demon's chest. I pull my knees to my own chest.

My God, where are they all coming from?

After finding the shifter pup locked in that room...I don't know the details of what happened to John's mum and sisters. I don't want to know. I have enough nightmares. But that moment in the hospital, when the demon revelled in their deaths in delighted, whispered words, I knew, without a doubt, that he was responsible.

Even with that knowledge, I still can't watch another creature suffer.

I can't. It's not in me to sit and watch someone be hurt. Not after having suffered the same fate of being subject to John's ministrations.

With determination, I place my palms on the floor, ready to roll onto my knees so I can stand, but a firm hand pushes me back down.

"Emma, no. This has been a long time coming." I flinch as the demon screams. "Do not interfere, don't you dare get up," Eleanor says.

"You used me," I whisper. My voice is hoarse from my tears. "While you pretended to guard me, you were in here making a demon circle, in his home. Weren't you?" I shake my head in disbelief. I throw my arms up in frustration. "I don't know how Arlo let this happen. It was never about guarding me; it was always about gaining access. How could you do this, why would you do this? I can't watch this. I have to help him." I attempt to rise again and she pushes me forcibly back down.

"You will do no such thing. He was going to sell you. If we hadn't interfered, one of those men would have bought you."

"No—"

"Yes. Don't be such a silly little girl. This is how the world works." Eleanor's hand returns to my shoulder in warning, and her fingers dig in. "What do you think you could do? Against John?" She shakes me.

"I could get the guards—"

"What guards? The entire estate is crawling with hellhounds. Wake up, Emma. The demon's rule has ended. You need to pick a side. The right side. The demon would have let you die. John saved you."

I knock her hand away from my shoulder. "John hurt me," I shout. At that declaration, Eleanor shakes her head with disgust. She looks away and blatantly ignores me. "Please, don't let the hellhound do this, Eleanor." I beg, "Please make him stop, please make him stop. I don't want to be here to watch this, please?" The demon screams, and without my permission, my eyes flick back to Arlo. I look.

The floor of the circle is now awash with blood. No-no-no. I shake my head and press the back of my hand to my mouth in an attempt to stop the frightened keening noise as it spills from my lips.

Each time the hellhound uses his knife, my own skin burns.

Oh, God. I don't want to be a witness to this.

Traumatised flashes of my time in the basement superimpose themselves over what is happening to Arlo. I rock from side to side and hug my knees. I could have kept pretending that what John did to me wasn't as bad as my memories. That it was embellished by pain and trauma. Seeing this happen with my own eyes without my shock and pain to shield me, there is no burying the truth. *John is a ruthless monster.*

At the sight of all that blood, part of the innocence that I was doing my best to cling on to—dissipates.

After all the challenges I've had in my life, it comes down to the bare-bone facts. The demon has sheltered me. I heard things...I heard about the horrible things the demon had done. But before I rode out that morning on Pudding, I still thought the world was fair.

I never wanted to see the bad. I wanted to see the light. The beauty.

I wanted the bad things to fly above me, completely over my head, unrecognised in the bright bubble of my life. I wanted to be untouched, untainted.

On purpose, I misinterpreted intentions and situations. I didn't want to see it. I didn't want to see the horrors of what people are capable of. Especially when I could do nothing to help. Powerless.

I held a silly, fixed black-and-white view where I trained myself to see only the good. To see evil and recognise it around me...I didn't want to. I thought it would break me.

Then I met a frightened shifter pup.

After I looked into those green eyes...to ignore the terrible things and to not acknowledge them, it made *me* culpable. It made *me* accountable.

I patted myself on the back for doing the right thing in helping her...when I should have been doing the right thing on countless other occasions.

It is my shame that I didn't act sooner.

Bad things do not stop if *you* don't see them or when you stop watching or stop listening to the whispered *truth*. They are still there, even when you deny their existence and put your metaphysical fingers in your ears.

I'm a hypocrite.

You don't need power to do the right thing. No, doing the right thing *gives* you power.

I struggle again to stand, and Eleanor mercilessly holds me in place.

I watch as the hellhound turns Arlo into pieces of bloody meat, destroying the once-proud demon. As I watch, I remember my pain and my fear at the hands of this man.

I cry.

I cry for the demon who nefariously sheltered me.

I cry for my own inadequacies—my uselessness.

And I cry because deep down inside I know...I know John is *right* and I *hate* him for it.

It takes a monster to destroy a monster.

When it is over, all I can hear is the steady drip-drip-drip of blood. The rough breathing of the hellhound and my own twisted, beating heart. The girl I once was has died, but by God she was clinging on. Clinging on to foolish hope. But in this world full of monsters?

There is no hope here.

CHAPTER THIRTEEN

Glistening raindrops spatter against the window, beading the view. I trace them with my finger.

"Where do you go?"

I turn my head and look at Sam blankly. She frowns and then pokes me. "Where do you go? As you haven't come back yet. I need you to come back. *Bob* needs you to come back."

Well, if my horse needs me...

"Also, Emma? Stop stroking the hellhound, yeah? It's fucking weird. You realise there's some big, handsome, sexy, muscly man underneath all that fur...Oh?" Sam wiggles her eyebrows and gives Riddick and me a lecherous wink. "Never mind, carry on. You keep stroking, girl."

She bounces away, leaving a trail of white shavings like wooden snowflakes behind her. They must have fallen down her boots when she was mucking out and stuck to her fluffy socks.

I quickly snatch my rogue hand away and I blink at the massive hellhound that is leaning against my leg. "I apologise, Riddick. I didn't mean to treat you with any disrespect." My voice is rough from disuse. I twist my hands in my lap and give him what I hope he interprets as a contrite look. He blinks back at me. His head bumps my elbow, and when my arm flops towards him, his cold nose butts at my hand.

Huh, okay then. I put my hand back onto Riddick's head and continue running my fingers through his soft fur.

Since the move to the new house, I've been stuck in my head. John has employed my vampire friend Sam to help me with the horses. The cost of a full-time groom must be excessive, especially with only Bob and the new pony, Munchkin. Sam is used to managing a team of grooms and a yard of over forty horses. I bet she's so bored...but I don't know because I haven't asked her. I sigh and rub my face. I've been a terrible friend. I need to snap myself out of this unhelpful mental darkness.

I am grateful for Sam's help. I can't do much with the hindrance of Bert, and most days I am exhausted. The tiredness hits me at odd times, and so quickly. One second I feel as if I can do everything and the next second, bam, my energy has gone, vamoose; it's vanished like I've hit a brick wall, and there is no way around it. It is so frustrating.

Hopefully I don't have long to wait until my reversal operation with Mr Hanlon. Once everything is back in place, perhaps this horrible tiredness will end.

I shake my head. Some powerful creature I've turned out to be. Every time my mind drifts, I am back in the library doing nothing while the hellhound kills Arlo. I feel ashamed.

I could have fought, tried harder, I could have done more. I hate myself for my non-action, and I hate myself for thinking that the world is a better, safer place without Arlo. It might be true, but who am I to decide that?

Now in my nightmares, Arlo watches on as I relive my time over and over again with John in that basement. He pouts and his black demon eyes glare at me when he tells me, *"You didn't help me. Why should I help you?"*

"Sam's right. I need to spend some time with Bob," I say. I scratch behind Riddick's ear and like a giant dog, his back leg goes. I huff out a laugh. I know he is doing it on purpose to make me smile. "You are one strange shifter."

I groan as I reluctantly get to my feet. I wobble as it takes a second to get my balance. I leave the room and Riddick pads behind me. He patiently waits as I stuff my feet into my boots.

Then we both go outside. Riddick is like my faithful shadow. I don't know when he sleeps, as he always seems to be awake and one step behind me, watching me, watching out for danger. His green eyes are always watching. Instead of it being creepy, he makes me feel safe.

My shadow keeps me safe.

The house. Dear John, of course, came to the *rescue*. My guards moved me and Bob into a pretty five-bedroom house with good equestrian facilities. The sprawling, modern home is on a quiet cul-de-sac. It looks like a doll's house from the front, with white render and a bright red door smack-bang in the middle with windows spaced equally on either side. It's pretty. I believe, from half listening to Sam's gossip, the house used to belong to a professional footballer.

John's continued help is bizarre. I don't know why I am here. It's disconcerting to sleep under his roof and eat his food. I'm forced again to allow my enemy to take care of me. It feels wrong. The last thing I want from the hellhound is any kind of care. I can't get my head around why he feels the need to help me. He did what he needed to do. He got his revenge by killing Arlo. Surely my usefulness is at an end? Yet, here I am. I now feel like the guards are here to keep me from leaving. Ha, they're not here to keep me safe, that's for sure.

I shake my head. I'm so naïve. They've always been a method to control me...I just didn't realise it until it was too late. Arlo didn't realise it either. I shuffle my feet a bit with that thought.

I haven't even been able to look at Eleanor. She makes me sick. She's nothing like the warrior elves in the stories—they protect the innocent and fight for justice. No, she's a hired mercenary, a hired thug. At the snap of the hellhound's fingers, she wouldn't think twice about taking me out. Killing me. In her eyes, I'm filth. Demon-loving filth.

Listen to me. I annoy myself as I'm a hypocrite. I'm quite happy to hate Eleanor but I *stroke* Riddick. Perhaps it's because Riddick wasn't around when things kicked off at the estate? I've noticed he's never about when John is. I've never seen them in the same room. John has probably got something on Riddick—perhaps that is the reason he is being forced to stay in his wolf form. I flick my eyes to regard him with concern. It must be uncomfortable to stay in animal form for so long. I grind my teeth. I wouldn't put it past John to do something so barbaric.

I wander aimlessly around the small, brick, L-shaped stable yard. It has four large stables, With one room for tack and feed. I trace my fingertips across the wooden doors. The stables are immaculate—Sam has already done everything.

A raindrop lands on my cheek. I didn't think to put a coat on and it's still raining. But I don't mind the rain and the nip of the wind on my face reminds me I'm still here, that I am still alive.

Bob and Munchkin are out in the field. Bob saunters over to me when I approach the fence. He checks to see if I have anything for him to eat. When I produce nothing tasty, and his snuffling inspection of my hands and pockets leads to no result, he turns away in disgust and wanders off.

As he snatches at the grass, he gives me a side-eye. "Human, visit only if you offer sustenance," his angry chomping seems to imply.

Munchkin, the cheeky black Shetland, stuffs his entire head through the fencing and attempts to bite me. I step away from his teeth, and when Riddick growls at him, Munchkin pulls his head free, rears up, and waggles his little hooves at us. He then turns and kicks out with both hind legs and runs away with a squeal.

"Little horror." I can't help my laugh; he makes me smile. Sam has him in a tiny lightweight rug and he looks adorable.

"So you've finished moping over the demon," Sam says, wiping her hands on her pant legs as she walks towards us.

Riddick pads away, to a dry spot underneath the overhang of the stables. He is giving us some semblance of privacy to talk. He settles down, head on his dinner-plate-sized paws. I see a flash of tongue and his bright white teeth as he yawns, and then he closes his eyes.

The fine mist from the rain settles on my skin, and a piece of damp hair sticks to my cheek. I scrape at the wood of the fence with my nail. "I wasn't moping, Sam." I grumble, "The hellhound pulled Arlo's head off in front of me. It was...it was bloody grim." I swallow and rub my chest with my knuckles. "I can't sleep without it replaying behind my eyes over and over again. All that blood..." I shiver.

"Yeah, I can understand. That green shit gets everywhere." Sam shudders and wrinkles her nose. "You can't even call that stuff *blood;* it looks and smells bloody awful."

I roll my eyes toward the sky. Not quite the point I was trying to make. Gah, vampires.

"You're better off without him, though...you know that, don't you? He was an evil twat." Sam digs me in the side with her elbow to make her point.

I give her an incredulous look. "Yes, I know he was a bad guy. I'm not used to that level of violence." I lower my voice to a whisper. "I don't know what's gonna happen. Sam, I'm so scared."

"Hey, we are living in a delightful house and you've got your Bob. Just take each day as it comes, Em." She shrugs. "That's all you can do. If the hellhound kicks you out, I've got a place for you. So keep your chin up, kid. It could be worse."

I lean against the fence, my chin on my arms. "Yes, it could be worse," I whisper back.

CHAPTER FOURTEEN

I potter around the stable yard and find a light job of scrubbing the automatic water feeders. They are bowls in the corners of the stables that automatically fill with water. I scoop handfuls into a wheelbarrow I've parked below to catch the water. Then I scrub the already-clean bowls. The bowls do have rubber plugs in the bottom, but they are sealed so tight, I worry that if I even managed to get the stopper free, it wouldn't go back. So I scoop.

My hands are red and almost going blue from the cold water, but I'm determined to do something. I've been trying my best to keep moving without lifting or doing anything heavy. I sigh. To be honest, I get in Sam's way.

Next, I'm going to do the horse feeds.

I hear a strange noise and the hairs on the back of my neck rise. I rub my wet, stinging hands on my jumper and pop my head out of the empty stable.

I count at least a dozen vampires outside the property line. They are heading towards us. "Oh bloody hell. Sam, friends of yours?" I shout. Sam appears from Munchkin's stable with a grooming brush in her hand. She takes in the situation and shakes her head.

"Nope, I don't have friends. Apart from you—only you seem to like me."

Eleanor appears around the corner. With grim determination, she grabs hold of my arm and guides both Sam and me into the feed room.

"Emma, do not move." There is the telltale glow of her warrior mark and with a wave of her hand across the doorway, she sets a ward around the feed room.

Whoa. Two short swords appear in her hands from out of nowhere. I watch with trepidation and a bit of awe as Eleanor goes into warrior mode.

"Vampires, you are trespassing. I suggest you leave with haste or otherwise prepare to die," she shouts as she heads towards them.

"I wonder what film that's out of?" Sam asks as she pokes at the solid, clear fae ward. It looks entirely different from the witch-made wards that I'm used to seeing. I shrug. Eleanor is so badass she can pull off the cheesy line.

"We have no quarrel with you, elf. We just want the girl," a vampire shouts back.

"The girl is my charge. If you want her, you must come through me."

"That's defo bad dialogue from a movie. Ooh, I can't wait for the heads to fly. I love a good fight." Sam claps her hands together and grins. Then she literally presses her nose against the ward. "I bet she gets at least seven before the rest run away. I wish we had popcorn."

"You don't eat popcorn," I say, distracted as the vampires invade the land at the back of the house. Hmm. I can't help thinking, *why* hasn't the house and stable yard got a boundary ward? With an established ward, they wouldn't be able to get so close. It makes little sense.

Eleanor twirls her two swords, perhaps warming up her wrists or as an intimidation tactic. Why she does it isn't as important—it's how impressive it looks.

The vampires flood the grass field and I watch as Eleanor engages them. Suddenly she begins to dance with her twin swords. That's the only way I can describe her movement and fighting skill: a dance. I'm in awe of her talent. Both swords work independently of each other, yet they still work together. The vampires don't stand a chance. Their once-human bodies, although stronger, are no match for the warrior elf as she swiftly cuts through them, one slice at a time. They fall at her feet. I cringe. It's so brutal. At one point Eleanor fights five vampires at once. Instead of it being an advantage to the vampires, they get in each other's way. It makes Eleanor's fluid dance even more dramatic, and it also makes her job easier. Slash, stab, twist. She jumps, and at one point she even rolls, avoiding a deadly strike from behind when a vampire tries to sneak up on her.

"Whoa, she is like a ninja," Sam says in awe.

I feel sick. The hairs stand up on the back of my arms. It is like watching art. Deadly, horrible art. Yet I still can't help worrying about her—the odds are overwhelming.

Even though Eleanor's impressive display and her fighting prowess are making me feel a little queasy, she is risking her life to keep *me* safe. The petty things I have felt about her fade quickly and become insignificant. I respect the hell out of her.

My silly empathy makes me sad for the vampires, though. Whoever sent them, totally sent them unprepared, and the massacre unfolding is a tragedy.

"Ooh," Sam says, her hands now pressed to the ward as well as her nose. I cringe as Eleanor serves a brutal slice across the torso of a big vampire.

"Will some of them recover?" I ask as I twist my hands.

"Yeah, if they get blood in time. As long as they don't lose their heads or get a direct hit to the heart, it's all good," Sam mumbles back, distracted by the gore outside.

There is a growl and a flash of red fur, and Riddick joins the fray.

The vampires scatter then as Riddick's fur—like he has struck a match—lights up with blue flames.

Oh my God. Flaming fur.

Sam lets out an appreciative *ooh*. I won't be able to look at him the same way again. And here I was wondering if he could do a tiny flame on his human hand like John. When he's got enough fire magic to light his fur on fire. Wow.

The fire magic lights up the entire garden with a blue glow. Riddick is like a mini blue sun as he burns and tears into the surrounding vampires.

Yet they keep on coming.

It's then that we hear the voices: "While everyone is busy, why don't we kill the horses?" My eyes widen with horror.

"Oi, if you harm a hair on those ponies, I will rip your ugly faces off," Sam snarls, banging her palm uselessly on the ward. A face appears, and it looks Sam up and down.

"What you gonna do, stuck behind that ward? You can't do shit. Charles, you do the little'n and I'll get the big'n. Horse blood is a proper treat." He licks his lips.

"You fuckers. Leave them horses alone. I will hunt you down, I promise. I will fucking hunt you down. Them horses are not for eating." Sam again slams her hand against the ward with a growl.

With a chuckle and a wave, the vampire stomps away. The other one has already slipped into Munchkin's stable.

The vampire's hand goes to Bob's stable door.

Without me thinking, my own hand lands on the sharp knife, the one we use to open bales of hay and bags of feed. I grab the black handle in my fist.

I'm so livid my vision has gone hazy, almost black. An inhuman growl rumbles in my chest and leaves my throat with a roar.

Whatever Sam is saying—shouting—is totally outside the bubble of my rage. At the forefront of my mind is *Bob*. My full attention is honed in, and all I can see is that vampire.

I growl again and shoulder Sam out of my way.

I step through the ward.

CHAPTER FIFTEEN

The vampire steps into the stable. Distressed by the stranger's sudden entry, Bob backs up against the far wall. His ears are pinned back and his eyes roll wide, showing the white. Bob snorts, nods his head, and paws at the ground. Instinctively, my boy knows this vampire is out to do him harm. "Be a good boy, let's see how you taste," the vampire says with a chuckle and a smack of his lips. He moves towards my Bob.

On silent feet, I slip into the stable and creep up behind him. No one threatens my horse. I hold in the angry growl that wants to rise and rip itself out of my chest. Without thinking, I lift onto my toes. I reach out and grab the vampire's hair. I grit my teeth, jerk him back, and with a tilt of my wrist, I run the blade across his neck.

I slice his throat.

I cut cleanly through his carotid and trachea. His only sound is a sharp intake of breath, then a gurgle.

His hands fly to his throat in an attempt to stem the bleeding. I let go of his hair. The vampire turns. His panicked eyes search for the threat and he finds me. When he takes in my expression, his hazel eyes go wide with fear. With a snarl, I circle him. Protectively, I put myself between him and Bob. I let the growl I've been holding in rumble.

I. Am. Livid.

Sweet Emma isn't home at the moment.

I boldly step forward and push him. He stumbles away from me, but not as fast as I would like. I shove him again, *hard*. I force him out of the stable, away from my horse. The vampire hits the doorway on his way out, wobbles for a second, and then sinks to his knees. Dispassionately, I note that he is struggling to breathe. He wheezes and chokes, and blood bubbles from his lips.

Another growl leaves my own lips. I kick away his legs so I can quietly close the stable door. Leaving him on the floor outside, I step over his prone, gasping form.

Munchkin.

My lips curl back, and I bare my teeth.

The second vampire has had little luck with getting hold of the feisty Shetland pony. My head tilts to the side as I watch him chase the pony around the stable...until he isn't and the pony turns and chases him. The vampire lets out a squeal. "This thing is nuts. Patrick, what do I do? It's trying to bite me," he shrieks, unaware that his buddy *Patrick* is a little preoccupied. Munchkin chases him towards me, and he runs into my knife.

He runs into my knife six times.

* * *

"Emma, are you okay?"

Sunlight streams through the stable door. One stripe catches my face and arm in its golden light. I blink. Sticky, warm, dark-red vampire blood clings to my hands and arms. One hand tightly grips the black handle of the dripping blade. My other hand drifts up. I hold it up to the sunlight. The blood glistens, and it makes sticky webs as I open and close my fingers.

"Emma, are you okay?"

Blood covers me. I pant with exertion.

My eyes drift down to the body at my feet. Munchkin gives the vampire a good kick, and his head rolls to the side. I get a good look at his glassy, dead eyes.

"Are you okay, stabber?" Sam shouts again from the feed room. Her words finally register through my slowly fading rage. The blackness clears from my eyes. I nod, even though she can't see me. My head keeps nodding on its own, it won't stop.

Oh my God. What did I do?

What did I do?

Uncontrollably, my hands shake. I must have stabbed him in the heart. I hold the knife out in front of me, extra careful not to stab myself. My knees knock together. "Bloody hell," I whisper. "Oh bloody hell, what did I do?"

Munchkin ignores me...and the dead vampire on the floor. He goes back to eating his hay as if nothing has happened.

"What the hell did I do?"

"Incoming," Sam shouts. Dazed, I walk out of the stable and encounter two more vampires. I wobble on my feet, and I clutch the blade in front of me in a tight, sticky fist.

Oh, hell. Where's the rage and the blackness now when I need them? I tremble. Oh no, I can't do this again...I can't do *that* again.

Riddick comes out of nowhere and barrels into the vampires. His teeth flash, and his massive claws rend the vampires' flesh. Blood splashes. The vampires don't have time to react. No time to scream.

My whole body trembles. I rock on my feet, heel-toe-heel-toe.

"Good job, Emma," Sam yells.

God, I feel sick.

Eleanor comes out of nowhere and gets in my face. "You were supposed to stay in the feed room," she chastises. "What were you thinking?" I continue to rock.

I wasn't thinking.

With a wave of Eleanor's hand, the ward on the feed room drops and Sam is released. "Oh, fuck—look at all the vampire bits. They're all over," Sam grumbles. Her nose wrinkles as she peeks over Bob's stable door. "Look at the stable floors. I'm gonna have to hose both the boxes down and disinfect." With her hands on her hips, she continues, "The field is also a mess. I hope I get a clean-up team to help with all the goo."

The words *vampire bits and goo* circle around in my head. I lean forward, and I only miss not throwing up on Eleanor by a whisker.

When I've finished, I go to rub my mouth...only to freeze at the state of my hands. My bloody hands. I can't wipe my mouth. I look forlornly at my trembling, bloody, murdering hands. "I better get cleaned up," I mumble.

"Yeah, killer, go wash your hands," Sam helpfully pipes up. "The heathens were gonna hurt the ponies," she tells Eleanor.

"Bob's a horse," I mumble.

"What arseholes. I got this, Em—I think you've had too much excitement for one day. I can hear your heart from here, it's going nuts."

"I am furious with you. Putting yourself at risk like that," Eleanor continues with a *tut*. It's as if I haven't just sprayed her shoes with puke.

"I'm sorry," I whisper. "I didn't mean to make your job harder." *I'm also sorry for the horrible things I've been thinking in my head about you.* But I don't say the words as it would only make the whole situation worse. I've been judgmental and unkind.

"Well, I understand your need to protect your horses," Eleanor says gruffly. At that moment, the vampire whose throat I first slit groans.

"Is he going to be okay?" I ask.

In response, a sword appears in Eleanor's hand. Light on her feet, she turns. There is a high-pitched noise as the sword sings through the air. She slashes the blade in a downward arc. It meets the vampire's neck at the perfect angle, just above his clutching hands. In its wake, the blade paints a fan of blood on the wall of the stable. The vampire's head topples to the floor with a *squelch*.

I wobble. Okay, urm, I guess that answered that. I cough to clear my throat. Pieces of loose hair that have escaped my ponytail blow in the slight breeze. I avoid looking at the vampire. Instead, my eyes fixate on the blood dripping down the wall.

My chest hurts. I killed a man today. I've stepped over a line and into the realm of being a killer.

The sound of paws padding, claws clicking on the concrete gains my attention. I lift my eyes. Angry energy swirls around Riddick. His ears are held flat to his head and his tail is tucked. He prowls towards me.

Blood covers the fur on his face. His nostrils flare as his nose meets mine. He snuffles at me. When I attempt to wiggle out of his way, his growl blows the wisps of hair back from my face, and I make the mistake of inhaling and get a mouthful of Riddick's *meaty* breath. I gag. "Eww, your breath smells of dead vampires." Riddick growls again and shows me a mouthful of enormous teeth. My entire face scrunches up in disgust, and I turn my head away. I'm sure I saw bits of vampire stuck between his teeth. "Riddy, I'm going to puke again if you don't get your bloody face away from me." Riddick huffs out another stinky breath as he continues his smelling inspection. "Stop it." I smack his nose away from Bert. "Stop it, I'm fine, they didn't hurt me. Stop breathing on me...stop sniffing me. It's gross."

"Em, fuck...urm, maybe you shouldn't smack the *hellhound* in the face," Sam squeaks out, her voice full of horror. I wave her concern away.

"I left Emma inside the feed room, behind a protective fae ward. She then left the ward of her own volition, to intervene in an attack on her horses," Eleanor says.

Riddick growls, again showing me his teeth. Not caring about my bloody hands, I grab his muzzle and close his mouth. I look into his angry eyes.

"I'm not sorry. I couldn't let them hurt Bob and Munchkin. I used the knife in the feed room, and I…" my voice drops to a whisper and my eyes fill with tears…"I stabbed them, stopped them. I'm…not…sorry." I swallow a sob, wobble and rock again. "Riddy, I killed someone." Riddick looks at me with understanding. His green eyes are full of compassion.

My hands fall away from his nose as he moves his colossal body to my side. His soft fur brushes against me, and he wraps himself around me. Warm, supporting. I take comfort in his nearness. After a few minutes, I gently pat his head. "I need a shower." I wobble away. My teeth chatter, and with each step, my body screams at me to rest. Nobody stops me. I can only assume that it is now safe. I need a shower.

This newly made *monster* needs to wash the blood from her hands.

CHAPTER SIXTEEN

I'm quietly reading on the sofa, diligently doing my best to ignore Riddick, who is attempting to get my attention. Nope, it's not happening, this book is way too good. The throw cover that I have over me jerks and ever so slowly moves. Out of the corner of my eye, I see Riddick has the cover gripped between his teeth. My lips twitch. I roll my eyes, grab it, and hold on.

Ha, I don't stand a chance in a one-handed tug of war with a hellhound. Riddy does a big jerk and the cover flies from my grip and pools on the floor. His dinner-plate-sized paws stomp all over it. I huff to cover my giggle and turn my entire body away.

Way too close for comfort, Riddick moves so he stands over me. Nose in the air, I continue to ignore him and pretend to read my book. Instead, I watch him. He has a glint in his eye and an evil doggy grin on his face. From this angle he looks even larger, which is a neat trick considering that he is already huge.

In revenge for my non-action, weirdo Riddick leans across and licks my face. His great dirty tongue licks me from my jaw to my forehead, catching the side of my mouth. I dramatically spit and scrub at my mouth. "Eww. Eww. Eww. Oh my God, you did not just do that. Eww," I wail, shuddering as I frantically rub at the rest of my wet face with my sleeve. "Riddick, you are a minga. That was so gross...you are a shifter, not a dog." I attempt to smack him with my book, almost falling off the sofa in my zeal. Riddy jumps from side to side, avoiding my blows, a smug and delighted wolfy grin on his face. "Bloody Riddick," I grumble, doing a poor job of hiding my smile.

Hellhound or not, I love the stupid creature.

"John has arranged a meeting with an angel," Eleanor says as she glides into the room.

I stop my assault on Riddick and blink up at her. I am currently hanging off the sofa. I huff and blow at a piece of my hair that's fallen from my ponytail and is now sticking in my right eye. I sit up with wobbly arms and give Bert an apologetic pat. Eleanor now has my full attention. What? An angel?

"Me? Why do I need to see an angel?"

"To heal you, of course," she replies. Heal me? An *angel* can heal me? Huh.

I wiggle and my book falls to my side, forgotten. Excitement and disbelief thrum through me. I've never seen an angel. Like demons, they have to be of a high level of power to be on Earth. They aren't native creatures of this world.

The ley lines that form the witches' transport gateway system are also gateways to other worlds. It's all a bit hush-hush. I only know this because I listened to the whispers at the estate, and I spent a lot of time with a demon. Only the powerful come to Earth, as they have to have the political clout in their world to do so.

Angels aren't like religious depictions of angels, but some believe that both races, angels and demons, had input into early human and creature history...poking their noses into our evolution, nudging us all in their preferred direction. Angels are as scary as demons. Perhaps if there is a creature that might heal me, an angel might be the one?

I scratch the side of my head. My ponytail is lopsided and more hair has come loose. To gain an audience with an angel is an impressive feat. I pull the bobble out of my hair to re-do my ponytail. I don't know why John wants to waste the opportunity on me...especially as there is a high risk of the magic not working. Then again, John is a hellhound—I shrug as I gather my hair and pull the elastic tight—so maybe he's best mates with everybody and I'm just overthinking things. Perhaps I might get information...information about what kind of creature I am.

"I will go get changed," I say with a bright smile. The thought that I might be able to go to the loo normally is a huge motivator. I stumble on the cover as I get up and use Riddick's enormous head to steady myself. "Thanks for that, big-head," I say with a cheeky grin. With a playful growl, Riddick nips at my bum as I hurry past.

"Ten minutes," Eleanor shouts at my scurrying back.

The house hasn't got a gateway, so we will have to drive to the angel. I make sure I have a fresh hot-water bottle handy. The heat will help me if I have any tummy pain on the way.

Twenty minutes later—as I had to check on Sam and the boys—we pile into the car and set off on a new adventure.

Thirty minutes into the drive, I'm fiddling with my phone, so I don't see the other vehicle when it hits us.

There's a sudden burst of impact. Time slows as my body slams into the seatbelt. My phone flies from my hand. I'm torn between protecting Bert and protecting my face. My stoma wins, and I hug my tummy protectively with my arms. Another bang. My head jolts to the side, and the pain in my side and stomach is excruciating. White-hot. My seatbelt keeps me painfully anchored in place, burning my shoulder and chest.

I whimper.

Crunch.

Weightlessness. I feel like we're in a washing machine as the car flips, over and over. I scrunch my eyes tightly closed as the window next to me splinters and glass flies, the tiny shards stinging my face.

My vision and hearing reverberate like I'm underwater as the car settles on its side. I blink and groan. It sounds distorted to my ears. My head throbs, and with a shaky hand I touch an incredibly sore spot on my temple. My fingertips come away wet with blood. I'm hanging sideways. I blink and try to focus my dizzy vision on the condition of the other occupants of the car, but both Eleanor and Riddick are *gone*.

What...where did they go?

With a *whoosh*, my hearing comes back. Outside the car I dimly hear fighting, the hiss and singing of Eleanor's swords, Riddick's growls. Then the tick-tick of the engine, the crackle of metal, glass, and plastic as the car continues to settle.

I take a deep breath to control the frantic beating of my heart. I'm unsure about modern cars and engine fires, and it might be my imagination, but I'm sure I can smell smoke.

Oh bloody hell. I decide it is safer to get out. I remove my seatbelt, grip it, and do a controlled slide across the seats until I stand on the crushed passenger door. The plastic and glass crunch underneath my feet and I use the headrests for balance. I slip my boot off and wobble on one foot as I surreptitiously use it to knock the shards of glass away from the broken side-window now above me. I feel like an idiot for what I need to do next.

I'm going to have to pop my head up into the line of fire.

Crap, it'll be like sticking my head out of a rabbit hole, hoping that a predator will not bite it off.

Boot safely back on, I tuck my hands into the folds of my jumper. Fingertips lightly on the windowsill, I take a breath, brave it, and peek out.

Vampires.

Oh bloody hell, the vampires are back.

It looks as if Eleanor and Riddick have drawn the vampires further away from the car and me. I duck back down and puff out a nervous breath. My heart pounds. *Thud-thud-thud.* God, I feel sick. *Come on, Emma.* I silently count down from three. When I hit *one*, I force myself to leave the vehicle.

I somehow manage to scramble out with no one seeing me. The car roof squeals as I slide down it, and I land on the road in a heap. I slam my back against the car. Then I let out a frightened squeak as the car rocks a little with the impact of my body weight.

Oh bloody hell.

Thud-thud-thud goes my heart. I pant, and my arms tremble from the exertion of getting out of the car. My head throbs and my crazy heart rate makes me feel dizzier. The residual pain from the accident throbs through me, and combined with my overwhelming panic, it makes it hard to think.

"It's okay, you're okay." I compartmentalise and swallow down my pain. I push it to the back of my head. I know pain, I can deal with pain. I can do this. I don't have a choice. I take a deep, shaky breath and force myself to be calm. I lift my jumper and do a visual check on Bert. Luckily, my stoma has no immediate issues. God, I am lucky to be alive.

I get on my hands and knees, tuck my head, and crawl.

The car that hit us is burning, and dark, rancid smoke billows around me. Shards of glass glitter on the tarmac like diamonds in front of me, and unavoidable they bite painfully into my knees and palms. I quickly crawl away from the fighting and the car, desperately searching for somewhere safe to hide.

Out of the corner of my eye, I catch a droplet of red.

Oh no, my head wound is dripping. With horror, I look back at the small trail of blood drops that lead away from the car. Oh God, I'm leaving a ruby-red trail of breadcrumbs. I swallow a sob. What a stupid mistake, with all the vampires. I rub as much blood as I can from my face onto my jumper and keep going. There is nothing I can do about it now.

Oh God, vampires, please don't smell me.

I crawl into someone's legs. I close my eyes and hunch over into a ball. I should have stayed in the car. "There you are, pretty demon," a male vampire says.

My heart drops. Oh bloody hell, not this demon shit again.

The vampire scoops me up. I don't stand a chance against his strength. Before I even think to scream for help, his hand slams over my mouth. My nostrils flare in panic as I try to get enough air into my lungs.

As he drags me towards a generic white van parked at the side of the road, he licks the blood from the side of my face. Gag. He hums and smacks his lips as if he is at a wine-tasting. "Huh, so that's what a demon tastes like. Not as bad as they have led me to believe. See you later, pretty demon." With a last lick and a creepy chuckle, he throws me unceremoniously into the back of the van.

I hit the metal floor with a *crack*, my knees taking the brunt of the impact, ouch. The van's back doors slam closed. Waiting hands grab hold of me, and a bag...they shove a smelly black bag over my head.

Darkness.

With every panicked breath I take, the thick material of the bag moves closer to my lips. I tremble as they tie my hands together in front of me. Painfully tight, the plastic digs into the scars on my wrists.

The click of chains. I shudder as a terrible memory tries to take me.

The van jerks, and suddenly we're in motion. I squeak as I'm thrown against the side panel. The impact knocks my already-sore head. I try my best to brace myself, protecting Bert as much as I can. But I slide and bump around. I let out a frustrated cry. My bruises will have bruises. Before I can slide again, I'm gripped by big, heavy hands, and I'm lifted. Warmth surrounds me from behind as I'm nestled into a stranger's lap. My kidnapper's lap. Solid thighs pin me against an equally solid chest. I shake with fear.

"I couldn't watch you bashing about anymore. You looked so pathetic. Settle down, lass, I won't hurt you. I won't let anyone else hurt you either, so just relax. This will be over soon."

"Where are you taking me?" I whisper. But this stranger with this smooth-as-chocolate voice doesn't answer. He just holds my shaking, frightened body tighter.

I'd like to say that when the doors of the van finally open with a grinding metal clank and a creak, I spring into action like a ninja and fight like hell.

But I don't.

If I hadn't been in a similar situation before, perhaps I'd be brave and be able to fight. But all I remember is the pain, and every day, all I see is the physical reminder of my last kidnaping stamped all over my body—in Bert and a network of scars.

This is all too soon. This is all too much. I can't do *this* again. I won't.

Everything fades: thought, worry, emotion. I retreat to a protective place in some deep corner of my mind that I've never found before. I stop trembling. The big guy who has held me steady during the journey guides me carefully out of the van. My body is being helped out of the vehicle, but I'm not currently here.

Like a coward, I've hidden in the dark recess of my mind.

My elbow is gripped, and I meekly follow. When I'm pushed down into a chair, I automatically sit. When the bag is tugged from my head, my eyes automatically respond to the bright overhead light. I blink.

I don't acknowledge the sound or the surrounding movement—I can't. Fingers click in front of my nose, but I don't respond. Hidden safely away in my mind, I curl into a ball.

My body sits in the chair, my eyes unfocused, my heart beating steadily in my chest. A hand slaps me across the face, and my head turns to the side with the impact.

A loud noise, yelling, crashing, banging.

Silence.

CHAPTER SEVENTEEN

Fur. Fur underneath my fingertips, so soft. *Safe*. My fingers twitch of their own accord, they flutter across the familiar softness. My head tips forward, and the darkness recedes.

I blink.

My senses rush back, the cold bite of the unyielding metal chair beneath me, the sharp smell of bleach.

I'm cold. I'm hungry. I'm thirsty. My body aches. How long have I been sitting here?

I blink. The sight of cream-and-red fur fills my vision. Riddick. He sits in front of me. There's fresh blood on his muzzle, and darker dried blood is mixed with his soft fur. Oh, no—I jolt when I see it. A silver collar is around his neck.

Shock and fear flood me, and with that potent hit of adrenalin, everything around me becomes more focused.

"Riddy," I whisper, my voice hoarse. I lick my dry lips. I hiss when I try to lift my hands to touch the collar and my wrists chafe against tight plastic. My frightened gaze drops to my hands. I can't lift them more than an inch as the vampires have secured them to the arms of the chair. I'm trapped. I'm trapped. Oh God, I need to get out of this chair. I need to get out. I struggle in vain and thrash about until the pain of my desperate movements registers. It bleeds through my panic and I notice that my entire body is screaming in protest. Ouch.

I pause, panting. My rapid breaths whoosh in my ears and I barely swallow down a scream that wants to bubble up from inside me. I force myself not to struggle and instead I close my eyes and compel myself to breathe through my rising hysteria.

No, breathe slow. It's okay, it's okay. Save your energy. I want to scoff at my thoughts. Energy? Ha. What bloody energy? Just breathe.

This is happening. I have to deal with it. I have to be brave. I have to think through the desperate, raging panic that is clawing at my insides.

If I don't, I'm dead.

Everything happens for a reason, even the horrible stuff.

But why me? the little voice in my head whines. Why not you—would you really want someone else to suffer in your stead? No, I would not. Riddick needs me.

God, please give me the strength to be brave. If not for myself, then for Riddick.

I slowly count down from ten. When I get to one, I take a shuddering breath in, and then I open my eyes.

Riddick limps away from me. He offers me no further comfort; he just whimpers and then curls into a ball in the corner of the room. He won't look at me. My lip wobbles and my heart drops like a stone. To see my growly, brave friend so defeated is *horrific*. He is the picture of total misery. I am suddenly ashamed, and so embarrassed at my panicked reaction. Riddick is truly suffering, while in reality I'm only tied to a chair. *You are pathetic, Emma.*

Hell, what have they done to him?

I know little about silver and its effect on shifters. I know that silver stops the shift. The memory of when I first saw the hellhounds with all their silver weaponry comes to me and only adds to my confusion. Why carry silver weapons when contact with it makes you weak? My head throbs. What is the silver collar around his neck doing to him? Can it kill him? If his whimpers are any sign, it must cause him pain.

"Riddy, are you okay? Is...is Eleanor okay?" In response, Riddick soulfully whines.

Oh my God.

As if his whine was a signal, a lock disengages and the bang of metal makes me flinch. The door opens behind me and the sound of heavy footsteps precedes two men as they saunter into the room.

The cell.

From his corner, Riddick growls.

My eyes flick about as I take in the bare cell-like space. My chair is the only piece of furniture and it is positioned in the centre of the room. I can't help the all-over body shudder that wracks me as my eyes take in and then skitter away from the drain underneath me. I clamp down hard on any thoughts on why they would need a drain. I shudder.

"Are you awake, buttercup?" Fingers click aggressively in my face. "I knew a little rub from the hellhound would get your attention." The guy who is talking has a horrific nasal voice. He isn't a vampire—no, he is a shifter, which is a surprise. Dark hair and sharp features. He gives the impression, as he looks down his pointed nose at me, that I am an inconvenience on what should have been a perfect day.

I keep my expression blank, take a shaky breath, and lift my chin. I can't help thinking: *Sorry, pal, undo me so I can leave. Sorry that my kidnapping and being here tied to this bloody chair has ruined your day.* But smartly, I keep those words firmly locked inside. I am in enough trouble.

"See the state of your hellhound? If you don't answer my questions..." He smirks, leans forward, and whispers in my ear, "I'll let you use your imagination on that one." His fingers brush against my left hand and I flinch. His eyes light up, and almost nose-to-nose, he purrs.

Oh, now he is interested in me. I lean as far away from him as I can. "Breath," I mumble, and I wrinkle my nose in distaste. His eyes flash in anger and he lifts his hand as if to hit me. There is an almost inaudible growl. I close my eyes in readiness for the blow, but it doesn't come.

"Just think, I was going to go soft on you, give you a time-out and a drink of water. Let's do this," he snarls.

He steps away. I gasp and my heart skips a beat at the sight of the trolly. He has a trolly full of *bad things*.

A wheel squeaks as it rolls across the uneven floor and the things clatter, clink and knock together. They glint in the harsh overhead light. I try to shrink away, but the unyielding metal chair I am tied to keeps me firmly immobile, as it's bolted to the floor.

I can't speak, I can barely breathe as my mind starts to shut down. More adrenaline and fear cloud my head, and I vaguely recognise that I'm going into shock.

He claps his hands, and I jump at the sound. "Oi, you disappear again and you'll never see him again, so stay with me." He nods in Riddick's direction.

Eyes gleaming, he runs his fingers almost reverently across the *things* on the tray. The shifter carefully separates each item so I can see them. Wide-eyed, I swallow.

His hands are delicate for a shifter, hands that are no doubt unafraid of getting dirty, bloody. He selects a knife, and he shows me the silver blade by waving it in front of my face. He smirks at me as he stands, his eyes now alight with cruel amusement. I tremble. His hand drops and he taps the Rambo-style knife against his thigh. It's big and solid, and the edges are serrated, with a blood groove down the middle.

Tap, tap. Tap, tap.

I nod, swallow, and lift my eyes away from the blade to his face. I look directly into his mean brown eyes. He is going to use that stuff to hurt Riddick, to hurt me. Oh, God. I shake, and my teeth chatter.

In desperation, my gaze skitters away from the threat of the man with the knife. I turn my frightened eyes away from him and focus on the other man who is in the room.

Is he safer?

My bound hands' jerk. He is John-level beautiful, but he doesn't stir me the way John's frightening beauty does. The way John makes me feel is almost magical—and I don't mean in a good way. Magical like a curse. It's like I've been cursed whenever I'm around him.

God, I hope the hellhound isn't angry when he realises his guards have failed. I worry for them if we're lucky enough to get out of here, to live through this nightmare. John is another scary obstacle to overcome. The man won't accept failure.

I drop my thoughts about John and focus back on the handsome face. Dark hair and pale honey-coloured eyes stare intently back at me. He stands quietly as he casually leans, resting a booted foot against the wall, arms folded across his chest as he observes me. I do the same and observe him right back, my head tilted to the side in contemplation. He isn't a shifter, a vampire, or a demon. I'm not a hundred percent sure, but I don't think he's fae either. The power coming off him in waves is...familiar. Even though I never saw his face, I'm pretty sure he is the man in the van that held me in his arms.

Angel? Could he be? What the hell is going on...

He pushes away from the wall and meanders towards me. The shifter backs away, giving him room. He crouches down in front of my chair. Being deliberate in not touching me, he grips the metal arms of the chair and leans forward. His honey gaze flicks up to my eyes, to the side of my head, my cheek, and then back. His eyes stop moving, as though he's focusing with everything he has on maintaining eye contact. Somehow I know he doesn't like what I presume is the smear of blood from my head wound and the bruises that are smattered achingly across my face.

"Save the hellhound some pain and tell us what we want to know," he says. As soon as I hear his voice, I know he is the man from the van.

I drop my eyes and look at my lap. I gnaw on my lip. It's a simple decision: I need to do everything in my power to keep Riddick safe. I lift my eyes. "You promised you wouldn't hurt me," I whisper. "You lied." His honey eyes flick again to my throbbing cheek. Someone, perhaps the shifter, hit me.

I push down my fear inside me and gather the tatters of my courage. "I will answer your questions...if I can. But I have one of my own." The honey-eyed man narrows his eyes in disappointment. Like someone's turned off a light switch, the softness in his eyes disappears, replaced with distrust. I shiver.

Crap, I've lost whatever rapport we had and I've disappointed him. *Way to go, Emma.*

"Go on," he growls.

Permission granted. Oh hell, in for a penny, in for a pound. I release my sore lip from between my teeth. "The warrior elf that we were with...is she okay?" I husk out.

The honey-eyed guy takes a sharp breath. I don't know why he is surprised—Eleanor is my guard, and she was protecting me. I need to make sure for my own sanity that she is okay.

"Yes. Last time I checked, she was fine."

I allow myself a deep, shaky breath of relief. "Okay, well, good, that's okay. Thank you." He stands from his crouch and moves away. He lifts his chin and nods at the other guy, the shifter.

Okay, let the questions—hopefully, sans torture— commence.

Riddick growls. My eyes slide in his direction. But the shifter with the knife, the guy who wants to interrogate me, clicks his fingers in my face to gain back my attention. "Eyes on me, demon."

Demon. I let out a sad-sounding sigh and look at him.

"Don't lie to me as this guy here will know..." He tilts his head and nods towards Honey Eyes "...and I'm very skilled in getting the truth." He smiles as he runs his fingertip lovingly against the shiny new blade of a box cutter. "Where did you come from? Who sired you?"

Oh, the straightforward questions. "I was born in Preston, Lancashire. Twenty-two years ago. I don't know who my dad is or what race he is." I shrug. My throat is so dry. I swallow the roughness and keep talking. These questions are simple. I can do this. "My mum wanted eternal beauty, so when I was five, she sold me so she could skip the vampire waiting-list. A first-level demon bought me." My wrists ache and I want to rub them, but I can't because I'm tied to this bloody chair. I drop my eyes and look. My thin wrists are red from my struggle before and the pressure of the tight plastic.

Fingers click again in front of my face. I lift my eyes. I wish he wouldn't keep doing that. "Keep talking," he snaps. When I don't answer him quickly enough, the shifter interrogator drops his hand and touches my knee. I let out a squeak of protest, and at the same time Riddick *and* the honey-eyed angel growl. The shifter looks in the angel's direction and smirks. He must see something hazardous to his health as within seconds he snatches his hand from my leg and he's backing away from me with his palms up in surrender. He lets out a creepy laugh. The skin underneath my leggings crawls from the memory of his touch. He gives me the creeps—there is something fundamentally wrong with him.

"Keep talking," he snaps again.

I lick my dry lips. I feel like I have a throatful of sand. "I was in the demon's household until a week ago. Then, Arlo, the demon died."

"Died or was killed?" the honey-eyed angel asks. My head swings in his direction.

"Killed. He was responsible for the deaths of a hellhound's pack and the hellhound took his revenge," I answer matter-of-factly, with a small, awkward shrug.

"John Hesketh?"

"Yes."

"He questioned you about his missing pack?"

I swallow and nod. He lifts his eyebrow; I guess he needs to hear the words. My whole body trembles, and my wrists scream in pain at the involuntary movement as my arms jerk. For a second, I close my eyes. "T-tortured me for the information, yes," I stutter out.

"Did you know anything about their disappearance?" God, this whole thing is like deja vu. I have answered these questions before—John's. I don't understand what the connection is and why these men want to know about John.

"Yes," I whisper.

"*What?*" The sharp-featured man snaps. Oh boy, it looks like he wants my full attention. I turn my head back towards him. He has moved closer, and the box cutter is pointing in my face.

Almost going cross-eyed with my eyes on the blade, the words spill from my lips. "I found a shifter female in wolf form locked in a room on the estate. I helped her to escape. When I handed her over, that was when I first met John..."

The questions keep coming, and I answer them. With each question, Riddick *paces*.

"Do you know what you are?"

"I'm half human."

On and on, more questions. Like some angelic lie detector, the angel interrupts for clarification or confirms to the other man that what I'm saying is the truth.

My head hasn't stopped throbbing since the car crash. The bright light and the almost-overpowering stench of bleach don't help, and my poor belly pulses with pain.

But I don't lie.

After what feels like hours, the angel finally gives me some water, and then both men leave the room. As soon as the door locks, my attention goes to Riddick. He isn't doing so good. The silver must be painful. He has stopped moving. He lies in the far corner of the room. Despondent, he stares at the wall. "Riddy," I whisper urgently.

Oh, crap. I have to get the silver collar off him. It must be killing him. Perhaps when he is free, together we can get out of here. I tug at the plastic binding me securely to the chair. Ouch.

I remember reading if you hold your hands up above your head and then quickly bring them down sharply while pulling your hands apart with a twist, you can snap plastic ties. But being stuck in this chair is a different matter.

I stare at my right wrist and grit my teeth, as this is going to hurt. I put on my brave pants and tug and twist my right arm. The plastic bites into my wrist. Blood dribbles. My poor abused abs scream at me to stop. But desperation makes me ignore the pain. I keep pulling. I keep twisting, keep tugging. Blood trickles down my wrist. *Come on, come on.* "Come on, damn you," I growl. The plastic on my right wrist snaps.

Bloody hell, I did it.

I wobbly stand up, my body screaming and my joints painfully crunching at the movement.

Ow. Gosh, I move like an old lady...I must have been in that chair for hours.

I nibble my lip; I need to be careful. With a painful stretch of my leg, I stick it out. Huh, the tip of my boot can just...just touch that awful trolly. My left eye squints as I slowly, oh so slowly, drag the handily left-out torture trolly towards me. I grab some nasty-looking clippers that I have been eyeing for hours. With a clip and a snap at the plastic on my left wrist, I'm finally free from the chair.

With a quick pants-rub, I smudge the dripping blood from my wrist. In a shaking hand, I grip the clippers, and with determination I limp across the room, intent on nipping that horrible silver collar apart.

"It's okay, Riddy, I'm going to make you better," I whisper.

My fingertips stroke Riddick's soft fur away from the atrocious collar. Before the clippers have even closed around it, a seamless catch hidden within the collar clicks and it swings free.

I catch the collar before it hits the ground, and as soon as my hand closes around it...I belatedly realise it isn't silver at all.

No, it's plastic.

"Riddick?" I ask. My hands shake and I stumble back, my legs weak. The cutters fall to the floor with a *clack*. "I...I don't understand—" Baffled, I look from the plastic collar in my hand to Riddick. Mournful green eyes meet my confused gaze.

Riddick shifts.

CHAPTER EIGHTEEN

Between one breath and the next, his wolf form dissipates, and a naked *John* stands in front of me. I stumble again, the shock almost sending me to my knees. John grabs me before I fall. My stomach tumbles, and my heart leaps. I feel sick. On instinct as I expect a blow, my hands come up to protect my face and quickly I back away from him. What the hell...what the hell happened?

I look *John* up and down with incredulous eyes. A naked John.

Oh, hell.

I rub my face, and my skin weirdly prickles with awareness as I stare open-mouthed at the beautiful, naked hellhound. I press my lips closed, unwilling to speak. I don't trust my mouth. It might blurt out every tangled, confused thought screaming through my head. The emotions I'm feeling are *nuts.* Even now my eyes find his abs. God was clearly biased when he made this man, because he is perfect. Every sloping muscle, every hard ridge is perfect.

Perfect, perfect, perfect.

The words bounce around in my head. I try not to think about my scars and Bert. I'm obviously *not* perfect. It makes me sad for a moment until I remind myself that there is beauty in my scars, in my imperfection. Beauty in the knowledge that I've survived.

John might be physically perfect. Yet inside he is rotten.

I tuck my hands behind my back, as I am still liable to reach out and run them up and down that bumpy torso. What the hell is wrong with me? A beautiful face and I'm enamoured—enamoured by a monster. A man who has committed atrocities against me. A man that has ruined me.

I hate myself. There is something seriously wrong with my head. There is something fundamentally wrong *with me*.

I wrestle with my libido and gather my crazy thoughts together. The question is, what is John doing here? Where is Riddick? What the hell is going on?

"Where is Riddick?" I ask. "If you've hurt him..." John drops his sorrowful green eyes and rubs his temple.

With that one look...I know.

Bam. Everything clicks into place.

Betrayal, sharp and bitter, hits me in the chest.

My heart feels like it has been eviscerated. Riddick...*Emma, you stupid cow, Riddick isn't real.* I close my eyes and rub my chest. God, it hurts. My shock is a ball of pain in my chest, it's stuck in my throat.

Ha, I dismissed the truth when it was staring at me in the face when I first met *Riddick* and I noted that he looked like a colossal version of my pup.

Of course there was a resemblance...he is her brother. Of course he stayed in wolf form; it was never about being forced. It was a disguise to manipulate *me*.

For a second I wilt, embarrassed by my obliviousness. How could I be so stupid? I let out a deranged laugh.

Riddick is *John.*

I continue to laugh. My manic, deranged laughter echoes around the bare room. My hands flutter to my mouth to try to hold the crazy in. I can't trust myself. I survived this man. Yet, look at me...still being punished. I tug at my hair.

"What? Why?" Oh my God, *Riddick is John*. "Why? Why?" I say again, more insistently. His expression is grim. He prowls forward and takes my upper arms captive, stopping me from pulling at my hair, but his hold doesn't stop me from pushing him away. "Why?" Another push, warm naked skin. "Why?" Another push. "Why? Why? You were my friend," I wail. Now, like I have turned a tap, the tears come.

I'm angry, God, I'm so angry, and I feel so sad. So, so helpless. I bitterly laugh through my sobs. Has this all been some elaborate test? A joke.

"Riddick was my friend," I whisper brokenly through my tears and my tight, straining throat. John pulls me to him and attempts to gather me into his arms. I struggle a little more against him, but it's useless. His arm around my waist is like a manacle, shackling me to him. My body sags into his warmth. I hiccup a sob. Was I so transparent? Give me someone in animal form, even a hellhound, and I hand over my trust like an idiot. "Why?" I ask.

"I had to make sure," John says, his voice rough, deep, *agonised*.

"Make sure of what? Why would you do this? Let go of me." What the hell am I doing, taking comfort from this man? This *monster*. I finally push away from him. My breath shudders and another stupid tear, a rebellious tear, slips down the side of my nose. Gah, my eyes need to stop leaking.

My friend wasn't real...Riddick wasn't *real*. This entire time, was it all a sick game? "What? Tell me. Was it all a trick? A game?" I say mournfully. "Did I pass? Did I pass your fucking test?"

"You truly don't know," John says with a swallow, his

evil eyes sad. No, how dare he, he doesn't get to feel sad.

"I don't know what?" I scream at him. "I told you *everything*, God, I helped your sister. I had nothing to do with anything beyond that. Didn't almost killing me satisfy you?"

"Demons lie—"

"I'M NOT A FUCKING DEMON!" I screech.

Silence as we look at each other. I shake my head and turn away from him with disgust; otherwise, I'm going to hit him. God forgive me, but I want to hurt him. The man is psychotic.

I rest my hand on the wall. The texture is sharp, jagged underneath my palm.

"Emma, think...your father was a demon. That means you are half demon."

"No—that's not true. No." I shake my head. "That is not bloody true." John takes my face in his hands. He gently cups my cheeks and brushes away my tears with his thumbs. "I don't believe you," I mumble.

"Please don't cry." He rests his forehead against mine.

My God, I can see the truth in his green eyes. I am a demon...how did I not recognise that I was a demon? To quote Sherlock Holmes, *"When you have eliminated the impossible, whatever remains, however improbable, must be the truth."* What a bloody silly idiot I am. I'm still that naïve, stupid little girl. Even after everything...I've yet to learn my lesson. I haven't changed at all.

"I'm part...demon...I'm a demon? Am I evil?" I mumble.

"Being a demon does not make you evil, Emma. It makes you powerful. Power corrupts. Demons as a race aren't evil, just as angels aren't inherently good. You are a lovely person. A good person." The hellhound continues to stare at me, into me, his green gaze intense. "Too good."

"All this time...all this time I thought you were wrong. I convinced myself that you made a mistake in taking me." My voice breaks. "I thought you were stupid, blinded. I couldn't contemplate how you could conclude that I was a *demon*. My God, you were right." I again push away from him. With a self-deprecating laugh, I wobble away to the other side of the room and sag against the wall. "Can I even use that word, 'God'? Will He strike me down?" My eyes drift up to the ceiling. Nothing makes sense in this world anymore.

I am bruised from the inside out.

"Why do you keep hurting me?" I whisper. "What have I ever done to you?"

"I had to determine what your involvement was in the murder of my pack. I had to ascertain that you did not know what you are. That you unequivocally told the truth."

I shake my head and laugh bitterly. "Your conclusion?"

"I absolve you. You are innocent." Oh, thanks for that, John, so kind of you to bloody *absolve* me. "You didn't know, you genuinely didn't know. Emma, how do you not know?

Sam said your eyes went black when you stopped those vampires at the stables."

Sam said that? I swallow down another bitter betrayal. Wow, they keep coming, don't they? "Why didn't Sam speak to me? Is everyone in on this?"

What a fool...I'm such a bloody fool.

I rub the back of my head against the wall as my brain struggles to line up all those little puzzle pieces together. I frown and tap my lips with my fingertips. "So...so you wanted to trick me? Force me to go all demon on you...to prove you right? You believed I was faking..." I rub the seal around Bert's bag. Was it *all* a setup? My eyes widen in shock, and I look at him in horror. "Killing Arlo in front of me...the vampire attack at the house...the lack of a ward. The car crash, the kidnapping, all those questions..." My lips part with realisation. "You killed all those vampires...to, what? Test me? Why...why would you do that?" I swallow, and my heart aches. "I killed that vampire. His name...was Charles," I husk out.

I grow agitated and my voice rises. "Those two vampires...did you set it up so those vampires would hurt Bob and Munchkin, to get a reaction out of me?" I tilt my head to the side. "But...you missed it when I went after them. According to Sam, my eyes went black, and you missed it. So you set this up as an elaborate hoax...of fake torture. With your fake silver collar, so you could sit all back of the bus as Riddick and have a front-row seat to my demon unveiling. My downfall. See my reaction first-hand with no distractions. Were you expecting a James Bond-style villain speech? Well, you horrible evil bastard, are you happy that you are fucking right?" I hold my hands out. "Aren't I the most pathetic, worthless demon you have ever seen?" I laugh bitterly. "I helped your sister, yet you tortured me. Not once, but *over and over again*. Riddick was my friend, and you used that against me. You used my love against me. I loved Riddick—" My voice breaks on a sob. John flinches. "What a stupid fool I am...did you have a good laugh? Have I finally passed your tests, or are there to be more? Now that you have your answers...am I expendable? Like the vampires? Are you going to kill me like you did those vampires? Didn't you think to ask Arlo? Before you chopped his fucking head off, but no, you didn't, did you? As you got it into your head that I was the mastermind...ha, I forgot it's always the overlooked blonde who is the evil genius."

"I'm sorry—"

"You're sorry? No—no." I raise my eyebrows and point a shaking finger at him. I rock on my toes. "You don't get to say that. You don't get to say *sorry* because you got caught."

"Emma, when I was with you as Riddick, our time together was genuine. What I feel for you is genuine." What? His beautiful green eyes plead.

The man is nuts.

I wipe the tears from my face with my dirty hands. "Genuine? You wouldn't know *genuine* if it slapped you across the face. You are so full of shit. You don't have any feelings for me, not without an ulterior motive." I turn away from him. I can't look at him; the man is pure evil.

"I still want the angel to heal you."

I huff and laugh bitterly. My sanity is fraying.

"Oh, how very magnanimous of you, let the angel fix your mess." I look at the honey-eyed guy tucked away in the corner by the door. Has he been here this whole time? "Will you do it, will you be able to heal me?" The angel's eyes widen. Yeah, I worked that shit out hours ago. The angel nods. I huff.

"Thank you," I say with gritted teeth. "If your magic can put everything back, I'd appreciate it." Sorry, Mr Hanlon, I know you were looking forward to the reversal surgery. "Just the internal stuff, not the scars." I glare at John. "If you can, please don't remove the scars. I've. Earned. Them," I bite out.

"I can unlock the rest of your demon powers—"

"My powers? I have blocked demon magic?" I interrupt the angel, staring at him incredulously.

Oh wow, there is more to come? Well, isn't that just dandy.

The angel nods and narrows his eyes. "Yes, it looks as if

they bound them when you were a child. It's a normal thing to do—children are by definition difficult. It's a simple but strong binding."

"Will I hurt anyone?"

"That would be unlikely," the angel replies softly. I want to say, *"Well then, let the bitch out."* I barely hold my tongue. I want to scream, and cry, *rage* at everyone, at the world. My head is rattled, my stupid heart is in pieces. I'm going through the motions of dealing with this shitshow.

Demon, demon, demon.

The word rattles around in my head, festering. How could I have not seen this? It has been in front of me this whole time. Now the honey-eyed angel is going to heal me, oh, and yeah, release my demon powers.

Ha, demon powers. Bloody hell.

Will my eyes go black like Arlo's, will I have scary teeth? Sharp, jagged things that will fill and poke out of my mouth? This is a nightmare.

A nightmare I'm going to have to embrace. John wanted to see, he wanted to see a monster.

Well, looky here, he has created one.

"Aren't you worried that I'll want revenge?" I ask John.

"No." Ha, he is so sure. Yet recently he was convinced that I was something evil hiding behind a human mask. Perhaps I am? I don't know anything anymore. What was up is now down...my whole life, my entire identity has been turned on its head. I'm no longer that elegant human girl, no no, I'm half demon.

"No, you are right—I don't want revenge. I didn't want to be hurt in the first place," I whisper.

I nod politely to the angel. His hands glow gold. "Okay, I'm ready." I don't want John here watching, but I don't have the strength to ask him to leave.

"You might need to sit." We both look at the metal chair. I cringe. He shrugs, and his glowing hands come closer and closer towards me. He gently takes hold of my face. His enormous hands cradle the back of my head, and his thumbs rest on my cheekbones. I blink up at his honey eyes. We both ignore John's growl. The small hairs on my arms and the back of my neck rise and my skin tingles. I shiver. Is this what magic feels like? Does everyone feel tingles and warmth? It's nice.

"So much damage, so much pain," the angel murmurs as his golden magic twists and sparkles through me. "This is a lot of healing to do at once, I didn't realise...you need to sit down—" They are the last words of his I hear as I crumple into strong, waiting arms.

Blackness.

CHAPTER NINETEEN

I wake. Sunlight filters through the bottom of the blinds and my heart sinks like a stone when I realise I'm back in my temporary bedroom at John's house. Am I a prisoner, or am I a guest? Oh, heck, do I have to make nice with that monster?

I sit up without pain—wow, that is a good sign—and slide from underneath the covers. Still dressed in my dirty clothing, I stumble into the en suite bathroom. I grip the sink and with trepidation, I look at myself in the mirror. I'm shocked to see the difference. Gone is the hollow-cheeked girl with the purple smudges underneath her eyes and the pale corpse-complexion. With a frown I poke at my face. I don't look like the girl I once was either.

There is a darkness, a hardness in my bright-blue eyes—a sadness that was never there before. I drop my eyes to the countertop, no longer able to meet the eyes of the sad girl. Huh, no wonder. My lower lip trembles.

When you hit rock bottom, the only way is up, right?

Right. I've got this...I look down at my tummy and puff out an anxious breath. I tap my fingertips against my mouth as I count down from three, and with shaking hands, I grip the hem of my stained, dirty jumper and lift it. I pull it over my head and allow it to drop to the floor with a plop. The ileostomy bag is still attached to my tummy, but Bert...Bert is gone.

Oh wow. I sag with relief.

I lock my knees as my entire body wobbles. I grip the side of the counter so hard, my fingertips turn white; I hold on so I don't flop to the floor.

The. Magic. Worked.

The awe I feel...wow, with a swipe of his hand and the warm golden glow of his magic, the angel healed me. It is mind-blowing. Magic has never been my friend, so it is surreal that an angel's healing gift has made this life-impacting problem disappear.

I empty the bag and then grab the adhesive remover spray, and with twitchy nervous fingers, I carefully spray and peel the sticky seal away from my skin. I tremble as I remove the bag for the very last time.

A sob spills from my lips. It's over, it is finally over.

Relieved tears stream down my face. Having Bert was lifesaving, and I will be forever grateful to the hospital and my surgeon, Mr Hanlon. I'm not sorry that because of magic, I avoided the scary step of more surgical intervention. I can finally get on with my life. I've hit a whole new level of *normal*.

Gah, I will forever hate that word. I laugh through my tears of relief. This "normal" is one that I can now get behind wholeheartedly. I hiccup another sob and allow a wobbly smile to tug at my lips.

"No more crying," I whisper to myself as I gently trace the scars on my tummy. As promised, my surgical scars and the scars from John's attentions are still there. Prominent. As I inspect them, I wonder if I've made a mistake, if I should have perhaps had a full healing.

My lips tug into a sad smile. I am at a youthful stage in my life where I should be able to safely make mistakes and learn from them. Learn what type of person I want to be. But in my world, I can't make mistakes; there is no room for error. You make a mistake, trust the wrong person, and you die.

I think I've proven that repeatedly. I hand my trust over like it is a meaningless commodity. I can't afford to make any more mistakes. I have to be more cautious. I have to ask questions and I have to be smarter, listen to my instincts.

These scars are a visual reminder.

When my memories fade over time, which is inevitable, the scars will be here. Hopefully, they will keep everything at the forefront of my mind.

They look years old—gone are the puckered, angry red gouges that painfully pulled at my skin and muscle. Instead, silver lines crisscross my tummy. My warrior markings.

I need a shower. As I strip off of the rest of my clothing, out of habit I move cautiously, almost protectively. I shake my head and straighten when I realise I don't have to be careful about Bert anymore.

It's the absence of pain that hits me the most strongly—it is so strange. Over the months I had Bert, I thought the pain levels had improved. But I guess I'd gotten used to it. Its absence now is profound. My body silenced.

I blow out a shaky breath. Internally I have been healed, but mentally, physically, I will never be the same. What's that saying? What doesn't kill you makes you stronger...I've always believed that everything happens for a reason, even the horrible stuff. Especially the horrible stuff. It impacts us the most. It forces us to change, to grow or to falter. You truly find out what you're made of when the shit hits the fan.

The way I see it, I've always had two options: option one, I can roll around on the floor wailing, "Why me, why me." Option two: I can woman the fuck up. I have so many things I've got to do. If I think about it too much, it becomes almost overwhelming. First step: I need to find Bob, Munchkin, and me somewhere to live. My independence starts now, this very minute. I will not depend on that arsehole John. The demon gave me an allowance that I managed frugally, so I have money in my name. Not a lot, but enough for me to pay for Bob and Munchkin and set them up at a livery yard, and sufficient to find me a place to live.

I'm not staying here in John's house for one more minute than I have to.

In this world, power is freedom, and I'm a shiny new half-demon. I need to learn what I can do—fast. I need to protect myself. I'm going to manoeuvre myself into a position of power so that no one, *no one* can have control over me again.

I slump. That sounds great when I say it in my head. I wonder how the heck I'm going to learn my new demon powers. I rub at my eyes, and the dirt on my face is gritty underneath my hands. I'm so gross. It's not like I can say to just anybody, *"Hi, will you train my demon?"* I snort.

I need a help book...or...I need a library.

I smile. Well...well, funny that. It just so happens I know of a private collection of demon books. I guess I need to visit one library in particular. Arlo's library.

He has a substantial hidden collection. I strum my fingers on the bathroom countertop in the rhythm of a horse's canter. It looks like I will be sneaking back onto Arlo's estate.

Dodging hellhounds and guards. Whee. It will be so much fun.

I shower and change, and before I head out, I pause. Perhaps I can start with something small, like my eyes. I go back into the bathroom, and I look at my eyes in the mirror.

I blink a few times.

I strangely hope my eyes will automatically go black, like flicking off a light switch. If I blink enough, they will change. Right? My rapid blinking makes me look a little deranged. Instead of my eyes going black, I look as if I've got something stuck in my eye.

I groan in defeat. This will never work.

I strum my fingers against the sink. How do I do this? I've done it before. Huh, perhaps the colour of my eyes is linked to my emotions? When they changed, I was angry. I want to smack my forehead. Of course—anger is the trigger. Arlo never had black eyes when he was happy.

Okay, think angry...I close my eyes and I focus on the moment when Sam said my eyes turned black. My heart drops at that betrayal, but I shove it to the back of my mind to deal with later. I remember the moment clearly. Yeah, I was angry.

The vampire's hand goes to Bob's stable door.

Without thinking, my own hand lands on the sharp knife, the one we use to open bales of hay and bags of feed. I grab the black handle in my fist.

I'm so livid my vision has gone hazy, almost black...an inhuman growl rumbles in my chest and leaves my throat with a roar.

Wow, the rage I feel. *That bloody vampire.* I growl and straightaway my eyes tingle. My eyes fly open and I stare at my reflection. I blink—my vision is hazy. I gasp. Whoa.

They are black. Boom, get in.

I've seen Arlo's eyes like this countless times. But nothing prepares me for seeing my own eyes completely black. It is probably the most freaky thing I will ever see. The urge to poke myself in the eye is huge, and I almost headbutt the mirror by getting too close. They don't look real. I drop the angry energy and like raindrops the black colour bleeds slowly down. It collects and pools at the bottom of my eyes for a split second and then disappears without a trace. I shudder. Creepy.

My wide, multicoloured blue eyes stare back at me. I blink. Wow. I need to do that again.

* * *

Sam is cleaning Bob's bridle in the tack room. I stand at the door and watch her as I gather my courage to ask her *the* question. I could ignore it and pretend I never found out, but I am done with lying to myself. I clear my throat. "Why didn't you tell me that my eyes went black?"

Sam turns her head. She tilts it to the side and silently regards me. "You look good. Better. The poo bag is gone then?"

"Yeah, it's gone. After John set up another kidnapping...he staged a car crash. Sam, why didn't you tell me? You told John, but you didn't think it might be worthwhile, to...I dunno, say something to me?"

"He set up a kidnapping? Who did he try to kidnap—"

"Sam, please answer my question," I implore.

Sam shrugs and looks down at the bridle in her hands. She rubs a clean spot vigorously with her sponge. I silently wait. My eyes narrow as the minutes tick by. Finally, she replies with a mumbled, "John pays well."

I flinch at her words. Oh, that's how it is?

I huff out a breath. "'He pays well'? You didn't think to speak to me...give me a heads-up? Sam, I thought we were friends." Sam shrugs again—unbelievably, she couldn't care less. I grind my teeth in annoyance. "Did you not hear me? John set me up. He staged a real-life car crash. The car flipped. Riddick and Eleanor jumped out of the smashed-up car and slaughtered a bunch of vampires." I wait for her to respond. "Do you not care?" I whisper.

Sam keeps scrubbing. I grip the wooden frame of the doorway. "I was thrown into a van and taken to what I can only describe as a cell, where I was interrogated. *Again*. They used Riddick as an incentive for me to talk...if I didn't talk, they said they were going to cut him into tiny little pieces. It was *horrendous*. I was so bloody frightened." I let go of the frame and hug my arms to my chest. I hunch and rub my arms. "Oh, and Riddick turned out to be John in his hellhound form. Did you know that? I was stroking my torturer this whole time." I laugh a little manically, my crazy peeking out.

I cut the laughter off and bite my lips closed. I need to hold all my deranged thoughts in; I need to get a grip on myself. I drop my arms and sag against the door. I close my eyes. When I have gained some semblance of control, I open my eyes and continue.

"It was all a trick to get information out of me. Ever since I fell off Pudding and helped that little shifter, the hellhound has been attempting to manipulate me into showing myself to be a raging demon—a demon that John knew without any doubt that I was, because you told him. You told *him*, not me, that I had black eyes when I confronted those vampires.

"I'm not saying that what happened wouldn't have happened anyway. I'm saying if you would have told me"— I slap my chest—"perhaps...perhaps I would have been more prepared." Sam continues to scrub in silence.

"Did you always know that I was a demon, Sam? Did you know John set everything up? He killed all those vampires to trick me into revealing myself..." I shake my head, my eyes water, and I sniff. I wait for her to answer me, but she will not look me in the eye. My heart squeezes painfully. "N-nothing? You won't say anything to defend yourself?" Sam shrugs. That's all the response I get to my heartfelt splurge of words.

I tap my fingertips on my lips and try to swallow the lump in my throat. In an attempt to get her riled up, I say, "You can get your stuff, and you can go. I don't trust you, not with Bob and not with our so-called friendship..." My voice cracks.

Sam throws down the sponge and places the bridle onto the side with a *clack*. "Look, Emma...you owe me money for buying Bob." I blink at her. That's it? That's all I get?

"I transferred the money last week. It should be in your account," I whisper through that same painful lump in my throat, my chest burning. I recognise the calculated move: Sam has neatly reminded me I owe her for rescuing Bob. Am I being too harsh? Or has my friend always been so manipulative?

"I'm keeping the Shetland," Sam says somewhat snidely as she barges past me, clipping my shoulder. I swallow down all the angry words I want to say. I've done enough damage.

"Were you ever my friend?" I ask her retreating back.

She pauses mid-stride, and with her back still to me, she quietly says, "Em, you are *the* best friend I have ever had...I just wasn't yours. I told that demon twat your every word, your every move. Then I told the hellhound." She shrugs, lifts her chin, and walks away. "I will do anything for protection, and I have bills to pay." Her last words to me whip around in the wind.

Wow, clearly all my instincts are seriously messed up: a ten-year friendship, or what I thought was a friendship, is over within seconds.

God, it hurts.

What is it about me that brings out the worst in everyone? Just when I thought I'd hit rock bottom, I instead have another meter to fall.

CHAPTER TWENTY

The taxi drops me off between the shop where I first met John and the estate. I hunch as I walk the remaining distance to the estate boundary wall, where I plan to sneak in. I can't seem to stop my shoulders from creeping up towards my ears. The memory of that shop...the hellhounds, of first meeting John...will be forever ingrained in my nightmares. Having it at my unprotected back creeps me out and makes me shiver.

I come to a stop at the boundary wall. I tilt my head as I investigate the glowing new ward. After the angel's golden magic-show yesterday and the supposed unlocking of my demon powers—if that's even what the angel did—I'm afraid of what will happen when I touch the ward.

Perhaps he blocked or altered my strange magic. I scratch my head—it's warm underneath my wool hat. Oh, heck, what happens if my immunity powers no longer work? I bounce from foot to foot. Oh, God, I should have worked out a way to check before I came.

I let out a self-deprecating breath, rub my hands together, and then tentatively stick my right index finger out towards the ward. I grimace, close my eyes, and wait for a nasty surprise.

When nothing happens, I open one eye to see my hand completely immersed in the ward. I want to roll my eyes at my foolishness. Note to self: I have no depth perception with my eyes closed.

My grin fades, and I glance about. I've been messing around out here for way too long. Confirming with a look that the coast is clear, I launch myself at the wall. Oof. In an ungainly move, I scramble over it. I wonder, when I gain control of my demon powers, will I become more elegant and prowly? I can't see Arlo ever having had to climb over walls.

I grunt when my feet hit the floor, and I land in the middle of a dense, thorny thicket of raspberry bushes. Oh bloody hell. I roll my eyes and raise my face to the sky in exasperation. Give me strength. The bushes tangle my legs and the thorns dig into the fabric of my leggings, biting my skin.

Ow, ow, ow.

I tiptoe away from the clingy plants without damaging myself or the thicket—I only sustain light scratches to my legs and hands. I groan as the old phrase "look before you leap" pops into my head. Trust me to choose the only stretch of wall with thorny bushes.

At least this time I'm somewhat prepared and wearing the right gear. I give myself a mental pat on the back. Today for my mission I settled on dark-green leggings, a heavy dark-green waterproof military-style coat, and a black (itchy) knit hat, all finished with sturdy boots.

There are guards everywhere, so it feels like it takes forever for me to slowly, cautiously sneak my way across the estate grounds to the main house. The bright sunlight dims and, luckily for me, the weather changes—the clouds roll in, and it starts to rain heavily. The rain lashes and visibility goes down to almost nothing.

I huddle into my jacket underneath a thick, ornate bush and squint at the guards as they patrol around the house. I watch as they battle the cold, stinging sideways rain. I work out their rotation and route; it's going to be challenging to get past them. When their shift changes, a few of the guards congregate together and in proper British fashion moan about the weather. I grin and use the handy distraction.

I hustle to the side of the house and the laundry room door. The lock has always been a bit temperamental. With a long-practised jiggle, a yank, and a sharp tug, I lift the door up ever so slightly, taking advantage of the loose hinges. The barely heard *snick* of the lock as it opens reaches my ears, and I'm in. I step through the door and close it behind me. I lean against it, and then I wait. The room is empty.

My heart is beating fast, and my naff human senses are tingling. I hold my breath as I strain my ears for any sign of danger. I count down from thirty in my head. When I feel it's safe, I take a small fortifying breath and move.

I creep past the empty, silent machines and grab a towel from a folded stack of clean laundry. I crouch down, grab the handle of the internal door, and open it a tiny crack. So far, so good. I peek out from the hinge side of the door. It gives me an unobstructed view of the hallway as well as the library, which is opposite.

As I unfortunately don't have X-ray vision or a super-sniffer or supersonic hearing, I figure I will have to do things the old-fashioned way. I will have to wait until I'm a hundred percent sure that the library is empty. So I sit on the cold tiled floor. I use the towel to blot the drops of rain from my skin and clothing, and to clean my boots. All the while, I continue to squint through the gap in the door.

I silently wait.

Well, sort of silently. My panting breaths are so loud in the small room. It seems almost impossible to control them with the adrenaline flooding through me, which makes my heart pound like a herd of galloping horses. I do my best to control my breathing, but when I try to quieten it, my chest burns with the lack of oxygen. I attempt to breathe through my nose, but the damn thing squeaks on my exhalation. I roll my eyes. Mouth breathing seems to be quieter.

Every time I contemplate what will happen if I'm caught, my galloping heart skips a beat, and I have to force the thought away. If it wasn't imperative that I access the demon's hidden books, I wouldn't be doing this. I'm so nervous, my stomach hurts.

My patience wins. Not thirty minutes later, the library door swings open and two witches exit. "I thought the library would have better texts," one of them moans. She has fluffy white hair—similar to the seeds of a dandelion before you make a wish.

"Oh, I don't know, Diana. The first editions are incredible."

"Yes, but what about all the references? Surely a first-level demon would have a better reference section..." They continue their conversation down the hallway and disappear around the bend. Conveniently they have left the door open, and based on what I can see from my position on the floor, the library looks empty.

I spring into action. I throw the dirty towel into an empty machine, slip out of the laundry room, and scamper across the hallway. Once in the library, I gently close the library door.

Without intending to, I take a deep breath. The library still smells the same as I remembered. It worried me that Arlo's death might have left an imprint in the very fabric of the room, spoiled it somehow. But it doesn't feel any different.

I guess I carry the wounds of that day within me.

I fix my eyes and ignore the area where he died. I don't look to see if they have erased the circle, or if the floor has been cleaned and repaired. I can't. Not even to show my respect. Heart thumping, I hurry across the room, my gaze firmly locked on the back shelves.

Instead of heading for a dusty dark corner, where any normal person would stash a hidden room, I aim for the centre of the solid oak shelves. It is the most prominent area of the library. Who would be mad enough to put the entrance door to a secret room in such a place? A demon would.

I place one hand on the most notable square of wood, above Lewis Carroll's *Alice's Adventures in Wonderland*, and my other above and slightly to the left on another panel. I push.

Nothing happens.

I duck, cringe, and adjust my hands. I bet the two witches only went for a quick break, and depending on how fast they can drink their tea, they could be back at any second. Oh, God...I feel myself shake. I'm panicking. If I get caught...I swallow down my nervousness, move my left hand an inch, and again *push*.

Oh, thank God. The relief when the panel clicks and the shelves swing forward towards me to reveal the hidden doorway. I open it enough to give myself sufficient room to squeeze inside. The nasty, crackling ward appears as soon as I pass through—it has killed trespassers in the past. I ignore it and gently pull the whole shelving securely back into place with a *clunk*. Once the door securely closes, I hit the old-fashioned light switch and the secret space is flooded with light.

Whoa, that was scary. I take a deep breath in, roll my tense shoulders, and jiggle my arms to loosen them. I then remove my wet jacket, stuff my hat in the pocket, and place it on the hook beside the door. My leggings are a little damp, but they shouldn't affect the environment in the room.

This secret place is...was...Arlo's pride and joy. What seems like unending shelves adorn the walls—they are as beautiful as the library's on the other side of the door, containing not only books but potions, magical weapons, and trinkets. Arlo stored everything of value in here, stuff that he didn't want anyone else to see.

I look about with nostalgia. The hours I've spent in this room...I shake my head. How on earth do I choose what to take? To remove everything from here would be impossible. I let out a sad sigh. It's such a waste. To have permanent access to these priceless treasures would set me up for life.

I've been in here hundreds of times, always while the demon was present. Growing up, this was my playroom. This is the first time I've ever been in here alone.

I drift towards his desk, and my fingers trail across it. My eyes drink in its beautiful wood and the well-worn leather chair. Sorrow hits me in the chest when I acknowledge that he will never sit here again.

I know he was a bad guy, but I still feel guilty for not trying harder to save him. I thought he was ageless, as unremovable as the mountains, as unending as the ocean tides—but he wasn't. I guess no one is. When it comes down to it, we don't know how long we have, even with the title of *immortal.* No one is unending, not even Arlo.

I don't know why that thought gives me a measure of peace. I guess I wouldn't want to live forever.

I might as well start my search at the desk. I lean down and open the nearest drawer. I sag when my eyes land on a note. I drag the chair toward me and sit, heavy with shock. I lift the letter addressed to me and place it with utter care on the desk. My fingers trace his words.

Sneaky demon.

Dearest Emma,

If you are reading this, you have either entered without my permission, or I am no longer of this earth. If it is the latter, you will be in danger as the sharks will circle. My gift to you is this room and its contents, as it is a pocket dimension —

I squeak, "A *what?*" I jump to my feet, knocking the chair over in my haste, and it clatters to the floor behind me. I back away from the desk. *Oh my God, oh my God.* I flap my hands. *A pocket dimension.* With my mouth open and my eyes wide, I spin and stare at the room, taking in the vast space with fresh eyes. I rub my face.

No wonder it is so big and has zero effect on the footprint of the house. Of course I knew it was magic, but a pocket dimension? I presume it's a similar magic to the gateways, strong enough to handle my weird demon magic and all the poking about I've done over the years. The room is a little world. An independent bubble within space and time that can only be accessed through a specific means. I glance at the doorway leading to the library. Wow.

That is how it fits into the space between the library wall and the rooms beyond. Wow, that is unbelievably…cool.

And it's mine all mine. Arlo has given the pocket dimension to *me*. I turn and stare incredulously at the letter, still on the desk. I cautiously tiptoe back towards it. I pick up the chair with shaking hands, sit, and continue to read.

— to ensure that nobody else can access the dimension, and to guarantee that you can access the space from anywhere, follow the instructions below to the letter.

The rest of the letter has instructions, and it also has the location of a reference book.

Huh. I wasn't expecting Arlo's last words to me to be anything special...hell, I wasn't expecting any last words. Yet he dropped that bombshell, signed his name, and that is it. There is no mention of my demon heritage. Not that I'm not appreciative, because I am...I'm shocked. The demon does—did—what was best for him. Manipulation, yes; outright kindness, never.

That's why I'll be finding this book, and I will make up my own mind rather than blindly following Arlo's instructions and willy-nilly doing pocket-dimension soul-tying magic. I don't understand *why* he left me this room of absolute treasures. Especially after I fell from his favour. Unless he wrote this letter a long time ago and had yet to update it... who knows? But I'm unbelievably grateful.

I hunt down the book, and when I find it, I let out a joyous laugh. I smile so big my cheeks hurt when I see it nestled within an entire collection of how-to-demon books. Well, they don't actually say that on their fancy titles, but the shelves surrounding the text on pocket dimensions have every demon book imaginable. More books than I will ever need.

Sneaky demon.

How can he be so thoughtful in death? It's nuts. I grab the book, and instead of heading back to the desk, I go to the squishy dark-red leather sofa that's tucked into a quiet corner. I settle down, open the book, and read.

After a few hours, I know everything there is about how this room works. The book doesn't explain how to make a pocket dimension, as it is more like a TV set-up manual. But it has everything else regarding keeping the pocket stable. The book talks about connecting the pocket to a permanent fixture—like the library—or having it linked to a person. As I don't have my own secret doorway and I don't want to unintentionally kill somebody by attaching it to a regular door, the best way to go is to secure the dimension to me.

The steps to do the transfer are the same ones Arlo had written in his letter.

I roll my eyes. Hours of reading and I end up doing the pocket-dimension soul-tying magic anyway.

Once I have read the steps another few times, I guess I'm ready to attempt the transfer. I get up, roll my shoulders, and march to a shelf full of weaponry. I grab a small, plain blade and a cleaning cloth. I clean the knife and then carefully nick the tip of my finger. I place the blade back on the shelf, and with the bleeding digit held aloft, I head to the doorway.

I smear my blood around the doorframe and say the words, "I bind you through time and space, I bind you to my soul, you are mine to command." I sense a tingle down my arm and a pleasant feeling of righteousness in my chest. When

I step away, the ward on the door flashes and the colour changes to a smoky black.

I cringe. Oh, crap. Okay...hopefully, black is good? I don't know, but there is now a tug, a heaviness in my chest. I rub the spot. If it doesn't sound too crazy, I can now *feel* the doorway.

The book was specific: since I've attached the pocket to myself, I can now open the door into *any* room. I have to have seen the room with my own eyes, but from what I can gather, I can exit and enter from anywhere. Like...like my own personal portal. Wow, how amazing is that? I guess if I haven't messed it up and I open the door and think of my room at John's...I should be able to walk straight into that room. I shiver. That's incredibly powerful magic.

I have absolutely no idea if it'll work. What I don't want to do is open the door back into the library. So being safe, I guess I should wait. Do some more reading, take some notes. If I don't have to sneak back out of here and out of the estate, I have time.

I back away from the freaky ward. I also need to treat my bleeding finger—I can't have my blood anywhere near those demon books. Heck, I can only imagine what a mess an unintended blood sacrifice would cause. I shiver. I wonder if there is a medical kit around here, with some plasters. I glance down at my poor finger...what the heck...I squint at it, turn it around to look at it from a different angle. I squish it with my thumb...*oh wow*...yeah, the wound, it's, urm...gone.

CHAPTER TWENTY-ONE

I check my hands and legs for the minor scrapes from the raspberry bushes. The scratches are gone. Holy crap, I healed. I healed myself...or did the pocket dimension heal me? I think back to when I was drying my skin with that towel. I can't remember the angry scrapes being there. No, the scratches were gone. I healed myself.

Bloody hell, that's amazing.

The revelation is mind-blowing. Will it be only the small stuff, or can I heal like a proper demon? I'm unwilling to test my theory and only time will tell. Ha, it was only a slight cut on my finger and a couple of scratches. No need to go crazy, but it's something.

I turn and head for the shelves and the demon books; time for some reading. Thinking of time, at least I know that time in here runs precisely the same as it does outside. Could you imagine coming into a pocket dimension for ten minutes and then leaving and ten years have passed? I shiver—magic is so dangerous in the wrong hands. That's why I've got to be careful.

I don't know why, but that moment when I asked John if being half-demon made me evil springs into my head. He said, *"Being a demon does not make you evil, Emma. It makes you powerful. Power corrupts."*

I have to be morally incorruptible, with my own strict moral compass. I have to have rules...that's something to think seriously about later.

I spend a few hours reading. When I get hungry, I know it's time to leave. I need to bring some supplies if I am going to be spending time here.

I leave the books I've been reading on the desk—I'm unwilling to take anything with me as I can't yet protect it outside of this room.

I look around Arlo's office. With its dark-green walls and low ceiling, it's cold and drab. The only things of beauty are the objects themselves and the shelves they sit on. I wonder why it was made this way. It's like a basement or a movie office for an old detective who has fallen out of favour and the police department has put him somewhere out of the way. I wrinkle my nose. If I designed a pocket dimension, I'd make it so homey and bright. I picture what that would look like, and I sigh and shake my head...that's never going to happen. I don't even know who makes pocket dimensions, let alone has one so nice. I'd have more luck decorating a cardboard box. Which might be in the cards if I don't get a finger out and find somewhere to live.

At the doorway, I put on my hat and coat. I blow out a nervous breath...I might need to be ready to run if this all goes pear-shaped. I close my eyes and focus on the en suite door of my temporary bedroom at John's house. With that image firmly embedded in my mind, I take a deep breath, open the door, and step through.

I whoop when I step into the bedroom. I then duck down and slam my hands across my mouth. Oops. My ears strain for any movement. When neither John nor Eleanor comes running to investigate, I sag in relief.

Perhaps I need to do less whooping in what is enemy territory.

I grin, wiggle, and do a silent happy-dance instead. Boom, I am a master...I then immediately freak out. Oh bloody hell, what happens if I can't get back in? My hands flap. I didn't even bring one book out with me...oh no...oh no, how could I be so stupid? No, no, no. My luck wouldn't be that bad, would it? I cringe and wring my hands. Yes, it would.

I will have to do a test.

I spin to the en suite bathroom door, close my eyes, and whisper, "Secret room, I need you." I snort, that sounds so silly, Emma. I force myself to concentrate. I don't know if the words will work, but anything to help me focus is good, right? It's not the words but the intent that matters, and it should help me focus through my panic and my thudding heart. I step through the door, and the smoky black ward clings to my skin almost lovingly. Huh, that's new. But I'm back in the secret room. Boom, fist pump. I'm so nailing this stuff.

I realise I've left the lights on—I don't even go there, thinking of how that works. The lights, the power...it's enough to blow my mind. I shrug; it's magic. I switch them off.

If all else fails, at least I have somewhere to live. Again, I concentrate and step back into the bedroom.

As I stand in the centre of the room, I tilt my head and strum my fingertips on my lips as I contemplate the bed. Huh. *If all else fails, at least I have somewhere to live*... Mmmm. I wonder if John would notice if I stole the bed.

I grin. I can so see myself dragging it through the doorway and into my new *home*. No, the key word is *stealing*, and I can afford my own bed, and the sofa in the storeroom is comfortable.

I grin wider. Stuff it, I'm going to move out. I know the secret room isn't ideal; it certainly isn't suitable as a place to live, but it would be incredibly handy and incredibly *safe*. My new home, it's perfect.

My bags are already packed. I've not been willing to get too comfortable here, and I never unpacked when I arrived from the hospital. So it takes me mere moments to gather my pathetic worldly goods together.

Oh, yeah. I smile smugly when I remember I have a room full of stuff. Important stuff. I can buy more clothing. Bags in hand, I go through the same routine of thinking of the pocket, and when I step through, I stumble.

The room has changed.

I drop my things at the door in shock, and my hands fly to my mouth. What the hell is going on? My eyes are so wide, I feel as if they're almost bugging out of my head.

Honestly, if I didn't know any better, I'd think I'd have come to the wrong place. This is not the same pocket at all—oh, all the stuff is here, so I know I've not entered some random doorway. There are still the unending shelves, my smoky, happy-to-see-me ward, but they have magically been moved to make way for a...*home*.

Total incredulity fills me as I gape at the surrounding room. I pinch myself.

Bloody hell.

All my favourite things that were hidden within the shelves are grouped together—displayed. Instead of Arlo's murky basement office, it's a homey space. The walls are a pretty, soft grey, the entire room is brighter. I tilt my head back; the ceiling looks higher.

Arlo's desk is now in the corner, and the leather sofa is now surrounded by floor-to-ceiling shelves and a reading lamp—it has been turned into a book nook. A beautiful, cosy mini library. I confirm with a glance that my favourite books and the demon texts I need are close at hand.

I stumble to an ample wooden cabinet with the word POTIONS prettily stencilled onto the door. I trace the writing with my finger and then take a peek inside. It is full to the brim with potions in beautifully crafted bottles.

Even though I cannot use these potions myself, the contents of this cupboard are worth a small fortune.

How can I be immune to potions but sneak through wards? Use the gateways and my pocket dimension without affecting the magic? I have no idea. That is the nature of magic. I smile in the direction of my book nook with all the demon books. I will do my best to find out. Perhaps with more control, I will eventually be able to use potions? I gently close the doors and continue to look around.

There's a weapon area, a kitchen. A dark-grey kitchen with a bright-white worktop and a white ceramic, deep Belfast sink. It has all the kitchen appliances I will ever need.

There are also two brand-new doorways, and when I peek into each room, I find a five-piece modern bathroom in the first room and a perfectly luxurious bedroom in the second. I stroke my hand across the bed and hum when I realise that the bed linen is super soft.

Back in the main room, I spin, my mouth agape, as I take in my new, magical home.

What the hell kind of magic is this? It is everything I imagined I would want for my own space, a proper home that no one can take away. Linking the pocket dimension to me must have caused this to happen. Wow.

I spin. I need to find that book. My eyes fly around the room, and my gaze lands on Arlo's—no, no, on *my* desk. There was a passage in that book...I rush to the desk and after a quick search I snatch up the book and carefully flick through the pages. There was an almost-offhand comment I had seen...there...*If the pocket dimension has ties with a powerful magic-user, over time the dimension can adapt within the original footprint for that magical user's needs.* Huh. I blink and look around again. Well now, that is interesting.

CHAPTER TWENTY-TWO

I'm almost in a trance as I unpack my clothing—I'm feeling a tad overwhelmed. When everything is put away, I decide I need to check on Bob. I also need to prioritise finding my boy a safe new home. It's a shame that I can't imagine equestrian facilities into being—the book said the changes had to fit in the original footprint. If I could imagine a few acres for Bob and a friend, I'd probably never leave the pocket dimension again. That would be, I guess, unhealthy.

I change into my stable stuff and step straight through the tack room door. I grin. Not the smartest thing to do, but no one is about. Bob's head comes up when he sees me. He whinnies and charges across the field. I'm relieved to see that Munchkin is still here. I grab both boys' head collars and get them in. Their stables are all ready for them. I brush both boys and leave them to chomp on their small nets of hay.

I take advantage of the late-afternoon sun and slump on the floor outside Bob's stable. I stab at my phone, which had been rescued from the car and conveniently left on my bedside cabinet, and search for a livery yard with a vacancy. Gosh, I also need to find myself a job. The money I have will not last forever—keeping one horse even in a basic do-it-yourself livery yard is expensive. Also, bad things happen to people with idle hands. If I'm planning to keep myself on the straight and narrow, I need to keep myself busy.

Bob's head pops over the stable door to nosy at what I am doing. He sprinkles the hay from his mouth into my hair. "Oi, Bob, stop it." He disappears to get another mouthful.

I shake my head and run my fingers through my hair. The little pieces of hay stuck between the strands remind me of Sam and my heart aches.

I feel lost without my cheeky friend, and I can't help worrying about her. I might have been too hasty. Was I too harsh? Mean? I didn't try hard enough to find out what was going on in her head. What kind of selfish cow does that make me? But I can't go back, I can only go forward. If she needs me, I will try my best to be there for her...*if* she ever needs me. Our friendship wasn't about what she could do for me. Being her friend made me feel good, and I'm going to miss that.

I allow another thought to whisper through my head. I miss...Riddick. Isn't that pathetic? I close my eyes and take a sharp breath as I'm hit with a boatload of pain. I miss him so much, those bright green eyes always watching, keeping me safe.

Ha, the silly things he used to do...My smile fades. I can't get my head around the fact that he was John. Who knew that John had that level of fun...that level of kindness inside him. Perhaps the wolf and John are distinctly separate entities. I don't think that's the case, but the disparity between the pair of them is so disconcerting. So confusing. Unless I ask John, I'll never know the answer.

I'm never going to ask John.

Gosh, all these changes. My life has changed so much in such a short space of time. I wiggle my bum; it's going numb with me sitting on the concrete floor. I guess I have to embrace my new life, and unfortunately, at this moment it doesn't include my friends from the old one. I hear a muffled snort, a stomp of a hoof, and finally, a lip-smacking, crunching sound above me. I tip my head back and close my eyes as more hay sprinkles down on me. Well, not all my friends. I reach up and tickle Bob's soft nose. "I still have you, Bob-cob."

I eventually find a few wonderful choices of livery yards. Most are in the northwest of England. I don't need to stay in the area where I grew up, but I think it's better to stick with what you know.

There is one expensive stable yard that stands head and shoulders above the others. It's posh and the facilities available are on par with the estate's. It's an all-singing and all-dancing yard, which means it will have an all-singing and all-dancing price tag. I gulp. It has outstanding reviews and fantastic security.

Not messing about, I ring and make an appointment with the manager in the morning.

"Emma, I didn't know that you'd returned," Eleanor says, appearing from around the corner. "Where have you been? You left like a thief, telling no one where you were going. You need to allow us to do our jobs. We didn't even know if your healing was successful," she chastises me, her hands firmly planted on her slim hips.

I avoid looking at her directly; I am still sore about her involvement in the whole fake kidnapping. I'm back to not liking her, and this time I won't allow my stupid empathy to make me feel bad. I also don't want to lie about my estate adventures this morning. If I look at her straight on, I'm sure all my sneaky endeavours will be written right across my forehead. Instead, I take a leaf out of her fae playbook and don't answer her question.

"My healing went fine, thank you. I am glad to see that

you're all right," I say instead, then smoothly change the subject. "I'm going out tomorrow; I've got an appointment."

Eleanor huffs and shakes her head at me with obvious exasperation. "Speak to John. He isn't impressed that you disappeared today. How can we protect you if you don't give us the courtesy of letting us know where you are going?" I can't help snorting at that comment. Wow, really?

I raise my eyebrows and shake my head at her. She hasn't got a clue about how hypocritical she sounds. She wasn't protecting me when the vampires knocked us off the road and the car flipped. That stupid stunt could have killed us.

"Excuse me," I say as I jump up and head for the house, "I'm going to speak to John to ask for *permission*." This will be interesting.

He's in the kitchen, making some food. The smell of cooking makes my stomach growl, and I remember then that I still haven't eaten anything today. It's a silly move; I need to take better care of myself.

Don't look at his face, Emma.

Yes, I will keep my eyes away from him. I don't trust myself. When I look at him, my brain short-circuits, it goes all gooey with my hormones.

Every. Single. Time.

Every time it happens, I hate myself a little bit more. So I will avoid looking at the hellhound. If I don't look into those sad green eyes, my hate can go entirely onto him, it can rest on his massive, broad shoulders instead of on mine.

Thinking of his shoulders...the man still has a body that belongs in a different time. There is a beautiful, brutal kind of efficiency about the way his muscles cord his frame. I forgot how large he is, not having seen him in a normal setting; he dwarfs the kitchen. There is no way to ignore it, the sheer physical power of him. I shiver.

He turns towards me and the eyes that I should avoid light up when he sees me. The hellhound has a mug of coffee in his hand. The mug has a pink, cutesy unicorn on it.

He is making dinner...something so normal.

In my head, I'd expect him to be in his hellhound form in some forest somewhere catching and killing and eating raw meat. But no, here he is, charming and untroubled, making food as he sips coffee. In a *pink unicorn cup*.

"Are you hungry? I made enough for you." Somehow this new John-on-his-best-behaviour version is scarier.

Abort-abort-abort, my instincts helpfully scream.

He smiles.

And my mind goes right into the gutter.

A man has no right to be so fiercely sexual without even trying, and now I have the hellhound's undivided attention, and it isn't frightening. It is...flattering. The way my body lights up when he turns his attention onto me. He turns me on by looking at me. I *enjoy* all that overwhelming masculine intensity focused on me.

I'm some special kind of idiot. Alone-time with the hellhound hasn't turned out so well for me.

I laugh under my breath, snort, and then laugh some more. I chuckle to myself like a loon. Perfectly mentally fit. I drop my eyes and I stare at the centre of his chest. Yeah, the hellhound will love that, he'll think I'm all submissive.

The wanker.

"How are you feeling?" I shrug; it's none of his business.

My blasé shrug looks silly when I glance down to find I'm rubbing at my right wrist. If that isn't a reminder not to trust the handsome bastard, I don't know what is. I can sense his eyes on my scars, so I snatch my left hand away and put both of my hands behind my back.

He tries again. "The healing was successful?" I can't stop my polite head from nodding in response.

Instead, I should swear at him. Scream. Smack him. Rage. But I can't force myself to do that. Screaming and shouting won't get me anywhere. I have to be smart, bide my time.

I know I need to let things go, move on. If I don't...I nibble on my lip, my eyes still firmly planted on his chest. I am not sure I will like the person I will become.

Pure hate is not an emotion I want to feel constantly. It rots. John Hesketh is not having that power over me.

"Yes, thank...you," I mumble.

He puts his coffee down and pulls off his hoodie. The white shirt underneath tugs up to reveal smooth abs before he pulls it back down again. The grey jogging bottoms he is wearing sit low on his hips. Forearms flexing, he tosses the jumper onto a nearby kitchen chair. He leans against the counter and crosses his arms over his broad chest. His top stretches tight across his broad shoulders and energy rolls off him, ferocious, alive.

I want to run my hands down that chest and feel the hard ridges of his abs.

Oh hell. I almost swallow my tongue. My attraction to him must be a mental impairment or something magical. *It's not real.* It can't be.

My thumb points behind me in the door's direction. "I need to go to an appointment tomorrow. I'm just letting you know."

"An appointment for what?" His voice changes from polite and chocolatey to deep and aggressive. I bet if I look, his eyes will be glowing orange. I have a strange urge to say, "A gynaecology appointment." Teach him to not be nosy. But I refrain from lying, even if it would be funny to see his expression.

"To view a livery yard for Bob."

"No," he growls. In John's mind, the conversation is finished.

He drops his arms and turns away from me in apparent dismissal. He continues with his cooking.

My mouth drops open...how rude. What. A. Nob.

My temper flares. "Am I your pet?" I growl at his back. I try to keep the venom and the frustration out of my tone, but I fail miserably. He turns back around to look at me.

"Of course you aren't. You're a demon—you are no one's pet," he bites out.

"A prisoner?"

John shakes his head.

"That's great, then you can't stop me. As soon as I can find a home for Bob, I'm leaving."

John shakes his head at me as if I'm a naughty, disobedient child. He steps closer to me, and I'm enveloped in his scent.

I'd like to say the hellhound smells of wet dog, but he doesn't, he smells of campfires and linen fabric softener. His scent tickles the back of my nose and throat. It makes me dizzy.

"You do not understand the dangers of the world out there—"

I lift my head and meet his green eyes with a glare. The edges of his eyes glow orange. My heart misses a beat.

"Oh, don't I?" I plough on, choosing to ignore the orange eyes that scare the crap out of me. I also have creepy eyes, so John isn't a special snowflake. "Well, from the viewpoint of standing here, the world looks mighty safe in comparison." I point to the floor in front of him.

"Emma, I apologised for our misunderstanding." *Misunderstanding?* Ha, the bloody crazy hellhound...he calls what he did to me a misunderstanding?

A laugh slips from my lips and darkness creeps into my vision. I can almost sense my eyes bleeding demon black. Now that I know what it is, it takes nothing for me to blink it away. I have a lot of work to do in controlling the demon part of me, but I will not start by letting it control me.

I huff and slam down on my accusatory words that are screaming in my head to be heard. I cross my arms across my chest and glare at him. I was going to sleep at my new place and pretend to be still living here, but stuff it, I won't do it—I'm not pretending anymore. I will not be a hypocrite like these two idiots that claim they are protecting me.

I have to live my life with my rules, and I'm not pandering to this...this hellhound.

For a few seconds, I clamp my lips closed, afraid to open my mouth again in case he accuses me of being overemotional. My nostrils flare with my building rage, and between clenched teeth, I carefully say, "Look, John Hesketh, I'm not your pet or prisoner, and if you've forgotten, I'm not a minor either. I'm a twenty-two-year-old woman, not a child. Frankly, I'm done. I will not live under your roof for one more minute. I don't trust you. I have a safe place to live, but to be honest, if I didn't, I'd rather sleep in the stables or on the streets then take any more of your *hospitality*." I spit the word. John's eyes flame more with his growing frustration. "I am not asking for your permission. I'm telling you out of courtesy, but you take my good manners, twist them, and demand more of me. I've had enough. Just so you know, John, I have already moved out. I do not need, nor do I want"—I curl two figures on both hands and do the annoying finger-quote thing to make my point—"your 'protection.'" I indignantly huff out an angry breath.

I turn to leave, then stop and spin back—I have another bone to pick with him, "Also, what the hell did you do to my friend? She won't even look at me. My only friend and you had her spying on me? Reporting back to you? What happened when Sam, my only friend, told you she'd known me since I was ten years old, that she watched me grow up? Sam practically raised me. Did you not think, 'Huh, grunt-grunt. Emma isn't a demon mastermind after all'? I didn't take you for stupid, John Hesketh, so don't take me for a fool. Leave my friend alone. Oh, and while you're at it, forget about me." He moves his arm and I flinch. His eyes soften. "I was angry with you and I took it out on her, blamed her. When I should have blamed you. You manipulative twat." I drop my voice and whisper, "Why do you ruin everything?"

John regards me with solemn green eyes. "Please, pay her what you owe, protect her if that's your agreement. Then please, for the love of God, leave her alone."

Now it's my turn to turn away, dismissing the monstrous hellhound.

Take that, you dickhead, I think smugly as I stomp out of the house. I slam the door as hard as I can behind me. I know it's childish, but I don't care.

I'm going to get a pizza, I'm starving. Huh, it hits me. Without Bert, I can now eat what I want without pain. Wow.

"Emma," John calls out from behind me. I jump with a squeak at the sound of his voice. Gah, I didn't even hear him follow me outside. Creepy hellhound.

I take my time in turning around. I school my face into a blank mask as I turn to face him. I do an Eleanor and plant my hands on my hips. Even though he is at least a foot and a half taller than me, I tilt my head as if I'm looking down on him. He is total scum. I am so over this man's shit.

When I look at him, all I feel is anger.

Anger is good, healthy.

"One thing I want to say in case we do not see each other again, is, if you are ever stuck, need a doctor, a solicitor, or a portal to get you out of somewhere...you know you can call me. I'll be there for you." His eyes have gone back to green, and he slumps his shoulders in defeat.

My left eye twitches at his words, and I slap my hand over it. My soft heart squeezes...No—I can't let his pretty words and solemn eyes sway me. I don't believe him for one second. His whole sad posture is a lie. He is attempting to manipulate me.

Too right, hellhound, you owe me, but it's not a debt I'm willing to let him pay. "I'm good. Oh, if you wouldn't mind letting me use the equestrian facilities for a few more days, a week at the most, until I can get Bob somewhere safe, I'd appreciate it. Please let Bob stay until I can find him somewhere, that's all I ask." John nods in agreement. Then he lifts his hands and rubs the back of his head. His top rises with the movement, flashing more toned skin and abs.

Gah. He so did that on purpose.

"You know that won't make us even." He speaks softly, his voice warm and deep. His energy trickles around me, playful and cajoling.

"We will never be even," I whisper as I spin away from him.

"No," he says quietly to my back.

CHAPTER TWENTY-THREE

After spending the night in my new home and sleeping on my cloud-like bed, I feel well-rested and confident. I arrive on time for my meeting at the livery yard. As I haven't been to the stable yard before, I couldn't zap myself there using my pocket gateway, so instead I got as close as I could and then got a taxi.

Everything was going so well until I was ushered into the yard office. "Your kind isn't welcome. You really should have been more transparent on the phone," the manager hisses at me. He lets go of my arm with a shudder and promptly pumps hand sanitiser from a bottle on his desk into his palm. Vigorously, he rubs his hands together.

What? Does he know I am part demon? Does everyone know, do I smell of sulphur? Oh my God, that must be it, I must have a demon stink.

"Our livery rates discourage humans. I have never had a human request a stable before—this is unprecedented. This equestrian centre is a human-free establishment."

Oh. Relief floods me. By my kind he means *human*. The yard is *a human-free establishment*—what a load of codswallop. I stare at him, grinding my teeth. I'm stuck, because if I tell him I am not entirely human and I am half-demon, he will laugh at me for lying, or worse, call the Hunters' Guild to arrest me.

To think I wasted taxi money to get here just to be insulted.

He is a boggart, an English fae. Sometimes people call them house-elves; in Ireland, they are called brownies. Tall, blond, and wiry, the fae sniffs at me with disdain. Even though he is wearing horse gear from head to toe, he looks like he hasn't seen or been near a horse in his life. He's so spick-and-span, the thought *"all the gear and no idea"* comes to mind when I look at him and his immaculate, shiny boots. But as he is the manager of an equestrian centre, he must have the experience, right?

What seems more likely to me is, the *human* grooms that are outside scurrying around are the ones doing all the work.

Human-free establishment, my ass.

I *almost* look back at him with a sneer, a rude reply on the tip of my tongue, but I stop myself. Whoa, what the heck is wrong with me? *My nana would be ashamed of me,* the thought hits me in the chest.

The guy is a boggart; they are renowned for being clean and tidy. That's what makes them so unique. Perhaps it's the owner of the yard that sets the no-human-client rules? Maybe he will get into trouble for even having me on the premises.

To protect myself from going all demon-evil I have to do better; I have to be morally beyond reproach. I tap my fingertips on my thigh rhythmically. The canter-strum calms me.

I need to nail the virtues...urm...when I look up what they are. Courage...and something...I squint at the thought. I think there are seven of them, or is that seven sins? I roll my eyes. It doesn't matter. In the meantime, it's time to set my rules...

Rule number one: Don't be a dickhead.

Rule number two: Be kind—always.

Rule number three: Don't lie to yourself.

Rule number fou...I need to write these down.

The boggart is looking at me as if I am nuts—I've been silent for too long. He points at the door with a glare and even taps his shiny foot impatiently.

Oh heck, it's a shame I have to break a rule right off the bat. "It's not for me," I say, scratching my nose. With a slight cringe and a shake of my head, I shove my hands behind my back and cross my fingers. "The stable is for my employer's horse. He is a demon, Mr..." I look at the guy's brown jacket that is placed carefully over his chair, "...Brown." The lie sticks in my throat, and I swallow down my nervousness. One small lie doesn't mean I'm evil...this is for Bob. "Mr Brown is a barrister for the guilds."

The guilds enforce the law and prevent crime and civil disorder. The dominant races have their guilds controlling their people, with everyone overseen by the Hunters' Guild. Which means the guilds are scary and important.

"Oh, Mr Brown...why didn't you say so?" the boggart says, nodding his blond head as if he and my made-up Mr Brown are besties. I barely refrain from rolling my eyes. "When will Mr Brown be able to come and sign the livery agreement?"

I huff out a breath, dramatically look around, and drop my voice to a whisper. "Mr Brown is incredibly busy, and he is currently off-world."

"Off-world?" The boggart whispers back, his voice filled with awe. I nod and put a finger to my lips as if to indicate it's a secret. He nods back and glances around his—apart from us—empty office. "Of course, of course, say no more."

"It also depends on whether I find the yard satisfactory. I'm unsure if we're going to stable Bob here. Mr Brown expects only the best." Oh God, am I laying it on a bit too thick?

"Of course, of course, let me show you around."

The livery yard ends up being perfect. It has sixty stables split over several yards. Some are the American-style barns with the stables enclosed under one roof, with the stable doors overlooking an internal walkway and an external window at the rear. My favourite yard is where I score an empty stable. The yard is one of the smaller ones, with only ten stables. Each large box overlooks a pretty central courtyard. Designed in a traditional brick style in a horseshoe shape, the adorable stables have a clock tower and a cockerel weathervane.

The facilities are also crazily good, with two huge international-sized indoor riding arenas and three smaller outdoor riding arenas. There is also a horse walker, a lunging ring and all-year grazing. There is also a farm ride, so like the estate I can hack Bob out without having to venture onto any roads. The place is incredible.

By the end of my visit, Stuart, the boggart yard manager, is eating out of my hand. He even arranges transport for Bob and all my horsey equipment to be collected from John's. I pay up front for the full year, and Stuart allows me to sign the livery documents on Mr Brown's behalf.

Phew.

Oh heck, I will at some point have to magic up a Mr Brown, but after reading a particularly interesting demon book last night before bed, I have a rough plan for that.

* * *

I lounge on the red leather sofa, a cover on my lap and a mug of tea in my hand, as I flick through the giant tome balanced precariously on my chest. I should do this at the desk. The book is so old that I should probably be wearing the fancy white gloves that historians wear to look at old books and parchments.

Instead, I'm sipping tea a little too close to it, and I'm in danger of dripping the liquid onto the pages. I am an idiot and I'm not thinking. My brain has short-circuited, and I can focus only on the words. The book has my undivided attention; it is absolutely fascinating. If I can do what the text indicates...if it is within the scope of my powers...I should...urm...be able to change my face.

Yeah, my face. It seems from further reading that not only can I change my face but my body type and sex...and if I want to, I could switch into an animal form, too. Wow. It's crazy.

This is one of the reasons demons are so dangerous. This is the reason John kept demanding to see my *real* face. According to this book—I tap my finger on a page—I can look like whatever I want.

Freaky.

Wide-eyed, I take another mouthful of tea and shiver. The book isn't an instruction manual. It hints at how to do things, but it doesn't give any clear directions or details. Ahh, magic users are so mean. With the whole, you could do this...but nah, I'm not telling you how because you should have proper people around you to show you. Reading between the lines, I think I have a rough idea of what I need to do. I gulp some more tea and my heart pounds in my ears.

The thought of being able to look like anyone is thrilling.

The possibilities are endless, as it's not just hypothetically shifting into a person or an animal. According to this book, it's *everything*, including clothing and weapons.

Can you imagine...

I'm in a scary situation, and bam, I look like John with all his muscles. Come on, who is going to mess with John? Or if I need to blend into a crowd or disappear into a small space? Being able to change my appearance to blend in is a game-changer. It's not like I'm unmemorable; you see my white-blonde hair and there is no missing me.

I've always been a pretty girl—oh woe is me, I have long blonde hair and pretty blue eyes, the universe is punishing me...sob...sob. Ha. I am not moaning about that, but being pretty in this world puts me at risk from the predators. It makes me an easy target. Add being half-demon without protection to the mix, and I'm doomed.

From my understanding, when shifters turn into animal form, they have to remove their clothing to do so. A friendly shifter guard at the estate once told me that shifters can use a witch's potion to shift with their clothing. But the potions are expensive and difficult to get hold of, and they're only really available if a shifter is on friendly terms with a talented witch. The guard sneered at the idea of taking a potion. I have no idea why...I guess most shifters are men and getting their bits and pieces out in public isn't an issue for them.

According to this book, demons don't need to strip. Everything...clothing, jewellery, weaponry...should shift with me. If I can just learn how.

I tap the book in thought. It all hinges on this question: was my father a first-level demon? If he was, there is a possibility that I will also have that level of power, or at least a small version of it anyway.

I have hope, as when the pocket dimension turned into my home, I realised I must be relatively high on the power scale. Why would it adapt so quickly if I wasn't?

My point is, I would enjoy nothing more than being able to go about my day unnoticed, without the risk of an inappropriate touch or comment. Ultimately, without fear.

Everything I've got to do to keep myself safe is almost overwhelming. I have so much to do. I'm so alone.

I've never felt so scared or so free.

The nervous excitement I feel at the endless possibilities, but also the stress of pending failure, gives me a mild headache. I put everything away and decide that what I need is to get some fresh air.

I need to go ride Bob and then get some food-shopping. Which is kind of exciting...I've never shopped for food before, and to me, going into the supermarket and filling the trolley with stuff is exciting. It is such a normal thing to do, a small thing that proves how controlled and insular my life with Arlo was.

Time will tell if my freedom is a good or a bad thing.

I hope I have the time to learn...as I have a horrible, nagging feeling that things are going to get worse.

CHAPTER TWENTY-FOUR

I've just bought my first-ever load of practical food. It was a challenge, as at one point I had a trolley full of random items, stuff that I like to eat but that didn't go together. When I realised that custard, mashed potato, and olives weren't really a good flavour combination, I had to turn around and start all over again, putting things back and picking up items that would not only work together, but was stuff that I might actually cook. Ha, at least I had the epiphany before I paid.

As I am leaving the supermarket, I see leaflets fluttering on the customer notice board. I guess not everyone can afford the internet. Nosily, I turn my head and scan the ads.

A flyer catches my eye. It is for a women's self-defence class at a local gym. Huh. Now that might be handy, and there is a new class tomorrow evening.

I put the trolley back and battle to free my pound coin from the locking mechanism that is holding it hostage. It has gotten dark while I've been inside, and the car park is strangely empty.

I hurry away from the supermarket; I avoid the car park and stick to the pavement. As I make my way around the side of the store towards a normally busy shopping area up the road, the hairs on my arms rise and a shiver works its way down my spine. My instincts scream at me, *I am being followed.*

My eyes dart about, my heart thuds. As I pass a dark shop, I glance in the window at the reflection of the street behind me. My heart misses a beat when I spot them tailing me. Three vampires are hunting me.

I'm sure there are more.

They move so elegantly that they almost float, compared to me as I shuffle awkwardly along the street, overloaded with my shopping. I hold the bags in my sweaty, tight-fisted grip, my still-weak arms trembling. The bags rustle and my heart pounds; sweat beads on the back of my neck. Somehow I don't think they have anything to do with John... the word must have gotten out about my being a demon, or about my unprotected status. Creatures love to gossip, and I am guessing these vampires are probably opportunists looking for an easy mark. A snack.

They mean for me to see them, so I'm more worried about the ones that I can't yet see. I think I am being herded. With so many eyes on me, opening my doorway is going to be a challenge.

With trepidation, I search the quiet street. I was going to go to a shop that I know well and use their doorway, but it's further up the road. Too far up the road—I need to get out of here pronto.

Unfortunately, I can't use the supermarket doors as they are automatic and they don't have a door handle. I contemplate abandoning my shopping, dropping it to the street and running, but I know the vampires will be on me within seconds.

A can clangs down the street, noisily scraping the ground as it rolls across the pavement. The sound spooks me. My heart jumps and I spin, my shopping bags painfully smacking against my legs as I abruptly do a sideways shuffle into a dark alley.

Not the smart-prey move.

Nice one, Emma. I am being hunted by vampires, so what do I do? I hop into a dark alley. I hope my crazy move will confuse the hunting vampires as much as it does me. If I'm lucky, it might gain me a few extra unseen seconds to find a doorway and escape.

I hurry past two huge bright-yellow bins full of rubbish and food waste. I breathe through my mouth so I don't get a whiff of the rotting garbage. Yuck...mouth-breathing doesn't help, as the stench is so bad it fills my mouth to the point where I can almost chew it.

The alley has rear fire doors for a takeaway and a nightclub. I head towards the closer nightclub door, which I know will be locked. However, I *hope* I can access my home through the locked door before the vampires arrive at the top of the alleyway and grab me. I've never attempted to use a locked door before.

Crap. Perhaps this is a thing I should have practised?

I jump almost a foot into the air when there is a crash, a bang, and a gurgling scream at the mouth of the alley. What the hell is that?

An echoing, angry growl reverberates off the tight walls of the surrounding buildings. A shifter has joined the party.

Oh hell, a bad shifter or a good shifter? Oh God. Oh God. I don't look back and instead I break into a run. I avoid a puddle of something unpleasant as my feet slap against the tarmac. When I get close to the door, my hands shake as I push the bag handles down my right arm to the crook of my elbow to free my hand. I reach for the handle and open *my* door.

Heart pounding, I rush inside and slam the door closed and slump panting next to my touchy-feely ward. My back thumps against the door.

Safe.

God, I feel sick. That was way too close.

I drop my bags in disgust. I bought too much stuff and I encumbered myself with the shopping—that choice could have killed me. I scrub my shaking hands across my face. I need to do better.

I remove my coat. When I go to remove my boots...eww...a used condom is stuck to the bottom of my left shoe. I almost throw up in my mouth. That is *nasty*. I am so glad I have gloves and that I bought bleach. I carefully remove my boot. That will teach me to wander into nightclub alleyways, I think with a curl of my lip and a full-body shudder.

I ignore my shopping and my poor boot for now. Dejectedly I wander over to the sofa and slump down. I stare up at the ceiling. One step forward and then two steps straight back...I'm rubbish at this. I can't even do a basic shop without messing everything up. I tug at my ponytail and then rub my face in frustration.

My real strategy hung on my being able to change my entire visage or being able to run. Crap, it looks as if hoping to have a handy doorway to step through will never be a foolproof plan.

I groan. This is no way to live, and at the moment I'm a demon that feels like prey. If I don't get myself at least halfway able to look after myself, I'm going to get hurt. Dead.

I need desperately to learn some self-defence so I can at least fight if needed or stop an attacker long enough so I can run away. The whole being-stalked-by-vampires has seriously upped my deadline. I need to be able to handle myself. *You dealt with vampires before when you went all stabby,* my brain helpfully pipes up. I rub my wrist.

God, I don't want to kill anybody. But I do need to add "learning to fight" to my growing list.

Handy that I now know of a place that has a class tomorrow.

Fighting wasn't something I ever had to think about in my old life—I was surrounded by guards. Dance, horse riding...I even had singing lessons, but nothing as uncouth as fighting. It would be silly to learn an actual useful skill to keep me alive. I roll my eyes.

Gosh, I have so much to learn. It's so overwhelming.

I lean forward to plant my elbows on my knees and rest my head in my hands. I rub at my temples. There was that one time that Arlo mentioned that I was immortal...bloody hell, I need to be immortal, to get through my piling-up to-do list.

My phone rings. This pocket is so weird—the internet and my mobile phone work, but how? Just like with the electricity,

I have no idea. Pocket-dimension free wi-fi and power. I just hope someday I don't get an enormous bill. I jump up, sidestep my boot, and grab my phone from my coat pocket. I groan when I see who is calling. I answer.

"Emma, are you safe? Your scent disappeared and I can't track you," John says.

Oh bloody hell, it was him. My frightened brain didn't imagine the growl...the gurgling. I shudder.

How on earth did he track me down at the supermarket? Is this another trick? A test? Gah, I want to tell him to get lost. I have the perfect rude words but I stop them from leaving my mouth, as I don't want to antagonise the scary hellhound.

Instead, I aim for diplomacy. "I am fine..." How can answering him be so difficult? Talking to him...I swallow. "Thank you for your help, but as I've said before...I'm not your responsibility. I can look after myself just fine, thank you very much." I say it primly, but my words are sour with dishonesty.

Liar, liar, pants on fire.

The truth is, I occupy a strange space between being a damsel in distress and knowing enough about the evils of this world to realise my vulnerability. I am doomed.

I know it, and the man on the phone knows it.

I am also stubborn, and I'm unwilling to allow my fear of the unknown, of what could happen, to curb me. I will have no one dictate my life going forward.

I don't want a man to come to my rescue. I want to be a hero, not a snack.

"You can look after yourself?" he scoffs, his tone incredulous. "Tell me then why you had vampires hunting you? Did you even notice them?" He lets out a patronising laugh and I grind my teeth.

"Yes, I noticed them. I got away, didn't I? Did I miss hearing the beginning of our conversation when you, the mighty hellhound, said that you'd lost my scent?" I say smugly. "So that was you? With the vampires...were you helping them?" I narrow my eyes and John growls down the phone at me.

I wait for him to answer. With a grunt, he says, "Stopping them."

"Oh, okay...well...urm...thank you?" I scratch my head and puff out my cheeks. "Do...do you, urm, know what they wanted?"

"Emma," he says, a warning in his voice.

"Oh, look at that"—a painful laugh slips out—"I can't even ask a simple question about my safety." He sighs and the phone rustles like he is smacking it against his head. "You don't have to help me out of guilt." As soon as the words leave my mouth, I realise how ridiculous I sound.

God, I want to smack my phone against my head, too. The idea of John reacting from any emotion other than anger is nuts. Ha, something as frivolous as guilt wouldn't motivate him.

"A master vampire has taken an unhealthy interest in you."

"Unhealthy?"

"Yes, for him. I am going to kill him."

Well, that is a little extreme. I open my mouth and no words come out. What can I say to that? "Thanks?" I slump against the wall and toe my abandoned shopping bags.

"I don't know any master vampires...oh, oooh, the crazy guy with the bow in his hair and the lace."

"Yes, Alexander," he growls out.

"Alexander...why? Is he going to keep sending people after me?"

"No. He will not have another chance."

"Why, 'cause he's going to be dead? Can't I talk to him, try to reason with him? You don't have to kill him."

"For fuck's sake, Emma, are you for real?" he explodes. "Do you think this is a game? He sent ten vampires tonight, and it's not the first time."

"Hang on...not the first time—"

"Look, I've got to go—"

"Was it him...did he send those vampires to the house? The ones that wanted to hurt Bob? The ones that hit the car?" Silence. "John?" I pull the phone away from my ear and check the screen. The bloody hellhound has hung up on me. I throw my hands in the air. Why is he so infuriating?

Arrrah, he is so annoying.

This is my life. Shouldn't I have some input?

I turn my phone off. I glare at the dark screen and grind my teeth. I groan, and with a throaty growl, I turn the phone back on in case the livery yard calls and Bob needs me. I can't risk missing that kind of call. I shove the handset back into my coat pocket.

I grab my shopping bags and head for the kitchen. Why does he care, why can't he leave me the hell alone? I slam the kitchen doors as I put the food away. This is my problem to deal with; it's got nothing to do with him. I got away fine and I hurt no one. I lean against the worktop. No. He will not handle my problems for me.

I spin and go back to my coat and grab the phone. I tap it against my thigh. I know two vampires; one isn't talking to me and the other...well, I've been avoiding her.

Is it wrong to call her? I hop from foot to foot. I thumb through my contacts and impulsively press the call button.

"Hello?"

"Hi, Mum, it's Emma. I need your help."

CHAPTER TWENTY-FIVE

Like with the supermarket, I've never been to a nightclub before. The music is blaring, and the flash-flash-flash of the lights makes my growing tension headache worse. The surrounding people are happily dancing, drinking, and shouting to be heard over the pounding bass. The club smells of sweat, old beer, and cloying perfume.

I thought my skinny jeans and pretty top would help me blend, but it seems I'm way overdressed. The rest of the patrons of the club are practically naked and I'm standing out, and not in a good way.

I shouldn't be here—it's a mistake. I know it's a mistake, but a big part of my life now is about moving forward, and I can't move forward with the chains of my past dragging me down. I could continue to ignore her, I could spend a lifetime ignoring her, but my anger isn't healthy.

I'd also like to somehow stop the vampire, this Alexander... before John pulls his head off.

A twinge pinches my stomach. *Nerves*. Gosh, I feel so nervous. I cross my arms over my stomach. The demon... although he disapproved, he never stopped me from searching for my mother. As soon as I was old enough to understand, I searched for her online in fury, and found...nothing.

Thanks to an old-fashioned address book that I found while digging through Arlo's desk, though, I've had my mum's phone number for a week. To think it was in his desk the entire time.

I creep around the edge of the room, avoiding grabby hands, and head towards the back of the nightclub to a bar area that stretches the full length of the back wall. I spot her immediately and grind to a halt, my feet sticking to the floor with shock. Like a statue I stand and just stare at her.

As I watch her work, I fiddle with the bottom of my blouse until my stomach tightens again, and my heart flips. She smiles and serves drinks to strangers as, laughing, she tucks a piece of blonde hair—so like mine—behind her ear. Vampirism has frozen her at twenty-four and we look like sisters...heck, we could almost be twins instead of mother and daughter.

I swallow a lump in my throat. I can't force my feet to move forward.

Is this what she imagined her life would be when she sold me to a demon so she could bribe the vampires to turn her? I try to push the bitterness away, but it hangs around my neck like a heavy chain.

My mum lifts her head and our eyes meet. A bright, blinding smile lights up her face. "Emma," she mouths. She drops everything and she is suddenly there in front of me. Her hands shake and she goes to touch me—perhaps to tuck a loose strand of my hair behind my ear. I flinch away and she drops her hand to her side. Her lip wobbles.

Oh bloody hell.

It takes but a second for me to be flooded with guilt, especially when her eyes flood with tears. "Hi, Mum," I say with a wave and a matching wobbly smile.

She looks about. "Let's talk somewhere quieter," she says as she grabs my hand and pulls me with her. We weave through the middle of the dancing, gyrating bodies and head towards a door that is marked PRIVATE.

When we step inside I find it's a staff room. As soon as the door clicks behind us, the throbbing sound of the club outside fades, and the thud-thud of the music disappears almost entirely. They have pushed a table and chairs against one dark-blue wall, and a leather sofa backs against another.

There is also a small kitchen, comprising a couple of cupboards, a worktop, a white under-the-counter fridge, a microwave, and a kettle.

"Would you like a cup of tea?" Without waiting for my answer and with shaking hands, she fills the kettle with water and clicks it on to boil.

She turns and perches on the edge of the sofa. Her hands settle between her knees, and she trembles. "What can I help you with, Emma?" she asks, blinking up at me. It is then that I realise that I'm looming over her. I grab a chair from the table, spin it around, and sit.

There are so many questions I have, but she looks so fragile. Her genuine, bright smile when she saw me and the tears in her eyes have thrown me off completely. She doesn't look heartless. My stomach crunches and flips. Suddenly I don't feel the need to demand answers from her. As I look into her teary blue eyes, I see worry and fear staring back at me, and it makes me feel sad. This lady is a stranger. I shouldn't have come here, and I shouldn't have even thought about involving her in my problems. I am selfish.

"You've grown. It's so strange...like looking in a mirror." She lets out a painful laugh and licks her lips and bounces her knees. "Your eyes, though, are so different, beautiful...I thought I remembered them but not clearly enough." She ducks her head and looks at her hands. "What kind of mother doesn't remember her daughter's eyes?" she mumbles self-deprecatingly.

"They change colour," I say, to make her feel better. "Every day they are different, depending on my mood and what I wear." I tug at my top and smile uncertainly at her. "Urm...thanks for seeing me so quickly." I cringe and let go of my top and instead twist my hands in my lap. "I'm sorry that the circumstances aren't better. As I said on the phone, I found your number and I needed some information." I shrug and attempt a reassuring smile.

It doesn't work, as my mum frowns and leaps from the sofa. She busies herself with finishing the tea. I sigh and continue anyway. "A master vampire is attempting to...urm, I guess, kidnap me? I'd like to find out why. I need his contact details so I can persuade him to back off before he loses any more of his minions or his life. There's this hellhound..." I tug at my hair. "I am not worth this amount of trouble," I finish lamely.

My mum pours the boiling water into the cups, places the kettle back on the side, and turns to face me. Confusion fills her eyes, and she shakes her head. "Sweetheart, you're not that naïve. You know what he wants." She gives me a sad smile and drops her voice to a whisper. "It is what all wicked men want."

Behind me, the door to the staff room clicks open. For a moment, the loud music from the club blasts inside, and I wince and rub my temple as my head pounds painfully in protest. The door closes and I swivel in my chair to eye the newcomer.

A pureblood vampire strolls across the room. A pureblood. A born vampire. My lips part in shock.

Born vampires are entirely different from turned vampires as they were never human; they never had mortal, human failings to start with. Born-vampire DNA produces exquisite-looking creatures. They are the supermodels of the creature world. There aren't many born vampires around, and the ones that are have an almost cult-like status among other creatures—everyone seems to worship them.

As I stare at him, the pureblood, I don't see the appeal. Yes, he is handsome, with his tailored bespoke navy suit from London's Savile Row that perfectly accentuates his wide shoulders and narrow hips. His floppy blond hair has a warm golden hue compared to my mum's ice-white, and his dark-blue eyes are almost the same shade as his suit. To me, he looks fake—airbrushed. Photoshopped. Perhaps even doll-like. Creepy.

I can feel his powerful energy and the monster inside him. On a danger scale from one to John, he is a level six.

My body twitches as if it wants to automatically stand in deference, but I firmly keep my bum planted on the seat. I pin my shoulders back, straighten my spine, and lift my chin.

I watch him approach with narrowed eyes.

I instinctively know that on the power scale, I'm somehow stronger than the pureblood. Huh, well, that's a recent development.

My eyes narrow further as I watch my mum deflate before me, her shoulders rounding and her body shrinking an inch at a time. He frightens her, even when he glides across the room and envelopes her stiff body in his arms and kisses the top of her head.

"Martine, who is this?" Huh, a game player. He knows who I am...unless my mum has other kids or clones stashed about.

"Luther, this is my little girl, Emma. Emma, this is Lord Gilbert, I don't think you remember, you were such a little thing..." her voice fades.

That's strange...I've met this guy before? "Hi, Lord Gilbert." I wave.

He tilts his head down, chin almost to his chest, as he assesses me. "Hello, Emma, how marvellous that you are as beautiful as your mother." He rolls his fingers in a wave of his hand and his nose goes up in the air with a sniff. "I didn't think that would be possible, what with all that disgusting demon DNA."

I huff out a startled breath.

What. A. Dick.

I slowly nod in acknowledgement of his words. My lips tug themselves into a small smile. *Oh dear, was I rude, not standing?* Yep, definitely. Arlo trained me how to greet other creatures, and not standing and giving the pureblood a formal bow is a real no-no. I know I shouldn't press his buttons and piss him off—I already have one vampire problem. But for some stupid reason, I can't help myself.

Mhm. I watch as he turns to the side, angling his body and face just so, highlighting his physique as if on a photo shoot. My eyes flick around the room as I search for the hidden cameraman. It's odd—normal people don't do that. This guy loves himself, and it's like he is in another world of his own making.

"Emma has an issue with a master vampire," my mum rushes to tell him.

"Who?" he asks me.

"Alexander."

"Ah, Alexander. The man is a lowly worm." I nod again. He narrows his eyes at me. I barely refrain from glaring back at him. I don't like this man. Something about him raises my hackles. "What is it about children? You only see them when they want something."

Huh. I squirm in my chair. The pureblood doesn't know me; he knows nothing about me. Yet I find myself looking down at my hands in embarrassment: he has a point.

I knew I shouldn't have come here. I just...I didn't want to be responsible for another person's death, so without proper thought, I jumped at an opportunity to gather information. Perhaps, being honest, I also used it as an excuse to see my mum.

No, I shouldn't be here, and I blame bloody John. I wouldn't be in this room if it wasn't for him.

I'd also be more scared of the pureblood. John broke something inside me...or...maybe he let something out? I lift my eyebrows. Wow, that's a scary thought.

Alexander is a centuries-old master vampire and responsible for his own actions. I remember the vampire's crazy rolling eyes...his giggling. You can't talk sense into that kind of person; it would be useless to try. I don't need Alexander's details, I don't need to talk to him. I'm reacting on impulse, an impulse to rebel against John and his ill-conceived protection.

If I got Alexander's details, what was I going to do? Say to him, "Please don't kidnap me...oh, and watch out for the hellhound that is coming to kill you." Ha, I didn't think this out at all. Being impulsive could get me killed.

I'm breaking rule number one: Don't be a dickhead; *and* rule number two: Be kind. I'm not being kind to my mum or myself. I was wrong. God, I shouldn't have come here.

I stand. I ignore the pompous Lord Gilbert and smile at my mum. "I can see you are busy. Thank you for your time—

it was lovely seeing you, Mum. I hope we can do this again, perhaps meet up somewhere quiet for a cup of tea?" Her eyes fly to the now-stewed tea on the side. "It's okay, I will ring you. I promise." I turn to leave.

"Didn't that demon I sent you to not teach you anything?" asks Lord Gilbert.

I stop. The demon *he* sent me to? What the hell?

Heck, look at that. He made that comment without even a hint of *mwahaha*. He doesn't even bother to villain it up— he just drops that bomb without care. *Boom.* I glance at my mum. She won't meet my eyes.

Okay, pureblood, I can play along.

My chest aches as I suppress the urge to growl and my eyes burn and go hazy as I fight to stop them from turning black.

My mum's introduction to Lord Gilbert, when she asked me if I remembered him, now makes more sense—how would I have remembered him if I hadn't met him before? According to my demon master, my mum didn't know any vampires before she sold me.

"*You* sent me to?" I say through gritted teeth. I raise an eyebrow. "Huh. You make it sound if you sent me off to school. So just to clarify, it was *you*, Lord Gilbert, who *sold* me to a demon's household?" He nods his head. I shake mine in response and my nostrils flare.

Un-bloody-believable.

"I didn't need the hassle of a five-year-old demon spawn."

What is it about powerful people? How they ruin lives without a thought. Without care. My eyes flick to my mum and she is crying. Oh, Mum. Silent tears roll down her face. All these years I hated her. What a waste of emotion: she never threw me away. "So it wasn't my mum's decision, was it? It was yours." I tap my lips. "As you know...what with all my disgusting demon DNA...the last time I checked, a demon was my daddy, not you. You had no right to sell me, Lord Gilbert." I want to scream and rage at him. Inside, I am livid.

The pureblood licks his lips, enjoying my reaction. I force myself to drop the anger and instead I contort my lips into a smirk.

He starts again to angle his body and face in weird poses, and I realise belatedly that he's peacocking. If he had feathers, he'd be flapping them about. He looks me up and down, almost like he's mentally stripping me naked. Eww. His attention makes me want to go straight home and have a shower.

"What's done is done. I clearly made a mistake in sending you away. You are a lovely creature, Emma. I can offer you my protection against Alexander, in exchange for you working for me." I scrunch my nose as his tongue again flicks out of his mouth. Eww. Does the tongue thing work for him? I shudder.

Out of the corner of my eye, I catch a movement. My mum imperceptibly shakes her head no. Her puffy, tear-filled eyes scream at me, beg me, to refuse.

I keep my eyes firmly on his. "No thank you, Lord Gilbert. I appreciate the offer, but I am happy on my own." I'm not at the stage where I am ready to deal with the Devil—demon pun intended.

God, I will have to somehow let John deal with the Alexander matter. I don't want people killed in my name. But it looks like it is out of my hands. I am out of my depth.

What I can do is work out how I can get my mum alone and perhaps away from this idiot. Impulsively I step forward, and fold her into a hug. I can't help the extra squeeze I give her. "I will see you soon," I reassure her.

"Okay, sweetheart." She squeezes me back.

"Oh, Emma, you don't have to worry about your admirer. He is dead. A team of hellhounds killed him and his inner circle"—the pureblood flicks his wrist and looks down at an ostentatious solid-gold-and-diamond watch—"about forty minutes ago." He smiles at me.

I close my eyes for a split second so I can absorb that nugget of information. I'm way too late. I would have always been too late.

John must have been ready to bust the door down when he called me. I don't understand what's going on in that man's mind; it's probably got nothing to do with me and everything to do with John using me as an excuse to settle an old score or old debts. He's fooled me so many times, everything he says can be taken as either half truthful or an outright lie. It's impossible to understand John's motivations. Perhaps rule number four should be: Don't trust the hellhound. John at least falls firmly into the territory of rule number one, don't be a dickhead.

If the pureblood wants a shocked response from me, he will have to wait a long bloody time. He knew Alexander was dead before he entered the room.

Instead, I give my mum a small wave, turn, and head towards the door. I open the door and blessed silence greets me—home.

I can't help myself: I look back over my shoulder at the pureblood and I'm gratified to see the confusion on his face. It confuses him, why his club is so quiet…ha.

To hammer my point home, I let go of the tenuous hold on my eyes and allow them to bleed black. "See you around, Luther," I whisper creepily.

I step through the door and disappear.

CHAPTER TWENTY-SIX

The gym is old-school in style and based within an ancient industrial building. The place looks rough, with its dirty, marked, off-white walls. But a good sign is that it smells like lemon cleaner rather than sweat and blood.

There's a reception desk with a small shop behind it, selling things like gloves and wraps, along with an office, two changing rooms, a weight room, and a room with standard gym-type equipment like running machines and bikes. There's also a room with over a dozen different punching bags, all diverse in shape and size.

I stand in the middle of a big blue matted area with nine other nervous women. My eyes flick about as I take in the padded roof-support pillars and walls. High on the off-white walls, there are national flags from all over the world.

"Okay, ladies, I am your instructor, Scott, and this evening I'm going to teach you some self-defence," the smallish redheaded shifter says with a smile.

I say *smallish* as, come on, shifters are never small...but this guy is under six feet. His dark-red hair is brushed away from his face—a handsome face with freckled, bold features, a broad forehead, and a short beard that hugs his jaw and highlights his narrow, pink lips. He claps his hands. "Let's warm up..."

The warm-up is brutal...or it should be. The surrounding ladies are all red-faced and sweaty, but my body is nicely warm. I don't know where my wobbly arms have gone. The instructor pushes us to work harder, but to no avail; I'm still not sweating like a pig, and I should be. Huh. Is this another demon thing? As in, it's weird. I've not been fit in months, yet I feel fantastic.

They pass pads and somewhat smelly boxing gloves around, and we split into pairs. One girl hits while the other holds up a square pad. Scott barks out instructions on our fighting stances and encourages us to use our hips to add weight to the punches. "Aim not to punch the pad, but through it."

When it's my turn, I try not to pull a face when I slide my hands into the damp gloves. I punch the pad and I grin, as this is fun. To add a little motivation, I imagine John's face superimposed onto the blue foam. *Take that, John,* I think as I hit his nose and then his chin. One particularly hard hit from my right fist and the poor girl holding the pad flies through the air and lands with an *oof* on her bum.

"Oh gosh, I'm so sorry," I say as I rush to help her up. She gives me a rueful smile, but before she has time to speak, Scott is there, pushing her towards another pairing.

"You okay?" She nods. "Double opponents," he says to the girl with the boxing gloves.

He turns back to me, and with a determined, angry look on his face, he nods toward a quiet area. I follow meekly behind his stomping form, and when he thinks we are far enough from the others, he spins back around and interrogates me. "Why you here? Are you from another gym? It's clear you're not a normal beginner." His head tilts to the side.

Boom. Instead of taking offence at his angry questions, I grin at him. He thinks I'm a fighter! I refrain from doing a fist pump. Instead, I bounce on my toes. I can feel the silly grin spreading across my face—my cheeks hurt from the strain.

Eat your heart out, Rocky. Eye of the tiger.

His eyes narrow. He looks me up and down, and then he nods. "You're the new demon," he says bluntly.

I stop bouncing, and my happy grin slides from my face. It's my turn to narrow my eyes at him. When he continues to stand there, I surreptitiously flick my gaze around the gym. No one heard him. But I'm busted.

I drop my eyes and stare at my feet. I toe the blue crash mat. "I will go, no need to chuck me out," I mumble. I remove the smelly gloves and hand them over. I turn to leave, but a gentle hand on my arm stops me.

Scott stops me. "Hey, no, don't be so soft...are you kidding me? A *demon* at my gym? Hell, demon, I'll train you for free—it would be an honour to train you. Look, we are almost done anyway for today. Why don't you come back tomorrow night, and we shall work out a real training programme." He sounds...excited.

My eyes narrow. If something sounds too good to be true, it usually is.

"Look, demon."

"Emma. My name is Emma," I grumble.

"Emma, I know the hellhounds. Well, I know *of* the hellhounds, and I know that they have a vested interest in keeping you safe.

"Times are hard. I'm not gonna advertise that you come here, but word of my training you will get out to the right ears, and it will be good for business." He smiles and gives a small shrug. He seems genuine.

I find myself nodding in agreement. I need the help. "It's a deal, but I'm paying you." I'm not using him—that is what bad people do.

Rule number one: Don't be a dickhead.

He slowly nods, and an even bigger smile works its way across his face. "Great. See you tomorrow night at eight."

* * *

"You killed the vampires," I say. John grunts down the phone at me. "You can't just go around killing people."

"Why not?"

"Because...because it's morally wrong."

"Morally wrong according to whom?" Honestly. Why do I bother?

"To me." He grunts again. "I met my mum last night," I whisper. I don't know why I tell him—maybe it's because I've got no one else to tell. How sad is that?

"How did that go?" he asks gruffly.

From our time together, he knows my history better than anyone. *Cold metal on my skin*. I shiver at the memory. I stop my free hand from frantically rubbing at the scars on my wrist. I swallow.

"She's with a pureblood, Lord Luther Gilbert..." I pause, waiting for some valid input to the conversation. All John does is grunt an acknowledgement. I roll my eyes. "...I found out tonight it was him who sold me to—"

"Emma, let me stop you there. You can't seriously be suggesting your mum didn't have a say in your being sold off. Come on, Emma, what mum would hand over a five-year-old child without a fight?"

Not being able to remain seated, I jump up from the sofa and stomp across the room. I growl with indignation down the phone, "No, you're wrong. Don't you dare tell me what a woman would and wouldn't do, John Hesketh. Last time I checked, you're a seven-foot monster of a man. You do not understand what being a woman is like in this world. So shut your mouth." I grind my teeth.

Why did he have to say that? He could never be in her shoes, never understand what happened. Neither can I.

"Did she confirm he sold you? Did she say the words, Emma?"

"Well, no...but it was insinuated."

"By the pureblood?"

"Yes."

"Before or after you turned down his protection?" How did John know he offered me protection? I rub my temple. I can't remember...before, I think. I turn and stare at my smoky ward.

"I want to help her."

"Like she helped you?"

"John," I growl out, a warning in my tone.

"Emma, listen to yourself for a moment. *She is a vampire.* She isn't human anymore. She left you at the mercy of a *demon,* with no clue about what kind of creature you were. If she is with the pureblood, then she clawed her way into that position. Vampires destroy weakness, Emma. You saw what she wanted you to see. Take it from a man who's seen and done awful shit: it's pure manipulation."

"You see the worst in people."

"Yes, and you see the best in everyone. That's what makes you a beautiful person, but thinking like that, it can get you hurt. Forget about rescuing your mother. She's made her bed, and she's fine. She isn't getting hunted by creatures like you are. It's a full-time job, keeping you safe," he grouches.

"No one asked you to keep me safe."

"How is your demon magic progressing?"

I sigh. His change of subject makes my head spin.

"It's fine," I grumble.

Gah, I can't see fault with his logic, and I understand what he's saying. Did I see what my mum wanted me to see...was she manipulating me? The shaking, the tears. Or is my mum another broken woman who is doing her best to survive in a broken world? I tap the fingers not holding the phone on my thigh. I don't know.

If I don't know, perhaps I need to find out.

"Emma, you still there?"

"Yes," I grumble again. "I was thinking...my demon magic doesn't do shit." I poke at my ward magic and it twists around my finger. I drop my hand and step away. I shake my hand out with a full-body shudder. Freaky ward.

"Try harder. You can disappear into thin air, so that's a good start." I don't take the bait—I'm not explaining my pocket. I grin; I bet it drives him crazy.

"Will you stop killing people in my name?" I boldly ask instead.

"No." Ha, a short and sweet answer. At least he didn't lie.

"I've got to go." I say.

"Will you call me tomorrow?"

I groan. "Whoa, no." I pull the phone from my ear. I wrinkle my nose and glare at it. I cautiously put it back to my ear and say, "I'm not going down the route of friendship with you, John. You make a horrible friend."

There's a long pause. I can hear him breathing.

Was I unkind?

"I don't want to be your friend," he answers in a low, guttural growl. Sexy. My body clenches and my heart misses a beat. I gasp and my throat makes a strange *eeep* sound. John laughs huskily and I quickly end the call.

I throw the mobile across the room like it's a magical hand-grenade. It bounces onto the sofa and the momentum carries it over the arm of the chair. It lands with a clatter on the floor, out of sight.

Oh bloody hell.

CHAPTER TWENTY-SEVEN

Everything was going so well. I moved Bob to his new stable yard, and I said a sad goodbye to the Shetland pony, Munchkin, who even gave me a farewell love-bite. I still have the bruise on my thigh. I will miss the little tyke.

Yes, everything was going well until Bob-cob developed a sore hoof. An abscess from running around his new field. A stray stone must have knocked his foot, causing an infection within the hoof horn. He was dreadfully lame.

Like a normal horse owner, when I got the phone call I freaked out. The world was ending because my precious Bob was in pain. The livery yard has its own emergency potions, but I am not the type of owner to allow someone to slap any old potion onto my horse without vet intervention. I waited, biting my nails, until the vet, Cathy—a talented witch— arrived to treat him.

I grin with relief as I lean against the stable door and watch a contented Bob happily munching on his hay net. Bob stands pain-free on all four hooves. My bank account will be lighter when I get the bill, but I don't care. Healing magic is incredible, Cathy is incredible. She has just left. It's late, dark, and it started spitting an hour ago. Now the rain is coming down in sheets.

In my panic to get to Bob, I didn't bring a coat. Now that I'm almost finished with my jobs and completely wet through, I wouldn't be able to put one on anyway without changing. I shrug and then wince as the movement causes the rain to trickle down the back of my neck—oh, that wasn't pleasant. Not at all. I do a full-body shiver.

With a final brush of the floor outside Bob's stable, I'm ready to go home. I empty the wheelbarrow and put the sweeping brush away and lock everything up for the night. As I am closing the feed-room door, there's a loud *bang.* I jump and clutch at my chest. "Shit, what was that?" My pulse pounds and my senses sharpen with the adrenaline that floods through me. I turn towards the sound.

Everyone else left hours ago. Perhaps it's Stuart doing a late-night check on the horses? I squint into the night. The rain and the powerful overhead floodlights blind me. "Hellooo?" I shout. I blink the rain out of my eyes and wait, straining my ears for a response, and weirdly I hold my breath. As if stopping breathing will make me hear better.

I shrug when I get no reply. I rub my face and I huff out a nervous laugh. *No one is here, Emma. What a scaredy-cat.* I berate myself for being so easily frightened.

I roll my tense shoulders, and my wet top sticks to me uncomfortably. I peel it away with a shiver. I need to get home and have a hot bath. I blink back out into the night. It must have been a horse. Bob isn't the only horse stabled tonight.

I look at Bob with a smile.

I freeze.

Bob isn't chomping on his net. Instead, his head is over his stable door. With wide, panic-filled eyes and flaring nostrils, his attention is firmly fixed on where the bang came from. My eyes drift to the other horses around us. The stables are in a horseshoe shape and they overlook a central courtyard. The other horses too are looking in the same direction, with an equal measure of fear and trepidation. All the horses are looking. One stamps, a few snort, and one horse lets out a frightened, shrill whinny.

A trickle of fear creeps down my spine and my heart speeds back up.

My body trembles as I back away from the feed room and towards Bob's stable. It would be so easy to use the feed-room door to leave. But I won't. I can't leave Bob and the other horses in danger. I pat my phone to double-check that it's still in my pocket. Should I ring for help? What if I'm mistaken and it's nothing?

That's when the creatures come out.

Fae creatures...the beithíoch. They look like deformed cats, hairless and big. Their skin is black and blends into the night. I estimate that they are around hip height and about five feet in length. The floodlights reflect off their huge white teeth, teeth so big they look like prehistoric lions'. As they get closer, their eyes glow with a freaky blue light. My back hits the stable wall as they prowl towards me on silent feet. Six, seven—no, eight. Eight huge beithíoch.

Oh bloody hell.

The bang must have been the ward failing.

I keep my eyes pinned on the beithíoch and slowly lift my hand. My fingers scrabble around as I scrape them against the wall, blindly feeling around behind the back of Bob's stable door. I blow out a relieved breath as my searching fingers meet metal. With a deft flick of my wrist, I unhook the top door and ever so gently swing it closed. With shaking hands, I bolt it, locking Bob inside. It's my only option to protect him. There is no way those beithíoch will clamber over the door now.

I sidestep slowly to the left, to the horse stabled next door, and do the same.

The cat-like creatures watch me, not yet moving to attack. I attempt to do another stable door, but a low hiss freezes me. I swallow down a moan of fear. The creatures want me to stay where I am. The surrounding horses are silent—the poor things are terrified. Trapped, vulnerable in their stables, unable to run.

Oh God, this is all my fault. I've never heard of fae creatures attacking a livery yard. You don't have to be a rocket scientist to work out that they've come for me.

I breathe out quick, panting breaths that fog the air, it's gone so cold. The cold is especially apparent to me given the wet, frozen state of my frightened body. I stand wide-eyed and shaking. My heart thuds in my ears until all I can hear is my heartbeat and the drip and gurgle of the guttering, the patter of the rain as it taps against the window of the feed room.

Footsteps. My stomach twists. At least three different treads are approaching.

Men dressed in black wind their way around the scary beithíoch. Their long hair and distinctive plaits identify them as fae warriors. My breath shudders.

Is this how I'm going to die?

"P...Please d...don't hurt any of the horses," I stammer out through my frozen lips. I shuffle forward and open my hands.

I hold my trembling arms out to the side to show I haven't got a weapon.

One of the fae steps forward. He tilts his blond head to the side and regards my shaking form with disgust. In a soft, lilting Irish accent, he replies, "We don't hurt innocent creatures." I briefly close my eyes and sag in relief. "That doesn't mean we won't hurt you, baby demon."

Demon. I'm not surprised that my assumption was correct. Why is every Tom, Dick and Harry out to get me? I've done nothing wrong...what the heck does everyone know about demons that I don't? I shoot him a small, wobbly smile. "Oh, I know. That's okay, as long as you promise not to hurt the horses." *Urm, Emma,* my inner voice shouts at me. *"It's okay?" Are you nuts? This is not bloody okay. They're going to kill you...*I shut down my unhelpful, screaming thoughts and—

A knife is at my throat. A heavy arm around my waist pulls me into a male body. A fourth fae warrior has me in his powerful grip. I have no idea where he has come from. I jerk away from the sharp blade and my head smacks into his chest, and the warrior's blade follows my movement. I lift my hands and with a panicked squeak dig my nails into his arm in an attempt to pull it away, but the knife moves closer and with a sting, it bites into my vulnerable flesh.

Ouch. I can feel my blood as it trickles hotly down my throat. It cools as it mixes with the rain.

Wide-eyed, I stare at the creatures surrounding me. Yeah, with my one self-defence lesson and my brand-new skill of turning my eyes black, I will have no problem fighting my way through four fae warriors and eight giant monster beithíoch. Right?

Oh my God, I'm going to die.

With these overwhelming odds, I feel so helpless. I should have run when I had the chance. *Coward, fight. Do something, anything,* my inner voice screams at me.

Oh God, if I don't fight, I'm dead.

I struggle in the fae's arms and kick his shin. He doesn't even grunt at my pathetic blow. In desperation, I drop my head to bite his arm, but with a tilt of his wrist he angles the blade so it pokes underneath my chin.

I freeze.

"You are a danger to us all," he says in a gruff voice.

"A danger? Me? Yeah, I was planning to take over the world on Tuesday, as Monday—" He strikes the side of my head with the butt of the blade and my vision goes hazy. I hiss out a pain-filled breath and my ears ring.

What the hell do I do with a knife at my throat? Defeated, I shake with useless adrenaline and my body sags in his tight grip. I could continue to struggle and fight, I could scream and I could beg. But I've begged before, and I know it doesn't work. I am reluctant to go down that path again.

I know...I bloody know that I need to get mad, get angry, somehow pull the sleeping demon out from hiding, but...but I don't want to hurt anyone, kill anyone.

I see the vampires' faces in my dreams—they haunt me. They are why I have my silly set of rules. It is kind of karmic that I'm going to die with my throat cut. Isn't that what led to the other vampire's death? Me slicing his throat? Eleanor only finished what I had started.

I will forever wonder about the lives I took, the man I stabbed. Did he have a family? A wife, children who relied on him, loved him? Realistically I know turned vampires can't have children. He most likely didn't even have a human family. Yet I can't help seeing his entire family in my imagination, in my dreams. They cry for him.

I feel as if it's marked my soul. I can feel it, the tainted blackness sitting there festering.

"Kneel, demon."

"My name's Emma," I whimper through my numb lips. "If you're going to kill me"—my voice cracks—"I'd rather stand than die on my knees." The wind whips up, snatching at my words, but the surrounding fae hear me.

I guess I can die with dignity.

The blond warrior in front nods his head and the arm behind me tenses. No villain speeches for me, then—these guys are professionals.

I lift my chin.

I slam my eyes closed.

I might be brave enough to stand. But I'm not brave enough to keep my eyes open. *Maybe…maybe I will heal?* Numbness spreads through me. I let go of the fae's arm so I don't hinder his movement. I remember reading that nobles used to pay the executioner extra to guarantee a clean blow. If I have to die today…Oh God, please, I am not ready…if I have to die today I'd rather it be quick.

In my head, I'm riding Bob. The sunlight is on my face and the birds are singing in the trees. The sound of his hooves as they clop rhythmically against the ground…it fills me with a sense of peace. "I love you, Bob-cob."

CHAPTER TWENTY-EIGHT

A faint, whispered *thunk*, a sharp intake of breath in my ear, followed immediately by a warm, wet splat against my cheek. The fae warrior who is holding me becomes a dead weight at my back. The knife slips from his grip and clatters to the floor. His arm becomes impossibly heavy against my neck. I let out a squeak as he drags me backwards while his body drops. On instinct, I franticly prise his arm away from my throat. I cough and choke.

"What the hell?" I gasp. I stumble when I see the silver knife sticking out of his pointed ear.

There is a thud and the sound of boots as they hit the concrete beside me. I lift my eyes to see a dark shadow. The enormous male must have jumped from the roof. With a flick of his wrist he throws another blade while simultaneously grabbing the third warrior's head, and with a sharp twist, he breaks the man's neck. Both bodies crumple to the floor at the same time.

He moves between one heartbeat and the next. With a flash of silver and a blade to the chest, the last fae warrior drops. Without hesitation or pause, he has ripped through the fae like paper. The silver blades in his hands wink in the overhead light.

I gasp as he turns his head and his eyes lift to mine, regarding me. Rainwater trickles down his face, a beautiful deadly face. Rain drips from his jaw. His strong cheekbones are highlighted by the orange glow of his eyes. "John." I mouth his name. My lips remain parted in shock.

The hellhound is like a war machine. All that took a matter of seconds.

Dead bodies lie around him.

A hiss and an angry growl draws my shocked eyes away from John, just as an angry fae monster springs towards me. I let out a squeak of fright. All I can see are glowing blue eyes and a mouthful of gleaming white teeth. I lift my arms to cover my face and take a quick step backwards. I trip over the body at my feet, and I go down heavily. As I hit the ground, a sharp pain in my hip and shoulder resonates through me.

"Bad kitty," John growls as he grabs hold of the skin at the scruff of its neck and yanks it away from me. I peek through my arms. Jaws snapping, the beithíoch quickly turns its attack onto John, and he grabs hold of its muzzle.

At first, I think he is trying to clamp its mouth closed. The beithíoch lets out a whimper—oh no—as John's forearms bulge and instead, he rips the beithíoch jaws apart. Blood splatters to the floor and I gag.

The other beithíoch converge. "John, look out!" Muscles bunching, John picks up the dead beithíoch and throws its body. It hits the other beithíoch, slowing them down.

John shifts.

It's a blink-and-you-miss-it kind of transformation. The magic re-forms his very cells. Intact clothing scatters around in the wake of John's hellhound form. Riddick growls harshly, so deeply, it's almost a roar. The sound echoes out into the night. Riddick. I watch wide-eyed as Ridd—I shake my head—no, *John*. As John crashes into the fae creatures.

I scramble back up to my feet, and my right hand lands on the warrior's chest. I yelp and shudder with revulsion. The whole idea of touching a dead person makes me want to puke. Bile rises into my throat. I gag again and my chest burns.

The seven remaining beithíoch circle him, their tails whipping from side to side. Each of them takes a turn at dashing in to attack the hellhound. Teeth and claws.

The hellhound is no mouse. He is bigger than the beithíoch, and his thick coat fur offers him a measure of protection that the hairless creatures haven't got. I don't want to watch him kill them. The beithíoch didn't bring themselves. Monstrous and scary, they are still innocent animals. I hate the fae for bringing them here.

John fights as if someone has hit fast-forward. His movements are so fast they are hard to track.

You are being pathetic. Do something. Help him.

I wobble on my feet and look around for the dropped knife. Oh, God, I can't see it anywhere. Instead, I turn to the dead fae and with trembling hands and a strange gurgling noise deep in my throat, I grab hold of the blade in his ear. I heave as I pull. When the knife doesn't come out, I wipe my hands on my wet pants and put my foot on his neck for leverage. Wincing, I silently apologise to my would-be killer for what is surely desecrating his dead body. I tug. The knife doesn't move. "Ew...come on...come on." I wiggle the blade as bile again creeps up my throat.

There are hisses and a yowl from the beithíoch.

I continue to half-heartedly tug at the knife still lodged in the fae warrior's head. "Please come out—I need to help him." Gah, I can't believe I am talking to an inanimate object.

A warm hand touches my shoulder. I fling my arms into the air and scream like a banshee.

"Emma, it's okay, it's me. You're safe, it's me."

I lift my eyes to see that John is next to me, and I cover my mouth with my hands. I hurriedly back away from him.

More dead bodies lie around us.

His naked body follows my frantic movement, and he prowls towards me. His beautiful body ripples with every step, and I almost swallow my tongue. I don't know if I'm more turned on or frightened. At least I'm no longer numb.

"Why did you stand there and allow that fuck to hold a knife to your throat?" he growls.

Oh, heck, the hellhound is pissed.

John growls again. "You lifted your chin for him." He reaches, and his massive hands grip both my shoulders. He drags me towards him, and as he does, he shakes me. "If I hadn't been here, you would be dead. Why didn't you fight? Why didn't you fight, Emma? You always fight. Yet you stood there...you just fucking stood there." He continues to shake me until my bones ache underneath the grip of his enormous hands. My teeth and eyeballs feel like they are rattling around in my head. "If you are ever in that situation again—you fight like fuck. Even if the odds are insurmountable. You fight."

Isn't he supposed to say, *"Do nothing—don't be stupid and don't antagonise the bad guys, Emma...call and wait for help."* I blink up at him with confusion. The rain hits my face and John moves closer. His huge body leans over mine, blocking me from the worst of the weather.

To be honest, I wasn't expecting the poke-the-bad-guys-in-the-eye speech.

Is this another trick? 'Cause if it is...I don't care how I do it, I will kill him. Dead John can haunt my dreams, no problem.

I think I am in shock. No, I know I'm in shock. This is all a little too much.

I open my mouth in an attempt to answer him and a keening, frightened noise escapes. I clamp my lips closed. Wow, where did that come from? Wide-eyed, I stare at John. The hellhound's eyes also widen and with no further words of reprimand he pulls me into his body. I bury my head in his naked chest, and his equally naked body wraps around me. His heat and comforting shifter energy surround me. The scent of him, bonfires and fabric softener, fills my nose.

His voice rumbles through his chest. "I will come for you, I will always come for you. But you don't give up like that. Even when you think there isn't a chance, you fight. You always fight, you silly fool. For fuck's sake, you didn't even attempt to run."

"Are they all dead?" I mumble into his chest. My lips brush against his hot skin and in response his entire body shivers. He groans.

"Yes. They are all dead. I am sorry about the beithíoch—

I had no choice. Without the fae to control them, they would have killed all the horses." I expect him to move away from me, but instead, he threads his fingers through my wet hair and strokes the back of my neck, offering me comfort.

"Why are the fae now after me?"

"They're not. They were paid assassins. Don't worry, it won't happen again." John drops his chin onto the top of my head.

"'Cause you'll kill them?"

"If I have too."

"I'm sorry you have to," I murmur.

"Don't be sorry. The fae warriors were bad guys. No one will miss them. The man who hired them was an old business associate of Arlo's. He's dead."

"Oh." What do I do, say thank you? I should...but I hate the idea he has to come and kill people because of me. "What do we do now?"

"I will get you home safe. I have the hounds coming to investigate and do a clean-up. I will also have a better ward installed." I nod, and shiver. "Do you not own a coat?" he growls out, tucking me closer into his body, into his warmth.

"Am I in trouble? Are you in trouble?" I mumble against him.

"No, Emma, the fae are the only ones in the shit. Neither of us is in trouble." He crushes me to his chest and drops his voice to a chocolatey whisper. "I've grown to care about you in the time we have spent together."

I lift my face from his chest. "Time?" It's as if John has flipped an angry-switch in me. What the hell am I doing cuddling with this *naked* man in the rain? "What time are you talking about, John? The time when you spent hours torturing me? Or the time when you disguised yourself as Riddick?" I snarl. I glare at him.

My hands come up between us and I shove him away. I squirm out of his hold. My back bumps into the wall of the stable and I use it to prop my useless, trembling body up. "If you think about it"—I flap my arms about—"we spent many nights together while you played hellhound bodyguard. But I'm not willing to spend any more *time* with a man who thinks it's okay to lie to me. What was all this?" I wave at the bodies. "Did you set this up too?"

John's torso tenses and he steps away from me. "I didn't set this up," he splutters incredulously. "I saved your life. While we're on the subject, I didn't intentionally set up the fake kidnapping or the vampire attack at the house. The lack of wards at the house was to encourage you to leave and to lead me to your accomplices. I didn't realise at the time that you could walk through wards."

I grind my teeth and narrow my eyes. I bloody told him I could do that when he had me chained to a bloody wall. What is it about this hellhound and his listening skills?

"The vampire attacks were Alexander. That was a real car crash, Emma, with real bad-guys." He rubs his face. "Did I take advantage of the situation? Yes. I used it as an opportunity to get more information out of you. The angel agreed to heal you and when we were ambushed, I asked him to come and get you. To set up an interrogation. I never set out to hurt you."

I huff with disgust and shake my head. His colossal body is blocking out the light, so I can no longer see his expression. "Well, you did hurt me. I sat in that chair over that drain for hours while you played with me. I can't shift and make everything perfect again. You had no idea if I had internal injuries. Yet you proceeded with your games anyway. I sat in that chair, frightened to death and in pain." I spin and undo Bob's top stable door. I open it and peek in. The fat cob is already settled and is back to eating his hay. I march over to the other stable and open its top door as well. "You, John Hesketh, are a stubborn grade-A dickhead. I have no idea what's going on in that head of yours. Thank you for saving my life tonight. Now leave me the hell alone."

CHAPTER TWENTY-NINE

Over the past few weeks, I've made no headway with getting my mum alone and away from the pureblood idiot. Frustratingly, she no longer answers my phone calls, and the one time in desperation I tried to visit the club to see her, the vampire doorman wouldn't let me in.

I am at a loss on how to proceed. Changing my face also seems an impossible dream. I have so much detailed research and so many in-depth notes on demons, some days it feels like I am doing a doctorate in demonology.

"Come on, Barbie," Scott yells, snapping me out of my musings.

He's right...I need to get my head in the game.

"Come on, Scott, that's not original," I gripe at him. "Bloody Barbie." Grr.

"Hit the bear shifter like you mean it," he bellows unhelpfully across the room. I grimace and puff out a breath. Okay, I can do this. I nod at Malcolm, the bear shifter in question, to check that he is ready for me, and then I punch him in the face.

Crap, it's less of a punch and more of a love tap. I groan in self-disgust and rub my face with frustration. Eww. I end up with a mouthful of the boxing glove.

"Oi, stop that. Come here," Scott says with thinly veiled exasperation as he waves me over. I'm perfectly fine hitting the bags, but when it comes to hitting people...I don't know, it makes me feel all icky. Pesky empathy. "What were you thinking about that day you knocked that girl on her ass?" Scott raises a red eyebrow. He nods and points at my frowning face. "Yeah, think that." He pushes me back towards the colossal bear shifter.

My face scrunches up with confusion. Yeah, that was an epic pep talk. I square up to the bear shifter and give him a wobbly smile. Okay, I can do this. Malcolm rubs his gloved fist across the back of his head; his dark blond hair, which is cut short on the sides and fashionably longer on the top, sticks up. The light stubble on his jaw adds to his overall roughness. Malcolm's kind brown eyes dance with amusement. He nods his head with encouragement and smiles kindly back at my grimace.

John. I superimpose John's face like a target. I squint, and it's almost too easy to imagine John's face on anything I want to smash my fist into. I bounce on my toes and punch him with a left, a right, another left. I bounce and roll my shoulders.

It's John's face that I'm hitting, and each punch becomes easier.

Malcolm drops his guard as he lazily swings an embarrassingly slow punch towards me. I duck out of the way and follow it up with my right hand. I twist my hips and throw everything I have at bear-John.

Smack.

I watch in horror as the bear's head snaps to the side. He spits and blood flies from his lips, and with a not-so-helpful shout of "Timber!" from Scott, the poor bear smashes down onto the blue mat, out cold. I knocked out a bear shifter.

I blink at the bear.

I blink at Scott.

Oh bloody hell.

"Oh my God, Malcolm, I am so sorry," I squeak out, mortified.

At the same time, Scott says, "That was brilliant! When he wakes up, I think we should start you on weapons."

"Weapons..." I silently mouth.

"Yeah, you're a natural," Scott says. He grins and his heavy hand pats my shoulder.

* * *

After the particularly hard training session with weapons, Scott and I sit on the floor guzzling down water. As I pick at the label on the bottle, I get up the nerve to ask him, what he thinks and experiences when he turns into animal form.

Perhaps I need a fresh perspective.

"Well, I just do it. Like scratching an itch—it's as natural as breathing." Helpful. I sigh and give him a smile of "thanks, anyway."

Malcolm lumbers over. I say *lumbers*, but it's still more like a prowl. I guess even bear shifters don't lumber anywhere. He sits on the floor opposite me, hands on his knees, his concerned brown eyes quietly observing me. "I couldn't help overhearing. I train the cubs." My ears prick up with intrigue. I stop messing with the label and focus my full attention on Malcolm, smiling at him with encouragement.

Come on, Malcolm. Please give me something I can use.

"The cubs first shift into animal form in their twenties. I help them. At first, it's all about focus. They have to learn to meditate, and then we work on getting them to imagine themselves in their true form, their natural self." Malcolm rubs his eyebrow with his thumb. "When the time is right, they shift. They know when the time is coming..." he huffs out a laugh and his face lights up with a grin…"we all know when it's time. It's a little like human puberty—they get all obnoxious and rude. Then suddenly you have a new bear knocking shit over and scratching the furniture as they get used to their claws. We normally take them somewhere rural, like the Lake District. It's hard work because they need extra help, but it's gratifying."

"So they think of their natural self?" I ask.

Malcolm nods. "Yeah. To shift back is the same thing— we get them to imagine themselves as human. You…urm, don't need any help with a young shifter, do you, Emma?" He drops his voice and looks about. "Be careful of the shifter council—they're a nightmare to deal with. Dangerous. It's best to let us shifters deal with our own."

I lean across and squeeze Malcolm's hand in reassurance. "No, I'm just nosy. Don't worry, I'm not harbouring a rogue shifter. I'm not about to do anything silly like stepping on the shifter council's toes." I do an exaggerated shiver. Malcolm's drawn, worried expression clears, and he returns my smile. "Thank you for explaining. The cubs are lucky to have you." When his ears go a little pink at the tips, I giggle at him.

"I'm happy to answer any questions you have—you only have to ask."

"Thanks, Malcolm."

I finish my water. I can't wait to go home and try his

suggestion. I need to think of my *natural self* and meditate more. Maybe I've been overthinking things. Perhaps my magic should be as Scott said, *as natural as breathing*? Everything seems to go tits-up if I overthink stuff. I've found that with my fight training, the less I think and the more I just do, the better.

With a wave at the guys, I head towards the front door.

"Emma, don't use the front door—that hellhound of yours is hanging around again. It's almost like you're his mate, the way he follows you around," Scott says with a chuckle.

My heart jumps. *John.*

I puff out my cheeks, spin on my heel, and head for the fire exit at the rear of the gym. John finds it hard to follow me, but when I'm in one place for a while, it doesn't take him long to track me down. He must have lookouts all over the city. Not that my evening trip to the gym is tricky to work out...I've been coming here for weeks and we set the time in stone.

"Thanks for the heads-up, Scott. Have a good evening." Scott shakes his head and laughs, then waves at his office.

"Use that door," he says. I turn my head and look at him. Oh, crap, does he know about my pocket? "Don't freak out. I know you are a demon, and I know you have magic. I also know that you don't walk out of here. The other day I was seconds behind you when you left, and you vanished into thin air." He taps his nose. "I am a fox. I couldn't track you— there was no scent. So I guessed you can *Step* like the fae or make your own temporary ley-line doorway like a witch." Scott shrugs. Powerful old fae can *Step*, which is how you'd imagine teleporting to be. They just "step" from one place to the next. "It's no biggie, and I won't tell nobody. I understand that there is shit as a demon that you can do. So if you want to just Step or if it's a portal thing, you can use my office door..." He shrugs.

I don't bother with any denials—what would be the point? Scott is my trainer and, I hope, my friend. There is no point in lying, but I will not explain what I do, either.

I smile and head for his office. "Thanks, Scott. See you tomorrow." Using the office door, I open my door to home.

CHAPTER THIRTY

When I arrive home, I can feel John's absence, the lack of his energy on my skin. John's energy is like what I experienced when I was around Riddick, inner peace—which is nuts. The thought makes me antsy. I need to learn to recognise this *inner peace* feeling as his energy, so I know when he's around and can avoid him. I've stopped answering his calls.

Yet John continues to follow me...I don't know how I feel about that.

It's all so strange. I can't help feeling safe whenever he is around. He saved my life, and in return, I was horrible to him.

Crap, when does being kind change to being a doormat? Or when does trying to protect yourself turn into unnecessary rudeness and cruelty? I don't want to be rude to him, but I also don't want him to walk all over me.

Heck, I don't want him to think that his actions have no consequences and what he did to me was okay, because it bloody wasn't.

He scares me.

My head tells me to run like hell, but something inside of me likes his attention...it tugs me back.

It is so confusing...Is it a demon thing? Is it an Emma thing? A hellhound thing?

Scott's words flash into my head. *"It's almost like you're his mate, the way he follows you around."*

Huh. I frown...demons don't have mates...do they? I vaguely remember that shifters have chosen mates, but I can't for the life of me imagine John choosing me as his mate.

There is nothing as silly as the idea of fated mates. Apart from in romance books, I've never heard of fated mates in real life. It might be some demony danger-warning system that I'm experiencing. Yet I don't feel as if I'm in any danger. It's more...contentment. Which is plain old freaky.

I stomp to my shelves and pick out *the* book. it's not like I've been avoiding this book...I just didn't feel the need to learn about demon *love*. Gag.

My life in pages...all I seem to do is read stuffy old books. It feels like I'm forever searching for answers, answers that leave me with more questions. Yay to freedom...I grin toothily. I am living the dream. *Not.*

I plop down on the sofa, still sweaty from the gym. I should have a shower, but my brain won't leave Scott's words alone. I skim the book and find what I need.

I read, and my hands shake as my brain slowly registers the words. When I've finished, I close my eyes tight.

Horror floods me.

Oh, no, no, no. I really wish I hadn't read those words. I slam the book closed, jump to my feet, and slide it back onto the shelf. I wriggle and rub my hands on my leggings.

Nope, it's not happening.

Every time I blink, the words are inscribed on the back of my eyelids, lasered onto my eyeballs, and stamped into my brain, never to be unseen.

Demons have soul mates.

Nope, it's not happening.

Soul mates.

Fate is really getting on my tits. A strangled giggle spills from my lips and I tug at my ponytail. No, no, no.

John is my *mate*. Ha, ha, mate—like in a romance novel. Insta-love. Soul mate.

Oh bloody hell.

I throw my hands in the air and look heavenward. "Okay, fate," I shout aloud like a madwoman. "What do you want from me? I will get on my knees and beg. I will roll on the floor and wail if that is what you want. What the hell have I done to offend the universe? Arrah...why him? Why bloody him? I feel so bloody fucked over." I let out my rage with a bloodcurdling scream. It echoes around the room. I pull my hair and then scrub at my face.

Nope, it's not happening.

That book, that bloody book. I lift my eyes and glare at it. It sits there innocently on the shelf. It dares to tell *me* how lucky and blessed I am. I grit my teeth. *Blessed.* My nostrils flare and my left eye twitches. "Blessed," I snarl.

My little mantra, "everything happens for a reason," isn't going to cut it.

My entire face twitches, and I vigorously rub it. The book talks about my symptoms: feeling his energy beyond the norm and an overwhelming attraction.

The whole overwhelming attraction on its own isn't a red flag. John is beautiful—he's on a scary level of beautiful, a walking, talking wet dream. But the book describes my strange feelings to a T.

My attraction to him has never been normal for me. I'm a reasonably sensible, well-rounded person despite my experiences and childhood. All this time, it's never made much sense — let's face it, the guy has been horrible. Yet, when I hear his voice...when I'm in his arms...I feel like I've come home. When that happens, my head screams at me to knock it off, and my heart...my soul? I gulp. Well, my soul wants to lick him.

I huff. Heck, the guy spent hours aggressively questioning me, he bloody stabbed me and my heart still happily skips a beat whenever I see him—that's not normal.

What has me worried the most is the energy thing, the ability to *feel each other's energy beyond normal senses*. I don't know...I don't want to know if he can feel my energy like I can his. His wild hellhound energy welcomes me; it is almost alive. Now that I can recognise it, I could probably pick his energy out of a crowd or feel him coming from down the street.

If that isn't enough, the book also describes *a zap,* a mixing of energy on the first touch. Considering John smacked me on the back of the head and dragged me away to a basement, I might have missed that step while I was unconscious. If I zapped him, John probably thought it was my bad demon juju.

I stomp to the bathroom and turn on the taps for a *relaxing* bath. I'm seething. But I smell, so I will have a bath, damn it.

While the tub is filling, I grind my teeth and stomp back to the sofa and the *love* book. "Hell's bells. I should burn it," I snarl.

Crap, that shows how angry I am, blaming a book for my situation.

I'd never intentionally harm a book: that's sacrilegious.

I gently remove the book from the shelf. I take a deep breath, ignore the mate stuff, and head for the chapter on progeny. I'm planning to never open this book again, but I just need to double-check one last thing before I forget about its existence.

Breeding with humans is best avoided. The offspring of such a pairing can be unbalanced and aggressive.

Huh. This right here is why I need to be careful and why I need rules.

Emma, the love content of the book is all about demon-to-demon pairings. No, there is nothing written that I can find about soul mates from other races. As John isn't a demon, and I'm only half...he shouldn't feel the same.

Ha, there is no way he feels the same. I know he's gone all flirty with me lately, but that could just be a normal attraction and not this soul stuff.

There's a fuzzy memory from the hospital...I narrow my eyes and tap my mouth with my fingertips as I try to remember. Arlo standing over my hospital bed, *"Poetic really, two broken souls twisted together by fate, forever entwined."* I close my eyes and groan. Arlo he bloody knew, he must have recognised the signs.

I lift my chin and square my shoulders. I can control myself; knowledge is power. This can only be a good thing. Now that

I know what's happening, I can ignore the whole thing.

I am not masochistic, nor do I have Stockholm syndrome. That's at least a relief. It explains a lot. I roll my tense shoulders and take a deep breath.

I swallow down my fear of John and the...*thing*. I will not think about that again.

The book goes back on the shelf, and I drift back towards the bathroom. I take another cleansing breath. Everything is going to be okay if I follow my rules, keep myself out of trouble, be kind, and *avoid* John. Everything is going to be okay. I nod. The direction in which my life goes will be on me.

I open a bottle of wine—I'm not much of a drinker, but, well, tonight I need a drink. The white wine is sweet and refreshing on my tongue.

With my glass, I slip into the steamy bath, and I close my eyes.

Once I'm wrinkly and relaxed, I set my empty glass on the floor and think about what Malcolm said about the bears and how they learn to shift.

Think of your natural form.

I shrug. I close my eyes and think, *Natural...natural—natural—natural demon.* My mind brings up Arlo's monstrous face in the circle, and I shudder. No, not like that. I dig deep into myself, into my magic, and I mumble the words *natural form.*

I feel an unfamiliar warmth on my skin, separate from the now-tepid bathwater. I open one eye and my smoky-black ward-magic is surrounding me and the bath.

I squeak and jump. A wave of water splashes onto the floor.

What? Oh my God...Oh, not my ward. What the heck is it doing here? I lift a shaky hand and the smoke drifts gently across my hand and twists between my fingers. I want to smack my forehead.

This smoky stuff is *my* magic.

Wow. I use my big toe to pull the bath plug, not willing to take my eyes off my magic. I stare at it in wide-eyed fascination as the bath drains. Wow.

"What can you do?" I whisper to it like a proper weirdo. The smoke seems to get thicker. *Natural form.* I aim the thought at my magic. It shimmers, and from one breath to the next...I have a cape around my shoulders.

A cape.

Ha, bloody brilliant. Useless. I roll my eyes and turn my head to see black fabric. The empty bath squeals as I stand up. The cape is heavy on my shoulders and hits me mid-thigh. What the hell? I don't need a bloody cape. I know the book said demons can create their clothing, but a cape is crap. "At least it could be designer horse-wear," I grumble as I step out of the bath.

I let out a bloodcurdling scream when I see myself in the mirror.

Oh bloody hell, hell, hell. That's not a cape. That's not a cape!

Wings.

I have wings. I panic. I wave my arms about in the air, and the bloody wings follow the movement of my hands as they open and flap. Ouch.

OhmyGodohmyGodohmyGod.

I run in a circle and they follow me; they smash off the bathroom walls, knocking stuff off the shelves and onto the floor.

Ouch, ouch, ouch, that hurt.

Oh my God, they are real. Oh my God, it's not my imagination. The freaky huge black *bat wings* sticking out of my back *are real.*

I slip on the wet floor, and only a desperate wing flap keeps me from falling on my bum.

Emma, calm down.

I stand, panting. I drop my arms and the...gulp...wings... relax down my back.

It's okay. I am okay.

Oh bloody hell.

I tremble. "*Natural form*...oh, for fuck's sake." I bury my face in my hands. "Nice one, Emma."

CHAPTER THIRTY-ONE

It has been two days and I've had to cancel my training with Scott as I can't go. I can't go anywhere. They will not go back in.

Oh, we're having a grand time bonding, the wings and me. I'm definitely learning the art of patience and the zen of keeping calm, as these things are sensitive.

I can't sleep. When I try to get comfortable, they do random things. Like smacking the walls, which is painful and causes bruises across the soft, silky membrane that covers the thin, bendable bones. I think I broke a small bone, but it healed before I calmed down enough to investigate. Both wings look the same, so at least it healed straight. Bones take seconds to heal, yet the bruises seem to take forever in comparison.

I have to admit my wings are beautiful. In direct light, they are purple. I sigh. God, I wish they would go away.

Malcolm said to shift back, all the bears had to think about was their human selves. I close my eyes for what feels like the millionth time and *think* human. Nothing happens. Nothing ever happens. I let out a manic laugh at the entire situation. What a clusterfuck.

I'm doomed.

I breathe one deep breath in and one deep breath out. I try my best to relax. *I bet my mate can help me.* I groan at the unhelpful thought. The entire left side of my face twitches. I don't want to rub it in case my wings go nuts and pop out from the movement of my hand. I much prefer them to be still.

Yeah, the thought I can't seem to banish, that is continually running through my brain, is: *I need John.* I need his help. With his experience, he must have an idea about how to help me. I have no one else to turn to.

I can't ask Malcolm or Scott—it's too much to ask, it's too much trust to give.

There is only John. How's that for irony?

My soul m—nope. John, the monster, has been texting me, demanding to know where I am. The missing time at the gym didn't faze him. But when I called the stables to arrange care for Bob, the demanding messages came in. I haven't replied, as I don't know what to say.

But after two days with still no headway, I'm admitting defeat. Each hour that passes, I step closer to breaking rule number one: Don't be a dickhead. I promised Bob that I wouldn't leave him for long and these wings are going to make a liar out of me. So I mentally pull on my brave pants, grab my mobile phone, and message John back.

We arrange to meet at his house.

I wear jeans, but my top half is an issue. Ha, I'm screwed. I carefully rub my face.

In the books, when a character has random wings appear out of nowhere, they slit two holes into the back of their shirts and thread the wings through. Voila. Hey presto all sorted.

Oh yeah, that's okay if you've got help and your wings are not trying to knock you out. There's no chance a tiny bit of fabric is going over my giant-ass wings, not a chance in Hell. I end up wearing a shirt backwards. I button it at my neck and my waist. It is not ideal, but if I keep my hands down, pinned to my sides, I shouldn't flash anyone. At least I'm covered.

I think maybe I'm making a mistake, going to John for help. But after days of pure frustration, I have no other options left. I step through my door and appear outside of John's house. When I think of leaving my doorway, I imagine stepping out of John's door so I don't step into his home. I could, but that would be rude.

I run my fingers through my messy ponytail. I turn. The driveway stone crunches underneath my trainers. I step up to the red door and tentatively knock.

My wings twitch at my back.

Moments later, as if he's been waiting for me, John flings open the door. I fidget as we stare at each other.

Oh my, he is still alluringly handsome. I haven't *seen* him in weeks and my eyes drink him in greedily. John's gaze flicks up and down as he takes me in, from my tired eyes to my wings. With a head tilt, he studies my new appendages. My wings rustle. I smartly drop my eyes and stare at his chest. He is wearing tight black fatigues, and his black combat top is so tight it almost gives way under the strain of containing all those muscles. I swallow and fiddle with my shirt.

"You're looking pretty demony, Emma," he says as he raps his knuckles on the doorframe. I grind my teeth. Why did I think he'd be able to help?

I reach up and cover my black lips. The strange colour is the least of my problems. With all my wing drama, that little detail I pretended to overlook. At least my eyes and mouth match.

"The wings are cute. Is that the biggest they get?"

I drop my hand and my lips part with shock. Cute? My eyes flick to his, and I growl at him, insulted. "What? They're massive."

"Oh, okay..." He coughs into his hand. "So I see you have a problem." And then the dickhead dares to smile. His bright-green eyes twinkle.

My nostrils flare, and I glare at him. After a few minutes, I break the awkward silence with a cough. "Urm...can I come in?"

"Of course." John steps away from the door and waves me inside.

As I walk over the threshold and pass John, a rogue wing *snaps* out and smacks him in the face.

Oops.

That wasn't intentional, but heck, I want to give my wing a high five. I do my best to hide my grin.

When we enter the living room, he circles me and inspects my wings. They twitch. I'm sure the little buggers are waiting for the ideal opportunity to smack him again.

"This is the reason you've been MIA," John says as he rubs his now-wing-red face.

Sorry-not-sorry.

I nod and suck in my lower lip. "Can you help me? I can't...I can't get them to go back in." John pauses behind me, and the heat of him sends shivers down my spine. I can feel our combined energy like waves battling against each other. Caressing each other.

He leans in closer. His warm breath on my ear. "May I touch you?" I shiver as his whispered words tickle the back of my neck. My mouth fills with saliva and I gulp; I can't speak. I gnaw on my lip and nod my head.

Even after I nod my head with permission, John seems to take forever to touch me. So I jump when his hand finally touches my back, landing gently between the wings.

My wings fling out with a *snap*. Flap-flap-flap. "They have a mind of their own," I say with an embarrassed whisper. John makes a noncommittal grunt, perhaps because he's dodging my wings.

I wish he wouldn't touch me. I like his hands on me, and that's bad, very bad. I swallow again. I force myself to stand still and not squirm. I like it and I don't want to. He runs his hands down my back and across my shoulders and neck.

"You need to relax—"

"I have been trying to," I bite out. I roll my eyes heavenward with exasperation. As if I can relax with John touching me...yeah, that's going to happen. Ha, I'd have more chance with Freddy Krueger standing behind me offering a head massage.

"Close your eyes." I huff. "Close your eyes, Emma. Think of your wings, think of how happy you are with them...how special they are." I scrunch my face in disbelief. What has that got to do with anything? I'm not bloody happy. I sigh and force myself to do as he says.

I am happy I've got wings...I grind my teeth. So happy. I puff my cheeks out. Okay, let's start smaller: I am happy I've got magic.

I have the means to protect myself, which is incredible. Seriously, looking at my messed-up situation, it could have been worse. I've got wings...I could have had a mouthful of serrated teeth and scary nails to go with them. At least I look like me. Me with black lips and dark-purple wings. I guess it's kind of cool.

The possibility that I might be able to fly is nuts, mind-boggling. I mean...how amazing is that, to fly...crash. I gulp.

Oh heck, what goes up must come down. Perhaps I'm not ready for that step yet.

"Shush, Emma, calm your thoughts. Relax, you are safe, now relax." John's hands continue their light attention to my skin. My skin tingles in response to his touch. He touches the membrane of my left wing, and it flutters. Wow, the wing is so sensitive. I can't help the small moan that leaves my lips. I cringe at the sound.

Oh God, that wasn't embarrassing at all.

John's hands move back to my shoulders and he digs his thumb into a sore spot. The wings are so heavy and my shoulders are so sore with carrying all the extra weight. His hands feel so good.

I allow myself this one moment to enjoy his attentions. I need his help and it won't do any harm just this once. I breathe in deep to fill my nose with his bonfire-and-linen-fabric-softener scent. My shoulders relax, my wings drop, and my chin drops to my chest. I let go. I let go of my fear. I forgive myself for being frightened of my wings.

I mentally release the tight grip that I have had on my magic. I let go of the ball of magic that I've been unknowingly, fearfully clutching inside me; I allow it out.

The black smoky magic pours out of me and gently caresses my skin. *Human...*I aim the thought at it. My magic shimmers, and between one breath and the next the wings dissipate. They are gone. *Thank you.* I sigh in relief.

"Well done," John says behind me, his hands still on my shoulders. He did it, he helped me.

I force myself to step away from his hands. With my back still turned, I remove my shirt and put it back on the correct way. "Thank you," I say as I quickly button it up. I turn and fix my eyes on John's chest. "Thank you for your help."

"You're welcome. Emma, why won't you look at me?" My heart misses a beat at his question. I gulp and attempt a blasé shrug.

"Thank you for helping me. I need to go," I mumble.

"Emma, what are you hiding?" My eyes fly to his, and his beautiful face almost makes me stagger. *Soul mates.* I fidget; he can't make me talk.

"I have two full days to catch up on. I need to go home and get changed and then go see Bob. Thanks again for your help."

Oh, and we are soul mates, bye-bye. I smile my bizarre, toothy grin, give him a double thumbs-up for good measure, and then with my thumbs still stuck out, I awkwardly wave goodbye. I hurry out of the room like my bottom is on fire.

The hellhound follows on my heels.

"Stay, talk to me. I want to know what you aren't telling me, what you are hiding. I know you, Emma. Tell me what's wrong, let me help."

"I've done nothing wrong," I squeak as I power-walk to the door.

Oh heck, I don't want to be in a situation where the hellhound feels the need to interrogate me. I need to get home. My heart hammers in my chest and my hands shake. The scent of my fear will be winging its way up the hellhound's nostrils.

I pant. I can't get enough air into my lungs. Oh God, oh God. Coming here was a mistake.

"What are you hiding?" He catches up, grips my shoulders, and spins me around. He deftly manoeuvres me until I'm pinned against the hallway wall. His muscly forearms land on either side of my head and I gasp as his massive body presses against mine. My blouse and his T-shirt are thin barriers between us. The clothes between us might as well be non-existent for how aware of him I am. My breasts press against him and with each panting breath and the friction it creates, my nipples harden. I feel my face turning bright red with embarrassment as his solid bulk against my softness reminds me I haven't got a bra on.

I swallow a mortified moan.

He cups my face, thumb under my chin as he angles my face until we are nose to nose. He looks into my eyes. "What are you hiding?" he growls. Something in his pupils flares and the orange flames flicker.

The clink of chains.

I shudder with fear. My body shakes as the lust that was dragging me down disappears. I feel nothing now but fear...it vibrates through his fingers.

He draws his knuckles across my cheek and I flinch. "Tell me what you are hiding."

I swallow. "You...are frightening...me," I stammer out.

"That is not what you are hiding." He glides his fingers down my throat and grips the back of my neck. His hand circles my throat. My pulse pounds underneath his fingers. No, I can't hide how much he frightens me.

"You are my mate."

Oh bloody hell.

My eyes widen with horror. No-no-no-no, *shut up Emma, say nothing else,* I scream in my head.

"You're my mate," I repeat, because saying it once isn't enough. "Demons have soul mates, can you believe that? Hahaha…" An awkward, nervous laugh spills from my lips. "Well…if you believe a crusty old book…I am not sure I do." I try to wiggle away.

If it's even possible, John moves *closer*, his eyes heavy-lidded and filled with awe. He dips his head.

"Mate…"

"No." Oh God, no. I turn my face away, John brushes the wisps of hair from my face and rubs his nose against the pulse at my neck, breathing in my scent. I tremble.

"You love me in my hellhound form…as Riddick, you love me." John speaks softly, coaxingly, his voice warm and low.

I wave my hands to the side to ward him off. I work them between us and try to push him away. I shake my head as if doing so will stop his words.

No, this is not happening. I voice my thoughts. "No, it's not happening, the soul-mate thing." I vigorously shake my head. He hasn't denied it, so John must feel it too. The awe in his eyes is freaking me out. "You aren't good…*we*…we aren't good enough for each other. Fate got it wrong." Rule number two: Be kind. "Yes, I loved Riddick as a friend, and I could have loved you too, John." My voice breaks. Being honest sucks. "Everything in me wants to love you. Yet I question your motives every second I'm with you. Even now you *scare* me."

Like I'd hit a switch, he sucks in a deep breath, and John allows me to push him away. A rueful expression flashes across his face, and my frightened brain takes in every detail. The subtle rhythmic movement of the veins in his neck, the tense muscles in his arms and shoulders, his hands clenching and unclenching. My chin quivers and I press my lips together. I can't look at him, his eyes...they are so sad.

"I don't want to frighten you, Emma."

"You do, though. You do frighten me, John. What is love without trust?" He doesn't love me, how could he love me? "Maybe in another lifetime, but not this one. I'm sorry. Too much has happened between us." I implore him to understand, and as my eyes flood with unshed tears, his face becomes hazy. "I didn't want to burden you with this. It slipped out. I am so sorry. Forget I said anything. Forget about me."

"I will not let you go. I will prove to you that we can be happy, that I can make you happy," John whispers as he closes the gap between us and his enormous hands gently caress my face. I look into his beautiful green eyes. "War is in my blood and war has moulded me. Times change for

some people, but not for me. I am a full-blooded warrior—
I'm expendable. I made peace with that a long time ago. But
for you, I can try. I can try to change." His thumb caresses my
bottom lip and dips into my mouth. The salty taste of his skin
floods my mouth. The urge to flick my tongue across his
thumb makes me groan. "You are the first thing that is mine."

With his words, my heart breaks and my tummy twinges
with stress. I drop my head to his chest and suck up the pain.

Ouch, it hurts. God, how this hurts.

"That..." my hand taps his chest, and I slide against the
wall and away from him. The tether between us stretches
thin. The tears I was gallantly holding fall. "...That right there
is the problem. John, you said, 'thing.' I am not a *thing*." I try
to lift my chin, but my head is heavy. I shrug and my lips
wobble into a semblance of a smile. A broken smile.

I am not strong enough to deal with this man.

I cringe away from the orange glow that is brightening
again in his green eyes.

He frightens me.

Rule number three: Don't lie to yourself. I am not strong
enough. I know that without even trying, without meaning
to...he'd destroy me.

So I walk away.

Everything happens for a reason. Pain rips through me
and I barely hold in my heart-wrenching sobs.

CHAPTER THIRTY-TWO

I do what I always do when I feel like crap—I go and spend time with my best friend.

Bob-cob is grumpy. He isn't impressed that his human hasn't been to see him for a few days. To placate him, I feed him a full packet of extra-strong mints and spend a good hour brushing him. I scratch all his favourite spots. I even take him for a lazy hack around the livery yard instead of schooling him in the riding arena.

When we get back from our ride, I untack him and then go grab a grooming brush. I leave Bob tied up outside his stable with his saddle resting across the top of the stable door. Brush in hand, I meander back across the yard. I narrow my eyes as I watch Bob lean towards his saddle. "Bob," I say in a warning tone. He looks back at me and then gives a deliberate nudge of his nose. The saddle on the door wobbles. I speed up. "Don't you dare..." I am a step away. With a wrinkle of Bob's nose and another strong push, the saddle thuds to the floor.

Gah. "You little sod, that saddle is a made-to-measure... why the hell would you do that?" I scoop the saddle up off the floor and inspect it. Phew, it's gotten away unscathed and there are no scratches.

I glare at him and he looks back at me, the picture of horsey innocence. If anyone that tells you horses don't or can't hold grudges...they haven't spent a lot of time with them. Bob seems more content now that he's got his own back.

* * *

I take the saddle and my cleaning kit and go sit on a bale of straw in the hay barn. A shaft of sunlight warms my face, and the rough straw digs into the back of my thighs. I've done all my stable jobs and a smug Bob is back out in the field with his friends. It's a lovely, warm day without a cloud in the pale-blue sky. With the saddle resting on my knees, and the comfortable heat in the barn relaxing me, my mind drifts as I apply the leather conditioner with a cloth.

"You moved out then, for real?" says a familiar voice. I cover my eyes with my hand and squint into the bright sunlight. "This is a nice place for Bob...expensive...that horse is so spoiled."

So I can see her better, *Sam* steps underneath the barn's overhang.

My lips part as I take her in. She twists her riding hat in her hands and looks at me sheepishly.

"Hey, yes and yes it's nice," I say, answering both questions. I glance down at the saddle on my knees and gather my courage. "I've missed you," I whisper.

"Yeah?" She steps closer. "I'm sorry, you know, about the whole"—Sam cringes and then does the *Psycho* film knife-move, with the screeching sound effect for good measure—"stabbing you in the back and stuff." I snort and shake my head at her antics. She plunks down next to me on the bale and nudges my shoulder. "I missed you too," she mumbles and shoots me a rueful grin.

"Did he send you?"

"Who...the hellhound? No. No, I don't work for him, not anymore. I finished up riding a client's horse and saw you sat here on your lonesome." She bounces the hat on her knee. "What's the hellhound done to you now?"

I shrug.

"You okay?"

"Yeah, I'm okay. You?" Sam shrugs back. "How is Munchkin?"

"He is a shit. The little tyke is teaching kids to ride...it's hilarious." I roll my eyes. Bloody vampire. I bet their parents don't think it's hilarious. I can imagine the poor kids pinging off the monster pony, crying on the floor while Munchkin tries to kick them in the head. Fun.

We sit in comfortable silence. I run the cloth across my saddle. Sam picks at some mud that's splatted on her breaches, peeling it off with her thumbnail.

"You know you can't trust me—I can't keep your secrets."

I turn my head and look at her, my eyebrows raised. Wow, that was honest.

"You know what? I'm sick of being afraid." I smile sadly and grab hold of her hand. I thread our fingers together. "I'm fucking sick of this world. It uses us and then it spits us out. To survive...we have to turn on each other, friend against friend." I squeeze her hand. "Parents against their kids. I don't want to be afraid anymore, and I'm sick to death of running. I don't want to hurt anyone, but I will not stand by and do nothing. I am done with standing on the sidelines...*snivelling*." I curl my lip in self-disgust. *I'm done with being a victim.* "I'd rather you didn't blab Sam. But you do what you need to do to survive—I trust you not to say too much." It might be a mistake, but it's a gut feeling I have.

I debate on whether to tell her about John, about us being mates, but I think it's better not to. It's private between us, and even though I should talk to someone else about it...I'm not going to disrespect John by doing so. Instead I change the subject.

"I've got wings."

"Wings? No shit...what type of wings?" Her eyes widen, and she almost shoves me off the bale in her exuberance to look at my back.

"Demony ones—bat, I guess. They're dark purple."

"Can I see?" she asks with a wiggle of her eyebrows. I grin and nod.

This...this is something I can share. I stand and prop my saddle against the bale. I open up the tenuous hold I have on my magic and it eagerly comes to my call. My black, smoky magic appears and Sam's eyes almost bug out of her head. "Is that your magic? Wow. I've never seen anything like that in my life. What can you do with it?"

I shrug. "I have no idea—your guess is as good as mine." Sam waves her hands in the air in an attempt to capture my magic, and as soon as her hands get near, they slip right through.

I mentally call for my wings. Sam squeaks, and it's only due to her vampire reflexes that she catches herself before she falls off the bale.

I giggle and allow myself a tiny bit of pride. Like with my eyes, I've been practising. Before I came to the stables I worked on releasing my wings and then putting them back away. Once I knew what I was doing and I wasn't freaking out over my magic, it became as easy as breathing.

Sam jumps up. "These are incredible, Emma," she says with awe. "Oh…" She holds a finger up and then digs into her jacket pocket. She pulls a potion ball from its depths and wiggles it at me. "…It's a 'don't see me now' potion, so we won't be discovered." She taps her ear. "I will also listen out with my vampire hearing." She flicks the potion ball onto the floor and it activates with a shimmer. As long as I don't go near that spot, it should work fine. "The wings don't tear your clothing?"

"Oh no, I forgot about that." I groan and rub my forehead. "I've never shifted with my top on." *Damn it.*

"Oh well, even if you have to shift with your boobs out…I still want a pair. Go on then, up you go." She nods at a rickety set of stairs in the corner that leads up into the hayloft—it's an open mezzanine area far above us. "Wait one sec…" she grabs her riding hat from the floor and slaps it onto my head. "Okay, champ, now go fly." Sam smacks my bum.

"Fly? Oh no-no-no, I am not going to *fly*. Are you nuts?" I shake my head so vigorously, the riding hat almost bounces off.

"You've got wings, Emma...what else are you gonna do with them?" She gives me a meaningful look and pushes me towards the stairs. "You're a demon...it's not like you're going to die."

I approach the dusty stairs, and thanks to the encouraging poke from behind me, I take a step up. The old wooden steps creak and the whole staircase wobbles. I glance back; the movement and the heavy weight of the wings unbalance me and I almost fall to my knees. "Okay, these things need to go, at least until I am up there." My magic springs into action and the wings dissipate.

So far, so good. I take another few cautious steps up.

"Huh," Sam says from behind me. "Your top is like brand new, it hasn't got any tears in or holes from your wings... looks like your magic fixed it."

"Wow, that's great." I grin as I continue my wobbly ascent. "How cool is that? I'm so glad, as I like this top." I step into the loft. The old wooden floor looks like it hasn't seen a brush in years. Clumps of dust and rotten-looking pieces of hay and straw crunch underneath my feet. I wrinkle my nose as I catch sight of a dead, mummified rat. The poor thing is so flat, it looks like it's been squished by something heavy. Eww.

I shuffle to the edge of the platform and peer down into the barn area. The ground looks like it's miles away. My stomach dips with anxiety. Crap, I know I can heal small things...so far, cuts and small breaks. But I can't heal bruises. I swallow a lump of fear; I don't know if I will be able to heal a broken neck.

"This isn't going to go well," I mumble. In response, Sam shrugs, rubs her hands together, and grins evilly. I roll my eyes. "Sam, that is quite a way to fall. I am not sure about this..." I wipe my sweaty hands on my jodhpurs.

"Yay, I have an idea." Sam scampers away and reappears with half a dozen haynets. Directly below me, she empties the contents onto the concrete floor, creating a hay landing-pad—a crash mat. Yay. I gulp.

"I hope you're gonna refill them and put them back later, 'cause I don't want to get kicked off this yard," I grumble.

Sam flicks a rude finger at me with dismissal. "It's all good. You always worry wayyyy too much...Miss Goody Two-shoes. Live a little, Emma."

Or die. Bloody vampire, it's not her who's going to be flying.

My wings return with a thought. I roll my shoulders and do an experimental flap. With the gust of air the movement creates, the dirt in the loft swirls around me. I close my eyes a second too late and a scratchy piece hits my right eyeball. It makes my eye water. Heck, do I need goggles? I rub my eye and blink like mad.

"Okay, fly," Sam yells.

Thanks, Sam, you're such a help. I adjust the hat and it wobbles. Sam's head is bigger than mine.

Why am I doing this?

This is so like the time she made me show-jump—which ended in disaster. No wonder I prefer dressage.

What the hell am I doing?

Is this going to be another thing to add to my "never try that again" list?

"Oh, no, wait!"

My heart rate picks up at her urgency; my hands tremble and my wings jiggle.

"Oh my God, what?" I yell back. "Is someone coming?"

Sam waves her hand in the air and then digs her phone out of her pocket. She'd better not be thinking of filming me.

No, after some button pressing, a tinny sound of music comes from the phone's speaker. "Is that…'Top Gun?'" I ask incredulously.

Sam nods and gives me a double thumbs-up. "Okay, we are good. Fly."

"Bloody Top Gun," I mumble as I back up as far as I can. *Sometimes the only way to learn is to throw yourself into it…*

I blank my mind, take a deep breath, and flap like crazy as I sprint towards the edge.

"ARRRAH!"

Let's say the fall down was quicker than the climb up. I land on my bum with a crunch and a puff of hay.

Ouch.

Sam stands over me. With a big, silly grin on her face, she claps her hands and bounces on her toes. "Perfect. Now do it again."

"Do I have too?" I whine.

She lowers her chin and in a deep voice says, "'Why do we fall, Bruce?'" She pauses dramatically. "'So we can learn to pick ourselves up.'"

"Batman?" I groan. Why am I listening to her, again?

"Yeah, love that line. Okay, again...again, more flapping... urm...less screaming. You'll give me a headache."

"Liar, vampires don't get headaches," I grumble as I scrape myself off the floor.

I go again. My wings flap like mad. I can't say for sure if my efforts keep me aloft any longer, but I fall as quick. I land on my face in the middle of the hay, and the pile doesn't cushion my landing, not at all. I don't like concrete.

To add insult to injury, the loose hat tips, cracking me across the nose. Blood dribbles down my face.

"More flapping"—she flaps her arms—"less falling, mmkay? Wipe your face, go again."

After another unsuccessful attempt, instead of running I stand at the edge with my heart in my mouth. My breathing is ragged and even though my nose isn't broken anymore, it's bruised. It's also blocked with crusty blood. My whole body is one big bruise.

Somehow, standing on the edge is *way* worse than doing a running jump. I close my eyes and I flap my wings, begging my magic to help.

At first, I try to flap them quickly, and then when that doesn't feel quite right, I try a bigger movement. I concentrate on moving the air like it's water, catching every little bit I can within the folds of my wings. I imagine I am swimming.

Eyes clamped closed, I feel...my toes leave the wooden boards.

I hover in the air for about twenty seconds, using muscles that have only just come into existence. My wings scream in pain and then my body drops like a stone. I whoop with triumph.

Sam is jumping up and down, a grin splitting her face from ear to ear. "You did it, you did it," she chants.

"Oh my God, I did it. I can do this." I grin back. I remove Sam's riding hat and brush clumps of hay from my face and hair.

"Okay, enough for today. I've gotta go." Sam grabs the riding hat from me and bounces away. "Same time next week?"

"Oi, what about the haynets?" I shout at her back.

She waves me away. "Yeah, you better get them refilled. Gotta go, I have another horse to ride. I'll send you a bill for the flying lessons," she cackles. I slump back into the hay and groan. "Oh, and Em, you are so badass." I huff out a laugh.

"No, I'm not." I drop my voice to barely a whisper. "But I'm going to be."

CHAPTER THIRTY-THREE

Eighteen years later

The years roll by in the blink of an eye.

I slam the door of the taxi and wave to the shellshocked girl huddled inside. I nod to the driver and mouth a thank-you. He returns my thanks with a cheerful smile and drives away from the loading bay. As the taxi disappears around the corner, I quickly check that I'm alone, and then I shift into *the girl*.

I mimic her perfectly, from her clothing to her hair. My magic is incredible. I can even remove an item of clothing and it will stay real for a few hours before dissipating, it's that complex.

No wonder John had an issue with me when we first met. The things I can do now with magic...I scare myself sometimes.

It's freaky.

John...I sigh. He's been off-world with a team of hellhounds for over a year, so I haven't seen him. The hellhound has thrown himself into work, doing more and more dangerous things; he puts himself at risk.

John is more renowned, more dangerous than he ever was before. I can't help thinking I've had a lucky escape, but a niggle in the back of my head tells me I am ultimately responsible. That I snuffed whatever goodness he had right out of him.

When I don't see him or hear about his antics for a while, I can't help the fear and the worry I feel. I know he's a grown-ass man, *a man who I rejected*, even if we don't talk about "the elephant in the room," he is still my mate. We gravitate towards each other. I catch the odd flash of pain in his green eyes, undoubtedly mirrored in my own.

Ha, I'm not one to talk about risk. People in glass houses shouldn't throw stones, and what I do isn't rainbows and kittens. John isn't the only one who has thrown himself into work. Daily I mess with people's lives, and there is nothing more dangerous than that.

With that fun thought...I turn and slip back through the fire-exit door into the shop's storeroom. I enter the changing rooms and nod at Penny, who has been my vigilant changing-room gatekeeper while Jessica was making her getaway.

The shop assistant twists her fingers together. "They are getting impatient," she whispers.

I give Penny a reassuring smile and I gently squeeze her shoulder. "It's okay. Thank you so much—you've done amazingly. I shouldn't need to ask for your help again."

I have a network of people I have helped over the years who owe me favours. I don't ask for much. It might be like today, a request to use the back door to a shop that they work in so I can smuggle a girl to safety, or for them to delay a bus for two minutes. Little things that add up like puzzle pieces in a sometimes-complex scheme that involves me helping others.

In a world full of monsters, I am the light in the darkness.

Mentally, I snort and I roll my eyes. Ha, what a big head: *I am the light in the darkness.* I am so glad I didn't say that out loud. I grab the clothes that Jessica has supposedly been trying on, and her small bag.

"Oh, no," Penny urgently whispers, "if you ever need help, you've only got to ask—I'm your girl." Her big brown eyes fill with tears and her lower lip trembles. "What you do...what you did...for my brother, for me. I can't ever repay you. So anything, *anything* I can do to help you..." her whispered words fade and she shrugs and rubs at a stray tear that's escaped. Impulsively, I give her a quick hug. "I've never met a witch like you—your illusion magic is incredible."

"Thank you." I smile, and I don't correct her assumption that I'm a witch; I let her think I am, like most people. Others think I'm a high-level fae. No one has yet to suspect that I'm a demon, which is how I like it. I scoop up and void the sound-masking potion ball Penny laid before the switch. The little ball crumbles to dust in my fingers and I rub my hands on my jeans.

I almost walk into the burly shifter bodyguard who is guarding the changing room door. "Mrs Philips, it is time to go," he says sharply.

"Of course. Thank you, Briggs." The voice that comes out of my mouth isn't my own. No, I look and sound a perfect copy of Jessica Phillips. I even smell like her. The shifter in front of me would be unable to tell us apart.

It took me a while to work out my demon magic. Transforming into a person took a little bit of finesse in the beginning. If I wasn't careful, I'd look fake, or worse, like a bad illusion. I spent days sitting and observing people, their faces, clothing, and their movements. I got good at mimicking people, and when I realised I could change not only my voice but my scent, I was hooked.

The satisfaction I feel knowing that the real Jessica is already safe and on her way to an entirely new life is addictive.

It is why I do what I do. It started with my pup, and then there was my mum and the frustration of not being able to help her. You don't have to beat people up or kill people to be a hero—sometimes you can uniquely, sneakily use your gifts. I am a silent hero and I don't care if no one knows. It's better that they don't. Every time I do this, my soul feels a little lighter.

Jessica is half-fae and unfortunately gained the attention of the wrong man, Henry Phillips. They met six years ago, and the cat shifter, a former member of the old corrupt shifter council, would not take no for an answer. He forced poor Jessica into a relationship with him.

No one realises what goes on behind closed doors, and with powerful creatures—especially powerful shifters—even if people know something is not what it seems, they still turn a blind eye. Too frightened. I guess they think it's not their fight.

When an associate gave me Jessica's information and told me she needed my help urgently, I didn't hesitate to step in.

I have to play the role of Jessica until I can safely slip away. The clock is ticking down and Jess is less than twenty-five minutes away from stepping through a portal into Ireland. Shifters aren't allowed in Ireland. The country is a haven for humans and the fae. It has strict rules, so I'm confident Mr Philips won't be able to track her.

Oh, and I don't just shove her through the portal. I have an entire identity established for her and a place to live, a job. Once Jessica finds her feet, she can decide what she wants to do, how she wants to live. For the first time in six years, Jessica is free.

Now I'm about to play a game to keep Jessica's bodyguards, and Henry Phillips, busy. Busy enough not to implicate any of the people that have helped me today. The game is my favourite: "Now You See Me, Now You Don't."

I follow the bodyguard, my back ramrod straight and my chin high, but my eyes are firmly, submissively fixed on the floor.

I meekly hand over the clothing to another shop assistant. "Just the white top, please," I say in Jessica's whispery voice. Mr Phillips loves the colour white. With the help of my hacker friend Ava, I have eyes all over the city, and I have done my homework. The shop assistant nods, and another bodyguard steps forward to handle the payment. Jessica isn't allowed any money of her own.

Once the guard has paid, we leave. The bell over the door chimes as we step out onto the busy pedestrianised street. Briggs tightly grips my elbow as the three other bodyguards that are waiting outside the shop join our small group.

Even though I've spent what feels like more time with other people's faces on than my own, when I catch my reflection in a shop's window, it is still jarring.

Like a living wall of shifter muscle, the five guards surround me as we head back towards the parked car. I chose this shop in particular to do the switch because they don't allow cars in this pedestrian-only shopping area, and the loading bay at the back of the store makes the perfect getaway.

When we get to the main road, which is heavy with fast-moving traffic, it's showtime. "Oh," I say. I rise onto the balls of my feet and peek around the bodyguard wall. I pretend to recognise somebody across the street. "That is my friend from school." I elbow Briggs sharply in the ribs, whip around the guards, and dash into the traffic. Chaos ensues as cars swerve to avoid me. The air fills with the sounds of screeching tyres and angry car horns. No damage.

Jessica's completely-out-of-character action leaves the five bodyguards stunned for a few seconds. A few seconds is all that I need as my feet land on the pavement on the other side of the road. I grin as I blend into the crowd.

I hurry into a department store, and I make my way through the store at a fast clip. With a wink at another shop assistant, I snatch my earpiece off a shelf and stuff it into my ear. I groan—this would work so much better if magic would work on me; a communication spell would be a godsend. I shrug. Unfortunately, using other people's magic is still not in my remit.

"They are tracking you outside. Turn left," Ava says in my ear as she follows me on the security cameras. I love this store, as it has various entrances that exit onto busy shopping areas. "Look up to your left, flick your hair, perfect...got you on that camera. The bus is at the stop and it will leave in three..." I step onto the bus and wave the bus pass at the driver. "...Two..." I move away from the doors and head to the back. "...One." I grab hold of the safety bar as the bus pulls out into traffic. "Okay, they have seen you and they are following."

I slide onto the bench seat and surreptitiously look about to make sure I have no one's attention. When I deem the coast is clear, I lean against the seat in front of me and I carefully wedge Jessica's small purse, which contains her phone, underneath the seat. I also leave the bus pass inside—dated today and dirty, with a footprint on it. It's almost as if it was dropped on the floor and Jessica conveniently found it. Fancy that.

"They're following, two cars back," Ava updates. The bus goes over the bridge. "The station is coming up in one minute—get ready." I stand, leave my seat, and make my way slowly to the front of the bus.

It is imperative that we leave a trail for them to follow. Over the next few days and the oncoming weeks, ex-Councillor Phillips will want to get his greedy hands on everything to do with Jessica's escape. No one can be implicated. The bus rolls to a stop and with a polite "thank you" to the driver, I jump off.

I head through a mass of people congregating around the station's monitors. "Stand there...okay, three cameras have got you...that's perfect. Look at the timetable. The next train to London is at platform six. Go, quick—you have three minutes, Boss."

I rush past and dodge the many travellers, some lumbering along with their bags and others chatting and stabbing at their phones. A few people are also rushing towards platforms. I run up some stairs that take me over the railway lines and then go down another set. I am glad Jessica listened and wore flat shoes—running in heels is not my strong suit. I arrive at platform six just as the train pulls in and the doors open. I head for the closest carriage and step inside.

"Okay, train camera has you. I can take it from here." I step behind a partition, and when I'm sure no one is looking...I shift and step off the train.

I tap my walking stick against the concrete as on doddering steps I slowly shuffle away. There's a beep-beep-beep behind me as the train doors close, and a whistle from the platform guard. I turn my head and watch in satisfaction as he waves to the driver, and with a hiss, a clunk, and a grinding sound, the train pulls away.

Three huge shifters barrel down the stairs, just in time to watch the train leave. One of them picks up a bin and throws it at the departing train with a roar. The others stand there, looks of disbelief on their faces. The rubbish flutters onto the floor and track. I frown. God, I hate littering.

"It's an express train to London. No stops, she's trapped. Come on, we have three hours to collect her from the other station," Briggs says with a snarl. He turns and almost knocks me over. "Watch where you are going, you stupid old cow," he spits out. He runs past me up the stairs. The other two shifters follow in his wake, not sparing me a glance.

I hum as I shuffle towards the lift, my walking stick tap-tapping. No one sees the old lady with her walking stick as she hobbles along. "Jessica made it, Boss," Ava says. I cackle with glee. Boom, mental fist-pump. Today is another good day.

CHAPTER THIRTY-FOUR

Stuart waves at me in a panic when I step out of Bob's empty stable. "Emma, I apologise—Bob should have already been in for his afternoon check and feed. I'm sorry to inform you he keeps running away from our staff. I even attempted to get him myself...but he would not come." He twists his hands and blinks at me with a contrite expression.

My lips twitch and I try not to laugh. Bob at twenty-eight is the same horse he was at three. The older he gets, the easier he should be, but no, he seems to get sneakier with age. "It's no bother, Stuart, I'll get him." I grab his headcollar from the hook next to his stable door, and with Stuart on my heels, we head towards the fields.

"How is Mr Brown—" Stuart puffs out. Mhm, Mr Brown, my demon barrister and Bob's *owner*...this situation right here is the reason I shouldn't lie. Eighteen years I've had to keep up the ruse. I think Stuart is aware that I'm not completely human, what with the not ageing and popping randomly out of thin air. I had to make Mr Brown up on the fly and now he is a renowned barrister who works tirelessly at helping people with guild issues.

To be honest, he is a favourite of mine. I thoroughly enjoy the havoc I can cause and the amount of good I can do when I wear Mr Brown's face. I have others do the legal stuff, as I'm not a barrister no matter what the paperwork says. But I can be a figurehead when needed, a legal advocate for the vulnerable and the lost. "—Are the new laws causing you much trouble?" Stuart continues, his eyes glowing with his excitement. He's such a gossip.

In response, I laugh and I shake my head. Truthfully I answer, "Oh, the law-makers are the people who deal with all that. My firm is doing what it can to help. If I am honest, I keep well out of the way—it is far above my pay grade." As Emma, I officially work as Mr Brown's personal assistant and Bob's groom. I think of it as my Clark Kent disguise. I go into a solicitor's office daily and disappear in there for hours.

In reality, the practice is mine and the very best minds are behind helping me help others. They know nothing about my gifts, and to them, Mr Brown is their boss and I'm his respected right hand. I let them do their jobs while I spend all my time planning my rescues of the people I can't save within the law.

I only keep abreast of the various legal situations of the races, as when big changes happen, the innocent can get caught up.

Also, there is a certain hellhound that I have a vested interest in protecting…I can't help myself.

Stuart is still chatting away, and I smile and nod my head at the appropriate moments. When we arrive at the field gate, I shout for Bob. His head immediately comes up, and he does an adorable high-pitched whinny that I translate to mean, *"My human is here."* He thunders across the field in my direction. The true love of my life.

"Hi Bob-cob, have you been naughty?" I ask him as he skids to a stop in front of me and gobbles up a couple of mints from my palm. I smile as his whiskers tickle my hand. I then frown as I catch sight of clumps of mud that are stubbornly clinging to the side of his face. I vigorously rub his face and left ear to clear the worst of it, and I get a mouthful of mud dust for my trouble as it transfers itself onto my face. Satisfied, I pop Bob's headcollar on and lead him out of the field.

I grin as Stuart scowls at Bob, and Bob flattens his ears and glares back.

* * *

I roll my sleeves up. My phone on the side is blaring out the local radio station and I dance around the living room. I'm setting up one of my safe houses, an apartment in the city centre. Apart from Ava and myself, and the few people that use a safe house, no one knows these places exist.

The money Arlo left in my name was a vast amount, and it amuses me, how I spend it. It would have made the demon rage. I normally choose the places I buy to be in busy buildings with young, transient residents who won't notice if somebody new arrives. I rarely use houses, as an empty house on a street is more noticeable. I have dozens of these apartments all over the country, and I try not to use the same one more than twice a year. Sometimes I will move a person in and it will become their permanent residence. It takes nothing with Ava's computer skills to bury the paper trail and keep the apartments hidden.

I also use my doorway to access them when I stock up, so I don't risk being followed and have the safe houses traced back to me.

I hum. The apartment is immaculate. I have stocked it with everything I can think of to make it comfortable. Unisex clothing—as I don't help just women—in various sizes, food, and toiletries. I'm not expecting to use this place for a while, but it's ready.

There is a bang behind me and the front door shudders. I have time to stop the music, send Ava a text message, silence my mobile, and shove it in my back pocket before the lock shatters.

I tilt my head and watch as three vampires barge their way into the apartment. Huh. I raise my eyebrows. What do these idiots want? "What the hell did you do to my door?" I ask incredulously, waving both hands at my poor dangling lock. "Ever heard of knocking? Why did you break down my door?" At least the door itself isn't damaged. What the bloody hell is going on?

Instead of saying anything, a vampire rushes me. His fists are almost a blur as they fly at my face. How rude. His form would mortify Scott, as his technique is awful. I step to the side and punch him sharply in the kidney. Vampire or not, that had to hurt. I kick out his knees and with a thump, he sprawls to the floor.

I shake my head as I step back away from his reach, and I keep his groaning, twisting form in my eye-line. I turn my regard to his friends, who so far, luckily for them, aren't as brash. I raise an eyebrow, cross my arms, and tap my foot...I wait impatiently for an explanation.

It better be good.

"Is this her?" one of them asks. He is tall and thin, with a dark blond comb-over.

"Yeah, the demon bitch. Girl, our boss would like a word with you. You are coming with us," his friend replies.

I make a meh-face. If I didn't have my empathy and I was a normal demon, I would pop his head clean off for being so rude.

This rude guy is broader, with an athletic build, and his hair is cropped close to his scalp. All three of the vampires are wearing variations on cheap combat clothing—although the tall blond guy's pants aren't quite long enough and they finish halfway up his ankles, leaving a bit of skin between his boots and pant leg. He sees me looking and glares at me. I smirk back at him.

I turn my eyes back toward the chatty rude vampire. "Urm...yeah, about that. I don't *chat* with people who send their goons to break down my door. I think I'll pass, thanks." The idiots are so paying to fix the lock.

"Bitch, you don't have a choice." The rude talkative one sticks his hand in his pocket and pulls out a magical Taser. Huh. "Come quietly—I don't want to have to hurt you, but I will." He wiggles the Taser at me and in response I hold my hands up.

Crap, I don't fancy being zapped today. Sometimes they are just magic and it slides right off me; other times they can have a spark of electricity. You know how in cartoons when a character gets electrocuted, you see a visible skeleton, a flash of bones? Yeah, I always imagine myself looking like that when I get hit by one of those things. It makes my teeth hurt.

"Before we leave, we need to confirm your identity." The tall vampire steps forward with a datapad. "Place your hand on the pad. It will take your fingerprints and a drop of your blood for DNA profiling," he says in a bored tone.

"Oh, I can't touch that thing..." I hold my hands up higher. If I touch it, I'll break it.

I can sense the magic in there—it's a fancy combination of technology and magic. The machine is like the medical ones at the hospital. A rip-off version of the ones that the guilds carry. The vampire with the pad ignores my protest and grabs my hand. He wrestles my arm down and with a heavy grip, grinds the delicate bones of my hand together painfully.

I wince as he slaps my palm against the screen and within seconds there's a beep and a burning smell. A puff of smoke comes out of the side of the machine and some poor pathetic-sounding beeps signal its death.

"What the fuck...you did that on purpose."

"I really didn't. I tried to warn you." I give him a toothy grin and shrug. "You put my hand on it." His face slowly morphs into horror and the hand holding the broken datapad trembles. I think reality has just caught up with him and he realises that I am a demon.

The vampire on the floor—whom with a smirk I dub "the Kung Fu Master"—groans and staggers to his feet.

Oh, here we go.

Like a wet dog, he shakes himself, and then a ferocious expression passes across his face. With a war cry of "Arrah," the bloody idiot attempts to rush me again.

I roll my eyes as I dodge his fist, and this time, I throat-punch him. Eyes wide, clutching his throat, he gurgles and drops back to the floor. I wince as his knees crunch. Red-faced, he sputters.

"Where on earth did you find this idiot?" I ask, looking at him with a frown. I'm not the best at hand-to-hand; even after years of practice, I'd say I'm proficient. I run my hand through my hair. Truthfully, I don't like hurting people. I will if forced to do so. But compared to Kung Fu Master, who is again rolling around on the floor, I'm practically a ninja. "He makes a terrible henchman."

I glance back up and cringe at the livid look Taser Vamp is giving me. I hope he hasn't got an itchy trigger finger. I give him a rueful smile and I hold my hands up again. I shrug. "Hey I was defending myself. You can't zap me for that."

"He's my brother," he says through gritted teeth.

"Oh, that sucks," I reply with another glance at the floor.

He nods to the tall vampire, who now cautiously side-steps towards me. He pulls out a magic void bracelet—it's a plastic magical band the guilds use. Aw, bless him, he has all the best toys today. I helpfully hold my arm out for him. With a trembling hand, he slaps it onto my wrist. With a snap, the plastic tightly wraps around. What it should do is deaden my magic. It voids magic completely, helpful if you have to arrest a magical creature.

I don't have the heart to tell them they don't work on me. Oops.

The two vampires back away and warily watch me. No doubt they are waiting for something dramatic to happen. Perhaps a good old head-spin? The third is still on the floor gurgling. I give them a toothy smile and tap my foot again...time's ticking, and we need to get this show on the road. I can't spend my entire day being kidnapped.

"Why hasn't she changed," the tall vampire says out of the side of his mouth. His buddy stares at me, his lips part, and he shrugs his shoulders haplessly.

"I dunno," he says.

I tuck a piece of my blonde hair behind my ear. "This is what I look like," I say, doing jazz hands. I rub my mouth to stop myself from smiling. Their confusion is adorable. "Were you expecting something different?"

"I didn't expect you to be so pretty," Tall Vampire mumbles.

"Oh...urm, thanks." I think. I'll take it as a compliment. At least he isn't trying to be creepy. "So your boss?" I need to get them back on track. Their dumbfounded expressions are now making me feel uncomfortable.

I've already decided that I'm going to go with them. I need some questions answered, like *how* they found this safe house and *how* they knew that I'd be here. It shouldn't have happened and I need to plug the leak. It's not just me I'm worried about. People are counting on me.

I'm also fascinated, so I will play along. I need to know *who* decided it was a good idea to come and...kidnap me? Ha.

"Yeah, our master has been after you for some time," Taser Vamp replies. I shrug. I do like a good bad-guy confrontation. Their boss doesn't know what shit he has dug up. Thinking about it, I've never done a confrontation looking like me before. I am like a walking trap. I might look like an easy mark, but I'm not...I am far from it.

"Terry, get the cameras." Terry, formerly known as Tall Vampire, scampers off to do Taser Vamp's bidding. I'm disturbed as I watch him pluck tiny cameras from obscure places around the apartment. Cameras are dotted all around. I cringe...that means someone somewhere has evidence of me attempting to twerk. I blame Sam for teaching me.

I wonder if this is the only safe house that's compromised. I doubt it. I groan. Crap, I'm not looking forward to all that extra work. At least that answers one of my questions, of how they knew I was here.

I am unceremoniously marched out of the building with the Taser poking into my side.

These guys have watched *way* too many films.

Kung Fu Master is trying desperately to intimidate me—he keeps knocking into me and growling. When he shoves me into the side of the car and I painfully bang my hip—ouch—I lose my temper; I spin around and smack him on the back of the head. "Knock it off. You're acting like a right wanker." I growl, "Knock into me again and I'll pull your bloody arm off." I poke my finger in his face. He growls back and flashes his fangs.

Oh no, he bloody didn't. If he does that again, I will pull his fangs right out of his stupid head.

Stuff it. I allow my eyes to bleed black.

His eyes widen in disbelief, and he drops them to my wrist and the void band.

He stumbles back away from me and glances about, opening and closing his mouth like a goldfish. His entire body shakes and he drops his eyes to the floor submissively.

"Your attitude is going to get you killed," I hiss at him. "Think before you act. Now get in the car." I push him for good measure and he hurries away to the front of the car and jumps in.

As I slide into the back of the car, I look up at the street CCTV camera. I give it a nod and mouth the words, "Track me."

CHAPTER THIRTY-FIVE

"She has black eyes. This isn't good, this isn't good...she's going to kill us all," Kung Fu Master whispers as his shaking body rocks forward and back in the front passenger seat.

"Shut up, Matthew, you're doing my head in," his brother, Mr Taser, harshly replies. Cringing, I sit in the back of the car with Terry. I feel a bit like a bully; I didn't mean to frighten him.

I wiggle in my seat. Okay, I meant to frighten him, but not as bad as I have.

We drive for around thirty minutes in uncomfortable silence. Kung Fu Master can't keep still. Every time I move, he shudders and his left leg bounces.

When we arrive at a familiar building, a familiar nightclub, I roll my eyes. This place has had many revamps over the years and its owner has stayed relatively quiet. I knew it was only a matter of time before the pureblood came for me.

My various attempts to rescue my mum from his clutches were in vain, and my relationship with her was stilted as a result. I close my eyes for a brief second, it still hurts when I think about her role in my life. The mystery of her giving me away hampered our non-existent mother-and-daughter relationship.

I don't trust easily, and I guess with John's words of caution churning in the back of my mind, it was difficult to give her the benefit of the doubt. I asked her; I brought up the painful subject a few times over the years, but she wouldn't answer. She'd quickly change the subject or she would cry. Then I would be left feeling like the bad guy. No one wants to make their mum cry. So I let it go.

I suppose I could have forced her into leaving him. But what kind of person would that have made me? I would have been no better than the wicked men and women I fight against. It's a lesson I learned quickly: you can only help the people that want your help. The people that are ready to move on. Otherwise, you are wasting everybody's time.

The club is closed as it's Monday afternoon. I get out of the car with a yawn and stretch. With a hand on my shoulder,

Mr Taser frogmarches me across the street. The frightened, wide-eyed brother disappears.

We pass bored-looking vampires that are standing guard outside. They have the look of elite soldiers, but they lack the menace of trained professionals. It doesn't help that their bright-red uniforms stand out for all the wrong reasons. I quietly count them as I pass. I give up when I get to over a dozen. I groan. Perhaps this isn't my best move, allowing Lord Luther Gilbert to have the pleasure of my company.

I'm shown up some stairs and we head through a door marked PRIVATE. Taser Vampire swings the door open without knocking and prods me to enter. We step inside.

The colour red assaults my senses. Glossy red tiles span the floor and gleam my reflection back at me—dozens of creepy, red, distorted versions of myself. Oh heck, that's not a flattering look. I refrain from the childish urge to grin or stick my tongue out.

I lift my eyes from the creepy floor and take in the rest of the room. I wrinkle my nose with distaste as the red theme continues. Red walls, curtains, blinds, and furniture. Instead of looking sensual, the shade of red chosen makes the entire room look tacky and gives the overall impression of trying too hard. Cheap. It's as if the designer was intent on screaming, "Here be vampires"...it's like a vampire threw up on it.

My feet squeak on the tiles as with another taser-nudge to my back we continue into the room and head towards a seating area in the centre. "The only thing missing in this room is a blood fountain," I mumble. Mr Taser grunts in response.

The floor-to-ceiling internal windows, which look out onto the club, is the only break from the colour in the room. I think they might be one-way glass, or perhaps mirrored. I can't remember seeing a window on the club side the last time I visited...but that was over eighteen years ago.

Mr Taser watches me and his eyes widen in panic, as without an invitation to sit, I plunk my bum down onto a bright-red leather chair, which is hard and unyielding. I wave his concern away as I slump back. I'm not standing on ceremony like everyone else; waiting for the pureblood to arrive can easily be done seated.

When the man of the house...club? glides into the room, I smile lazily at him. Vampires call their collectives *Houses*. Headed by a pureblood leader, the then-House rules over the smaller clans in the area. So perhaps I was right the first time with "the man of the house."

"Hello, Luther," I say with a small wave. I sit up and peer over his shoulder for any sign of my mum, but she doesn't appear. The pureblood is alone. Well, if you ignore his guards, that is...three of them flank him, plus Mr Taser. "My mum...not about today?" I ask pleasantly as I drop the wave and slump back into the chair. My elbow cracks against the arm. I frown, give it a rub, and then prod the cushion. Poke-poke-poke. I'd be better sitting on a slab of concrete or the floor. What was the designer thinking? Perhaps vampires don't have any sensation in their bottoms or lower extremities, so it doesn't matter if the furniture is uncomfortable. How on earth did they get this chair so hard? That is an impressive feat on its own. It's definitely not styling over comfort, as the chair is u.g.l.y.

"Emma," Luther says sharply. I glance up from my chair-poking to meet his narrowed, angry eyes. He takes in my overall slumped, unconcerned position on his rock chair. Was he expecting fear and tears? I haven't done that in a very long time.

"Why am I here?" I ask with an enormous yawn...gosh, the room needs a window open and some fresh air. The stale air and the smell of rot from the turned vampires in the room is giving me a headache. I rub my temples.

Yes, turned vampires smell of dead things. I never noticed it before, but over the years my senses have improved. It's no wonder that shifters, who have more sensitive noses, seem to hold their breath when around vampires—they stink.

"I've been biding my time, waiting for the ideal opportunity for you to be vulnerable. I'm a patient man. It is so handy to have eternity at my fingertips."

Yeah, yeah, you're immortal, aren't we all? Good for you.

With a dramatic sigh and an ostentatious pout, he looks at his nails. My heart misses a beat as he reminds me of—in that moment—Arlo. Although a poor version of the demon. Arlo would have done his villain speech a heck of a lot better. Luther smiles down at his nails as he misinterprets the jump in my pulse. "The opportunity presented, and I took advantage. Today I decided on a more direct approach as your hellhound protector is off-world and isn't around to rescue you," Luther continues.

My lips twitch at his words and I relax further into the chair.

I've never been, nor I have ever wanted to be, the girl who waited to be rescued. I'm a fighter, not so much with my fists but with my mind. The mind is the best weapon. I'm not a princess looking for her proverbial prince. Does he think I need John to save me? Oh boy, of course he does. I cough and cover my mouth to hide my smile.

"You refused my invitation once before and attempted to take away my favourite toy." He lifts his eyes from his nail inspection and petulantly glares at me. Someone had his feelings hurt.

I raise my eyebrows and give his words a small nod of acknowledgement. "How is my mum?" I inquire pleasantly.

"I haven't spoken to her for a while."

"She wants you in the fold. My House offered you protection with open arms and you turned me down." I barely refrain from rolling my eyes as the pureblood goes into a rant. "Do you know how many times I've offered protection in my lifetime? Yet you turned your nose up at my offer." He paces in front of me, his shiny shoes clicking across the tiles and his voice getting a little louder with each step.

Gosh, I agitate him. I do that to some people. It's a gift.

"You belong to me. You are in my House now," he declares, turning around to pace back towards me.

"How did you find me?" I ask conversationally as I trace the leather seam of the chair. My heart rate is steady, and I relax my body and belatedly ignore his manic words and pacing. Nothing upsets a pureblood more than a lack of fear or non-deferential behaviour. They love all that bowing and scraping. If you don't kiss ass, it freaks them out.

"Your new apartment was flagged in our system as having an unknown buyer. We have been monitoring the residents of that building, as a few of the clans have become..." he narrows his eyes and curls his lip, "...difficult. There is a rebel leader in that building on our watch list. When the sale for your apartment was processed, it was flagged by my security team, who ordered the cameras to be put into place. I was pleasantly surprised when you moved in today and my security team alerted me. I took the opportunity as a gift and sent my closest men to collect you."

Huh. If he is to be believed, Ava and I missed a vampire issue in the building. A definite oversight, but understandable as the politics among creatures is ridiculously complicated, and this is a small vampire dynamic in the scheme of things. If I do believe him, and I have no reason yet not to, I can rest easy that my other safe houses are...well, safe.

This rebel leader...I need to have a chat with them. Anyone willing to upset a pureblood might be someone I want to watch and possibly help. The enemy of my enemy and all that jazz.

"You could have called. Stalking and kidnapping is so cliché, Luther." *Crack.* The pureblood slaps me across the face with the back of his hand. The sound echoes around the room.

"You will address me as Lord Gilbert. You have not got my permission to use my given name—have some respect," he seethes.

Blood fills my mouth. Huh, I didn't see him move—he was fast.

I slowly blink at him, lift my hand, and run the back of it across my lips, smudging the blood across my mouth and cheek. I look down at my hand, at the evidence of his anger on my skin. I tilt my head until the dark-green tinge of my blood catches the light.

Lord Gilbert steps back and the guards in the room mumble. His eyes narrow as he stares at me. "Green?" he says with astonishment.

I tilt my head and smile. I watch him as he frantically wipes the hand that hit me on his suit trousers.

"Demon," I growl back.

He knows I am part demon so why is it such a surprise?

On purpose, I lick my lips clean. In response, his own lip lifts at the corner with poorly veiled disgust. Unable to hide his distaste, he shudders.

There is more mumbling from the guards. My blood tastes normal to me, but to a vampire, my green blood—my demon blood—tastes like shit.

The green didn't happen overnight. It started as a green glitter within the red and it became darker over time. Meh, I roll with it. I have wings and I can fly...heck, I can shift into a fly...so I decided early on not to freak out about my blood colour.

My tongue prods my lip. The cut from his blow has already healed. My lip was good as new seconds after he hit me. Shame I can't say the same for the bruising—my throbbing cheek will take a while to heal. He doesn't understand who he's messing with.

I can see the growing confusion in his eyes as he focuses

on my lips, as he looks for the evidence of the damage he caused. He shakes his head dismissively. He ignores his instincts, which I presume are screaming at him, with a shake of his blond head.

All he sees is a little girl he sold.

"Your demon parlour tricks don't impress me," he scoffs. "I have watched you for years. I wanted to see what of your own volition you'd amount to, and honestly, Emma, I'm not impressed. An administrator at a solicitor's firm? What a disappointment," he sneers at me, and paces away.

I can read him like a book. He's now using the pacing as an excuse to move away from me. My overall unconcerned demeanour and my dark-green blood have thrown him.

I do my best to keep the smile off my face as he starts what he thinks is an epic speech about my failings. I miss the majority of what he has been saying, but it's no bother. He sounds like a disappointed parent. A disappointed parent who lacks all the facts.

Not for the first time, I think about what kind of person I would have been if this man had been in charge of my childhood. If I stayed with my mum, lived with his vampires. I remember John's words, *"Vampires destroy weakness, Emma."* My stomach flips as I acknowledge they would have killed me or I'd have changed into someone unrecognisable.

"Guard," he yells. I don't understand why he isn't all

suave and vampy. You'd think a pureblood would know his vampires can hear everything and that there is no need to shout.

I've done my homework on this guy and he's supposed to be at the top of the vampire hierarchy, the top of the tree—at least in this area. Yet he's behaving like an idiot. No wonder his men were so gung-ho and ill-trained: his whole House is festering.

One of the elite-looking vampires marches forward. If it wasn't for the smell and the shocked muttering from before, I would have forgotten that they were in the room. It's that red uniform, with the whole red-on-red...they sort of blend into the background. "Dominic, please show Emma to the white room." I sigh at the clear dismissal.

Dominic, a guard in a neat red uniform, deferentially bows to Luther. He turns to me, and his expression is...zombie-like; his eyes are dead and void of all expression. Creepy. He snaps out his hand to indicate for me to go ahead of him. Okay, then.

I rise. As I escape the unyielding concrete torture chair, I frown and shake out my limbs. Pins and needles run up and down my thighs. I glare at the chair and give my bum a rub as it re-forms back into its normal shape. God, I feel as if my whole lower half pops back into place.

"I will talk to you tomorrow. For the rest of the day and

evening, perhaps you can have a rethink about your attitude and behaviour. Tomorrow we will discuss your new role in my House." I nonchalantly shrug in response.

Huh, not if I have anything to do with it. I'm planning not to be here within the next hour. I have all the information I need.

CHAPTER THIRTY-SIX

Aptly named, the room is white, everything is white. I wash my hand across my face and groan. Oh heck, I can see myself leaving dirty smudges everywhere. The more I try not to, the more it will happen. I'm the person who, when told to be careful while eating, gets all nervous and my face twitches and I miss my mouth. I will drop every crumb or spill my drink. Not intentionally. But the more careful I try to be, the less it works out.

Gah. I also cleaned the apartment in this outfit. Forcing a horsie demon into a fully white room amounts to torture. It's almost as bad as that red chair. I remove my boots and leave them by the door. Even with me as an unwilling visitor, some poor sod will have to clean up after me, so I can't drop my manners.

In my socks, I pad across the white carpet and look around the room...no windows. The door has a fancy locking mechanism; it is a combination of infused magic and technology. It also has a dangerous, buzzing ward over the top. I move to the closest wall and give it a tap. It clangs. I hum; they've reinforced the wall. There's a big white bed and another door leading to an attached bathroom.

I yawn. I haven't got a clue what I'm going to do about the pureblood—I can't let him get away with this, but I can't kill him either. I don't mess around in vampire politics, and killing a pureblood is equivalent to killing a king.

Flash-flash, flash-flash. I lift my head and spot the red light underneath the security camera as it blinks rhythmically. I spin away before whoever is manning the security camera can catch my bright, beaming smile.

I dramatically flop onto the bed and bury my head in the pillows as uncontrollable laughter bubbles up inside of me— I can't help my giggles. This whole situation is ridiculous.

Anyone watching the camera feed will see my shoulders shake and probably think I am crying, not laughing.

I allow a few more minutes for Ava to do her thing, and when I'm sure enough time has lapsed, I flip over and sit up. I lift my hips and pull my phone from my back pocket.

The naughty vampires really should have frisked me.

My mobile vibrates immediately in my hand. I get comfortable and sit cross-legged in the centre of the bed as I answer. "Hi, Ava."

"Hey Boss, I'm in their systems—I have been since I got your text message. I've got you on screen." I wave at the camera. "I've looped the camera feed so they can't see you talking to me. I've gone through their systems with a fine-toothed comb and I can't find any evidence of any other safe house being compromised. No more hidden cameras. I found and deleted the one from the apartment. But just in case, I'm doing a full security check as a precaution. I'm..." the phone rustles as Ava puffs out a sad-sounding breath. "...shit, I'm so sorry Boss, I messed up." I vigorously shake my head at the camera.

"No, no, hey...you haven't messed up, don't be daft. These things happen..." I push my hair away from my face and tuck it behind my ear, "...and I appreciate everything that you do. Thank you for having my back."

"I saw the void bracelet. Can you still use the doorways?" Ava asks. I glance down at the snap band on my wrist. Huh, I'd forgotten about it.

"Oh yeah, it's all fine. I can still use the doorways—my magic is still active; the bands don't work on me. I have some clippers at home that I can use to cut this sucker off.

I'm not happy about hanging around here for long—I need to leave."

"I will keep you on the camera loop, so you can leave anytime. Are you going to use your doorway?"

I grin at the camera and point at the warded door with my free hand and scramble off the bed and roll my shoulders. "Is it bad that I want to go out the front door?"

"Yes," Ava says, being the voice of reason. "I can see on the cameras that he has a lot of vampires hanging around."

I grunt in response.

I move towards the door with its crappy ward and the over-the-top magic lock. It would be so easy to walk out of this room. Going out there and beating up or frightening the vampires is going to make me feel vindicated.

In that awful red room, when I looked down at those glossy red tiles as they reflected my distorted, red face back at me, I felt inspired. It gave me such a great idea. I could shift into a demon, red, huge, and scare the crap out of them. A human against vampires wouldn't stand a chance, but a demon...

Walk away or cause a scene...apart from a bit of bruising across my cheek, I'm okay. I let them take me. I came for answers, and I got them.

But...Ava is right, it's not a good idea. I am not that person; it's not the vampires' fault that their boss is a dick.

I spin and mockingly glare at the camera, then shift my gaze to the room's bathroom door. With a disappointed sigh, I grab my boots from the floor, and like a sulky teenager, I trudge away towards the bathroom doorway. "No, it's not a good idea," I grumble, once I'm standing on the bathroom tiles and not on the dreaded white carpet. One-handed, as I'm still holding the phone in the other hand, I stuff my feet into my boots. "It's not a good idea at all. I hate you. It's not like you, being the voice of reason."

Ava snorts. "Yeah, I know. You must be rubbing off on me."

I know I'm doing the right thing. Luther has a lot of guards...poorly trained, but a lot of them. Perhaps we can take him on indirectly. "Mhm, so...what else did you find? Do we have any dirt?" I smirk up at the camera. "Of course we have dirt."

"Oh, Boss, I have access to so much dirt on this guy, I am surprised he hasn't got a team following him around with shovels. With the stuff on his computer network, he should have been more on our radar. There's a girl at the apartment building they took you from. In their communication, they call her *the rebel leader*." Ava snorts. "The girl is twenty. Bunch of idiot vampires calling her a rebel leader. I think releasing the information I have to the vampire council will help her, act as a distraction, and keep the vampires away from you. It should keep this Luther guy busy for years. I can make his entire House a priority for the guilds. He is going to be a pariah in vampire circles. It's a win-win on all fronts."

I tilt my head in thought. I'd prefer to see the information with my own eyes and plan things properly. But...we've done this so many times and I trust Ava's judgement. This situation calls for something different. Plus, he made it personal by sending his henchman to my safe house to kidnap me. And he slapped me.

Not that it wasn't already personal: the guy sold me to a demon. I nod while I rub my sore face. "Perfect, do that."

"Okay, done. I've sent the information out to the vampire guild, the vampire council, and a few Houses. I'll do the necessary explaining to the girl and get her someplace safe."

"Do you need me for anything?"

"Nope, I just need to ring the *rebel leader*." Ava snorts again. "I've already sent all the information out to the relevant parties. Lord Gilbert, your pureblood kidnapper, is about to have a very bad day."

CHAPTER THIRTY-SEVEN

There is a bang and a crash outside my office. Raised, angry voices filter into the room. "You can't see her without an appointment—" Suddenly the door flies open, the door handle impacts the wall with a crunch, and a puff of white dust rends the air.

"I don't know how you did it," he says as he stomps into my office, panting. He pauses at the edge of my desk and points a trembling finger at me.

With calm nonchalance, I gather the documents that are spread across my desk and slide them safely into my top drawer. I wave away my hovering, worried staff, rest my palms on the desk, and plaster a pleasant smile on my face.

"You disappeared from a locked room. It was supposed to be impenetrable," he whines. "You had a void band on. How the fuck did you get past five of my best guards? I stationed them right outside." He runs his hand through his hair in frustration, and his floppy blond hair awkwardly sticks up. "I had a visit from the vampire council's enforcers. Some questionable evidence has come to light. Evidence that was held on my secure servers. The information could only have been obtained by someone hacking into my computer system. Which I've been assured isn't possible. It is the same computer system that handles my security cameras, the same cameras that had you lying facedown on the bed. Yet, the entire time, the room was empty—"

I interrupt his rant. "Hello, Luther, what a pleasant surprise, it's so nice of you to visit my place of business rather than simply kidnapping me." I follow my words up with a patronising smile.

The pureblood is wearing yesterday's clothes. His once-pristine suit is now wrinkled. Perhaps I should have bided my time in sending out the information and not made it so obvious, the link between my escape and the data leak. Luther isn't certain of my involvement and he is still seriously underestimating me.

Oh heck, I am surprised smoke isn't coming out of his ears. He slams his hands down on my desk. The heavy desk squeals in protest as it is shunted a few inches across the floor towards me. I rest my elbows on the desk and prop my chin on my hands. I flutter my eyelashes at him.

He leans over the desk until our noses almost touch. "You little bitch, I am going to kill you—"

"Oh, okay. That's nice...um hm...you might want to work on that temper, Luther...eww...no one likes a spitter." I scrunch my nose, sit back in my chair, and wipe my face. "Humans use a saying: 'Say it, don't spray it.'"

"—I'm going to bleed you dry." So vampy, I almost shiver. "I have your mother—"

I gasp and press one hand against my lips and the other on my chest. I open my eyes comically wide. "Oh no, not my mum, your partner for almost thirty-five-years...whatever shall I do?" I drop my hands and give him a toothy grin.

"—and your hellhound."

Everything stops.

My silly quips freeze in my throat, and I almost stop breathing. Fear floods me. When I look into his livid eyes, the hair on my arms rise.

He has my hellhound.

"I am listening." It's not my voice that comes out of my mouth. It's throaty, dark, not human. I can feel my eyes going black. Instead of being hazy, like it was in the early days, my eyesight becomes pinpoint-sharp, magnified.

"You fix what you did." Luther prods the top of my desk with his index finger, and his voice drops into a low growl. "You send a retraction, admit liability. You tell them you lied." I've seen the evidence, and there's no retracting that shit—Luther is delusional. "Then you make sure you have all your affairs in order." He digs into his trouser pocket and slaps a business card on top of my desk. "Come to this address."

"When," I growl.

"Ten this evening." My eyes flick to the clock: it's eleven a.m....I have eleven hours. I nod and he turns on his heel and stalks out of the room.

Rein in your temper, Emma. Wield it like a weapon.

My nostrils flare with my poorly reined-in anger and I close my eyes for a second. In a poor attempt to get a grip on my wildly beating heart, I take a deep, shuddering breath. I force my eyes back to normal. Freaking out will not help John.

God, I'm so angry. I have an urge to run after him and pull his head off—with the increase in my strength over the years, I'm pretty sure I could do it.

Instead, I call Ava. "Have you got a location on John? Drop everything for a moment. I need a location on him and everything you have on this address..." I rattle off the address from Luther's card.

"Boss? That you? You sound...urm...okay. One sec." I wait. My breath rasps through my tight throat and my heart continues to slam into my chest as I wait and Ava plucks stuff out of the internet ether. I strum my fingers on the desk and rub the side of my face when my eye twitches.

It's a long time since I've been this angry, this afraid.

For John.

Our relationship is the epitome of complicated. Over the years I've attempted to date, sort of. One guy was nice, but after a few weeks, he ghosted me. I later found out the guy had a visit from John. To be honest, it was a kind of relief. Dating is naff. I felt so guilty...like I was cheating on the hellhound. Which is ridiculous...you can't cheat on a man that you've never had a relationship with. Can you?

I guess when you have had your soul mate handed to you on a silver platter and then you tell fate to go shove that platter...I compare everyone against John and they don't stand a chance.

God, how I've missed him.

I huff. It's not like he's breaking down my door—not that he can, what with my living in a pocket dimension—and proclaiming his undying love. I glance down at my strumming fingers. In my secret, shameful moments, I daydream he'll do just that.

Whenever I need him, he's always there. Grumpy, angry

hellhound. Attempting to fix problems that sometimes don't need fixing.

"Oh, wow, oh no, John Hesketh isn't off-world. He came through a portal within an hour of your kidnapping."

Why the hell did he do that? I let out a pained moan. The bloody stubborn man came to rescue me...he knows I can take care of myself.

"Can you send me everything you have, please, Ava?" I manage to whisper. We end the call and I place the mobile carefully down on my desk.

I bow my head, and grip the edge of the table so hard that it hurts my fingers.

He has John.

CHAPTER THIRTY-EIGHT

I stand in front of my desk, hands gripping the back of my neck as I eye the complete rescue plan that's laid out in front of me. Ava has pulled up everything she can find about the building. The live camera feeds are unavailable as the vampires have destroyed the cameras, but I have older CCTV footage and detailed building plans of the inside. My office is overflowing with pertinent information, but frustratingly, it might not be enough.

When the pureblood left, all I wanted to do was immediately go and rescue John. Off the cuff, figuratively storm the castle and kick vampire ass. But I told myself I couldn't do that as I'm not Rambo. No, I needed a plan.

Now, an hour later, I have a plan that'll work, but I have no way of pulling it off.

We've tried to contact John's team of hellhounds, but frustratingly—because of the time constraints—we can't even get hold of them, as they are all still on mission and off-world. Eleanor's on a bodyguard assignment and unable to leave her client. Ava even attempted to find the honey-eyed angel—not that I'd know if he would help, I haven't seen him since he healed me—but to no avail. If Ava can't find someone, no one can.

God, I am such a bad person. I've never bothered to find out about his friends. If he has friends outside of work, that is...I guess that like me, John is very much alone. I drop my hands and lean against my desk. I know everything about his enemies. He has a tonne of those. Yeah, such helpful information for this situation.

I huff and rub my forehead. What is frustrating is that off the top of my head, I don't know anyone I can ask to help me. I care too much to ask anyone to risk themselves in going against an entire House of vampires, vampires that I've already backed into a corner—it's suicide. I could pay mercenaries, but with the short time frame and the risk of collateral damage...heck, it looks like it's back to me playing Rambo.

I glare at the mounds of information and the surrounding plans—what a waste of bloody time.

John is my go-to person. How's that for irony? If I ever needed muscle I'd ask him, or he'd turn up uninvited with his shiny knives.

I have a better chance of doing this on my own—well, I won't be on my own, because I will have John—perhaps all I need to do is get to John and heal him. I know the only way to keep a shifter down is silver. If I can get him away from whatever silver they are using, heal him enough so he can shift...

In my cupboard, I still have lots of fancy healing potions. All I'd need to do is hand him a bottle and he'd just have to tip it...he could then shift into hellhound form and chew everyone's faces off. The pair of us might be able to fight our way out.

Gah, unless he's got silver in his system, and then a healing potion isn't going to do shit. His body has to process the silver and that could take a while. The odds aren't good.

I could hand myself over at ten tonight and hope that Luther will let John go, but when does that ever happen? Bad guys don't let men like John go.

I look at the clock. Time is quickly ticking away...every second he spends in the vampire's clutches is a second too long. I wring my hands together and dig my nails into my palms. I fight against the almost-overwhelming panic that is gripping my throat and squeezing my chest.

The little voice in my head is screaming, *I did this*.

God, I feel so guilty—this is all my fault. If I hadn't allowed myself to be taken, he wouldn't have come back to rescue me. Time and time again he helps me, and I let him.

I just use him.

I rub the back of my neck as my heart continues to ache.

I point John at the bad guys, and I use him. Memories flicker across my mind like a film with the countless times John has saved my life. It more than makes up for our poor beginning. I was so hurt, so bloody angry for such a long time, it became a habit to grudgingly accept his help and then push him away. I didn't even realise how cruel I was.

Oh God, I didn't mean to, I never thought—I attempt to shelve the disturbing thought to deal with later, as now isn't the time, but it won't go away. I use him just as everyone else does. A tear runs down the side of my nose and I angrily swipe it away.

John Hesketh is renowned in creature circles...his reputation is practically legendary. We see him as the hellhound, as an extremely deadly weapon. I remember his words on the day I rejected him: *"War is in my blood and war has moulded me. Times change for some people, but not for me. I am a full-blooded warrior—I'm expendable."*

But he is also a man.

All he has known is war and violence.

And what did I do? I showed him he is also expendable as a mate.

I sink into my chair and I tuck my knees to my chest and hug them as if I can stop the pain from leaking out of my heart. I want nothing more than to slump to the floor and let my body shake from the anxiety and the heartache that I feel for John.

I have another epiphany. I realise something quite profound, and it rocks me to my core...I'm *not* afraid of him, and I've wrongly been clinging desperately to that excuse for *years*.

I know...I bloody know he will never again hurt me. He can't. Something inside me, deep down, knows John didn't hurt me on purpose and he has allowed me to slowly torture him through the years.

Bloody hell, Emma, he's been punished enough.

God, I have been so bloody selfish. I've spent this entire time rescuing strangers when the man who needed me the most—

I grit my teeth. I slam my eyes closed and rock on my chair, as my thoughts berate me. I tug at my hair in realisation. His power terrifies me, our past terrifies me, but it's a deep-seated, instinctual kind of fear that has no hold on me. Not anymore. No, I'm not afraid of John Hesketh.

There is lust, there is always lust...and yearning. But the fear that rattled me for so long is *gone*.

I've grown. The person who I am today is different from the frightened girl that I once was. I'm not who I was years ago, and that brings me a little peace.

No, I'm not that girl anymore. I'm better, stronger.

I'm strong enough.

I almost disbelieve my thoughts...I let go of my knees and flop back in my chair in shock. I'm strong enough. I've been strong enough for *years*. Now, if John hurt me, I'd hurt him back. Yeah, that's not healthy, but I'm not human.

I'm a demon and John is my mate.

My mate needs me to fight for him. I cover my mouth with my hand and rock in my chair.

Oh bloody hell.

I am going to rescue the shit out of him. I laugh lightly through my pain; I sit up and square my shoulders. Even if I have to take on every bloody vampire in this world. I am going to rescue the bloody hellhound, and I'm going to keep rescuing him until he is mine. *Mine*. Until he knows he's loved.

Love...wow, I do, I do love him, and I am strong enough to deal with his shit.

My eyes drop back to my plans. I just hope I'm not too late.

CHAPTER THIRTY-NINE

The vampire runs straight at me, and his meaty fists fly at my face. I block his right arm with my left forearm and jab the heel of my right hand into his nose. He staggers back. I sidekick him in the ribs and follow with a punch to his liver. He grunts in pain. Ow. My hand screams as a small bone snaps, then instantly repairs itself. My poor fist burns. I hit him in a supposedly squishy part of the body, but what the hell? His vampire muscles broke my hand. I shake my hand out and I whirl to the side with seconds to spare. I laugh at the near-miss to rile him. The vampire flashes his fangs at me and lunges. My temper flares when a punch gets through my guard and he hits me in the boob. Ow.

I grab hold of his shoulders for leverage and knee him in the side to hit his liver again. Once, twice—vampire bodies hate their organs being bashed about; it's particularly painful. The vampire clutches his side and falls to the floor. For good measure, I grab his hair and knee him in the face. His eyes roll back in his head as he goes unconscious. He won't be out for long, though.

I grab hold of his shirt and with a huff and a puff, I drag him across the hallway and prop him up against the wall. I don't want to trip over him when we leave.

It was all going so well. As soon as I arrived, I could feel John's power, the energy that is all him emanating halfway down the road. It only grew, the closer I got to him. I shifted into a mouse and squeezed into the building undetected. The problem arose when I became a little cocky and ran down the middle of a hallway without caution. I could feel John behind the door at the end of this hallway...my magic shivered in appreciation and I got excited.

A surprise attack of a stomping foot ruined my hallway dash. The boot missed me by a whisker. I had no alternative but to shift into my human form and kick his ass.

I groan as two more vampires run around the corner. The one ahead of the other comes at me with his fists swinging. I step into him rather than making space, and his eyes widen with surprise. I'm hoping the move will make it more difficult for vampire number two. Unless he wants to hit his colleague, he has to wait his turn. I grab his arm, block the blow, and land two quick jabs underneath his chin. I follow that with a kick to his side. He stumbles back but doesn't go down. I kick out again, my boot hits his chest, and the momentum shoves him down the corridor and past the other vampire.

The other vampire takes his place, barrelling into me with brute strength. For a vampire, this guy is huge. With a squeak, I try to jump aside, but his arm catches me in the throat and we both tumble to the floor. I land on my back and forget to lift my head as we crash down, and my poor head smashes into the unyielding concrete. I groan and my ears ring. The vampire is halfway on top of me...at least I manage to get my leg between us so he can't pin me. I use the strength in my thigh to shove him off me. I roll away from him and scramble to my feet. With a growl, I kick him in the face. I must have hit the sweet spot underneath his chin, as his eyes roll into the back of his head and he slumps unconscious.

I feel the movement in the air behind me. I duck and the remaining vampire's arm swings above my head. I grab his wrist with both hands, bend, pull, and twist my hip. I use my smaller frame combined with my strength to flip him over my head and onto his back with a *thud*. I boot him in the ribs twice and skip away when he tries to grab my leg. When he attempts to roll to his feet, I jump into the air and Superman-punch him with everything I have. The bones in my hand shatter as I hit his face.

Ow-ow-ow.

At least three bones in my hand rapidly repair themselves. The pain makes me feel dizzy; I clutch my hand against my chest as I glare down at the bleeding, unconscious vampire.

I huff and puff as I shake out my healed but bruised hand.

I hate fighting. It hurts.

Unfortunately, our fight wasn't quiet, and now I can hear more incoming vampires. The entire building has come alive, like a nest of angry wasps.

Oh, God. I bounce from foot to foot. What to do, what to do.

I can't do this all night.

Scare them. Go big or go home, Emma.

Well, it's more like "die" than "go home"...but perhaps I can shift into something scary. I allow myself a cheeky grin, and then without preamble, I shift into a seven-foot demon.

Inspired by the reflection of the red tiles, my demon comes to life with a little added theatre. Red skin, horns, the whole shebang. I wobble on my hooves and brace myself against the wall. My horns scrape the ceiling.

My real wings hurt, so I keep those bad boys tucked away and instead choose wings of fire. I make them the same size and shape as my natural wings, but without substance, so there is no risk of them getting hurt just in case this doesn't work. I am sick of hurting my hands punching vampires, so I also produce a ruddy great sword; it forms solidly in my right hand. I flex my impressive red bicep as I twirl the enormous sword to warm up my wrist and arm.

Okay, showtime.

A vampire guard in his red uniform dashes around the corner. When his eyes land on me he skids to a stop and his arms comically windmill. His eyes widen, and I see the fear ignite in their depths. He fumbles with something in his hand, and then with a war cry he throws a potion ball at me. It hits me on the chest and the glass breaks. I tilt my head down and we both watch as the noxious orange substance gets to work.

The vampire's mouth opens and closes. He makes a strange squawking noise in the back of his throat when the potion dissipates harmlessly into the air. I shoot him a toothy grin.

He promptly wets himself.

I frown. Oh no, that's not good. Having peed myself in fright, I can't help sympathising.

He spins, and in his haste to get away from me, he bounces off the wall. As he runs away down the corridor, droplets of wee follow in his wake.

Oh crap, I feel terrible. I cringe and tap my hoof as I wait for more guards to arrive. Heck, his reaction to me makes me feel like a big bully. I know he chucked what was probably a nasty potion at me. Nevertheless, I've never made anyone so frightened before that they wet themselves. I scratch the base of my right horn. Perhaps the seven-foot demon—eight and a bit with the horns—was a little too much?

The first guard—the mouse stomper—wakes up. He takes one look at me and with a gasp, he flips onto his hands and knees and motors off down the corridor.

Wow, look at him go.

There are crying, screaming, angry voices. Should I take a peek around the corner? I lower the sword and push the point into the floor. I cross one hoof casually over the other and lean against it as if it were a cane. I can't hear what they are saying, but I can imagine the potion guard pantomiming what happened to his colleagues.

The stomping footsteps quickly *retreat*. Huh? Urm...I think they are running away from me. I shrug and move back down the hallway.

I carefully step between the two unconscious guards. I *finally* get to the door and without even checking to see if it's unlocked, I lift my leg and kick out with my hoof—I am no longer messing around. The door shatters into satisfying pieces.

I clop through the doorway.

I rapidly take in the room, and I immediately find John. You would think a year of not seeing him would make a difference, and it does. It makes whatever wicked fate-magic that pulls me to him *worse*.

With widening eyes I take him in, and my heart pounds with my growing panic.

This is worse than I imagined.

CHAPTER FORTY

The difference between this situation and our previous fake kidnapping set up all those years ago is *huge*. They have chained John to the wall with silver. Attached to the short chains are silver manacles that have *spikes*. Like an inside out-dog collar's, the spikes dig into his skin. I did a lot of reading over the years and I now understand that silver only harms a shifter *if* it gets into the bloodstream.

He has thick collars around his neck, wrists, waist, and thighs. The nasty combination pins him literally to the wall. Everywhere the silver touches, he bleeds, and the skin around the wounds that I can see has a black tinge. To me, it looks as if his skin is dying. I swallow the bile that is attempting to claw its way up my throat and I bite my lip so I don't make a sound.

This archaic way of keeping him secured is not only stopping John from shifting to heal, it will painfully bleed the shifter magic right out of him.

He's shirtless, and his blood-crusted black pants are tucked into his black boots, which come halfway up his ankle. His hair isn't long enough to be tousled, but it looks unbrushed and messy, and dark stubble highlights his jaw. Chained to a wall, he's lost some of that killer efficiency that makes him so terrifying.

I hate this. How the hell am I going to get him out of those chains without hurting him further?

Women up, Emma.

I wave. "Hi, I am here to rescue you," I say, slurring around a mouthful of demon teeth.

John lifts his chin from his chest and raises an eyebrow as he slowly takes in my red demon form. His lips twitch and he huffs out a bitter laugh. "Why did you come?" Wow, that's it? No, *"Hi sweetheart, you're looking fetching this evening. Thanks for the rescue..."* I roll my eyes.

I clop closer and between one step and the next, I allow myself to shift back. Everything dissipates, including the sword. My shift leaves me dressed in leggings, boots, and my favourite black T-shirt that has a bunch of flowers and a knuckle-duster on it and the words *fight like a girl.*

I am trying my best to remain blasé, but inside I'm freaking out. A younger, less powerful shifter would have already been dead.

The muscles in his shoulders and arms tense as he leans forward towards me, and the chains on the wall clank and groan as they hold him in place.

"Please..." I squeak out, "Please don't move, you will hurt yourself." I swallow. Oh, this is bad, this is so, so bad. My bottom lip wobbles but I force myself to speak. "So you have a vampire problem? You seem to be in a bit of a pickle, John. Urm...how do we do this without hurting you further?" My voice cracks, revealing the panic I'm trying my damndest to hide.

My hands flutter. I don't know where to start. Blood is running in rivulets down his arms and neck; it trickles down his chest. This shitty situation is going to give me nightmares for a very long time. I tremble as I inspect the horrific, archaic setup. I gnaw on my lip. Oh, God, he must be in so much pain.

John lets out a gruff laugh. "It's not me that has the vampire problem—I came to rescue *you*."

"Screw you, I rescued myself," I say back with a fake angry huff. "I'm not the one chained to the wall, Hellboy. So, the whole rescue attempt worked out well for you...I thought you were off-world. You shouldn't have come back to save me, John—I had everything in hand. What did you think you were doing?" I glance at his poor wrists. "Please tell me how to get you out of these chains." My voice breaks.

"I will always come for you," he mumbles, his eyes closed. "Get out of here, sweetheart. I am too weak. What were you thinking, coming here on your own? Go before they catch you. You need to get as far away from me as possible...I keep making mistakes. I've lost my edge and I've slowly been losing control for years. Look at me, I can't even do a basic rescue without fucking everything up...It's fucking shameful."

I ignore him as I intently study the manacles. There is so much blood on them, on the floor. John's blood. I need to get them off.

"Yeah, yeah, and you've lost man points 'cos you're being rescued by a girl...have you heard yourself? That's a little hypocritical, John. Where has my fighter gone?" I mumble.

My heart pounds in my ears. I flick my wrist and a long, thin pick appears between my fingers. I think it's better to start at his feet. I don't want to practise on his neck or wrists. As I drop to my knees, I decide I'll use the pick and my smoky magic on the spiky cuffs on his legs. It's a shame I can't imagine a key that would fit...yeah, that would be way too easy.

"Didn't you see my badass demon form? I'll get you out of here before the vampires get brave enough to intervene. I'm pre-warning you...if I have to shift and throw you over my shoulder, I will. Isn't that the way it goes when you rescue someone? The damsel always gets carried by the hero." I grin up at him and wiggle my eyebrows. "You're the damsel."

I smirk. If that doesn't motivate him to move his bum when I free him, nothing will.

"Will you find my sister? Tell her...that I'm sorry."

I clamp down hard on a sob that wants to smash its way out of my lips. No, I've got no time for that. "Tell her yourself," I growl back.

"This world doesn't take any prisoners. If you're weak, Emma, you die. Tell her our pack wasn't weak. Our father was one of the first of his kind, a hellhound. In the beginning, they called him a fire wolf." John coughs and his strong voice becomes a rasp.

What on earth is he going on about? I spare a moment to peek up at him. His bright green eyes have gone dull, unfocused.

"He was an incredible warrior..."

Oh bloody hell, my hellhound is doing his death speech. He doesn't think he is going to make it. John grimaces and black blood seeps from between his lips. My heart thuds in panic and I force my attention back to my task and focus. I narrow my eyes and bite down on my tongue, which is sticking out the side of my mouth. With shaking hands, I dig my magic and the pick into the locking mechanism.

Bloody hell, what a time to learn how to pick a lock.

"The world of shifters you know today differs completely from the world that I was born into almost a thousand years ago...nine-hundred and twenty-two-years. There was equality between the sexes, with no difference between men and women. We had female warriors and male caregivers. In those days, shifters were all about pack. Wolf, bear, even the dragons—it didn't matter. We coexisted peacefully."

"Perhaps you should save your strength—"

"My father said the beginning of the end started with a group of rogue fae. They decided the shifters were getting too strong. I was young when they started killing our females. It took us a while to notice the pattern. That shifter women were not dying in normal circumstances...no, they were being targeted. At first, it was one or two, and then dozens as more races joined in on the cull.

"In horror, we attempted to keep our remaining females safe. We adapted, and we changed for the worse. The carefree shifters became dangerous and in many ways incredibly selfish. We lost our dignity, and with that, our strength. Our women suffered the most, losing not only their friends, their mothers, and their sisters...but also their freedom. Many fought the changes and were beaten down and forced. Others embraced it, as everyone was frightened. I never experienced again the joy, the comfort of being a shifter. All I saw was pain, war, fighting, and oppression.

"Before my eyes, as a race we changed...I changed. My pack, my sisters Nessa, Clare, Gwen, and my mother became targets. Hunted not by the other races but by other shifters, because as our women became rarer—a commodity—shifters became more aggressive in their pursuit for mates. My father worked tirelessly over the years to keep them safe. Until one day on leave from battle, I came home too late, and I watched helplessly as they ripped apart my pack. I destroyed the perpetrators. But I couldn't save them. My smart, funny, incredibly talented sisters were gone. My father, who was a better man than I'll ever be, was killed. Not by an outside enemy, but by friends. Jealousy, panic, and fear rot. Only my mother survived.

"In the aftermath, she discovered that she was pregnant...with another female shifter. Another fucking problem." John lets out a sad-sounding laugh. I lift my eyes from my task as he drops his head and his eyes plead with me to understand. The spines of the collar dig further into him and I watch helplessly as more blood trickles down his neck. His sorrow is palpable and my heart aches.

"They denied me leave, so I had no time to grieve. I compartmentalised the best I could, did what I could to keep my mother safe, but I distanced myself from her and my new replacement sister. When you've seen everything that you love ripped away...I guess it's natural to avoid having to deal with that shit all over again. My mother ended up meeting another man, having *another* girl." John's fists tighten as he laughs bitterly. "I was livid. You have to understand, our remaining females couldn't produce girls. The birth of a female was rare. No amount of scientific or magical intervention worked, nothing. We were cursed—it seemed as if even Mother Nature herself wanted us to go extinct." John coughs again and his entire body shudders. I keep my eyes on my task.

"Yet there was my mother, popping out girls for fun, for all to see. Couldn't she see the world as I did? Understand the dangers? Fuck, it's not like any of the other girls lived. It's not like she enhanced or saved a dying race. I knew...I fucking knew they'd die anyway, Emma. Born to die. It was senseless. Selfishly, I couldn't take it. I avoided the problem...to my shame. If I didn't care about the two girls, it wouldn't matter when they died in the end.

"With my mother having a new pack, a new mate, I was relieved to finally be able to wash my hands completely of them. My mother's *new* pack could deal with the problem. I was done. Then as you know, it all went to shit. When they were taken, it hit me, how much I had failed them. To find them was an impossible task, the proverbial needle in the haystack. The possibilities of who could have taken them were endless. Because of our status as protectors, my team and I were assigned to the task. We chased our own tails until a call came in, a shifter claiming that he had eyes on a young female." John sags further into the chains and bitterness flashes across his face.

"Seeing her wolf form in your arms, I lost what little control I had. I could tell that you were a demon and I convinced myself it was all a trick. There is no excuse for what I did to you, and I will be sorry for the rest of my life." That might not be very long if I don't hurry. "No wonder you rejected me." John lets out a bitter laugh. "I can't keep the women in my life safe. That's why I let you go...I am a selfish bastard and I still couldn't leave completely. Seeing you safe and helping you...I told myself it was enough. It was what I deserved. All the strength that I possess, the shifter magic, the fire magic, being a trained combatant...it doesn't do shit."

With his words, I'm done for...I silently cry. I tuck my head down and hide my face so he can't see me.

"I'm an evil man. Even after you rescued her, my little sister...I...I let her go. I couldn't bear to even look at her. She survived, and I hated her. I hated her for it. I still wanted Nessa, Clare, and Gwen, not her. I wanted my mother, not the useless, weak shadow of a wolf. My fear and hate blinded me...yes, fear and panic rot. I am the most rotten of us all."

My tears drop onto my hands. I can't stop them from falling, and every tear is for John.

"Please, Emma, tell my sister I was wrong. Tell her I love her and that I am proud of her. I've tried, but...her mate said he'd rip my head off if I attempted to talk to her before she was ready. Now it's too late, but she might listen to you."

If I could swap places with him, I'd do it in a heartbeat. This is horrible. I hate how useless I feel. On the day I admit my love for him I have to see him like this, hear his confession. I can feel his energy slowly ebbing away, a wisp of pattering raindrops compared to its usual crashing wave. It's not bloody fair.

"You will tell her yourself. I promise I will speak to her, and we will have...urm...dinner."

My guilt thrums through me. *I did this...* I need to get him out of here and somewhere safe. My determination feeds energy into my magic, spurring it on, and the cuff clicks open and releases its grip on his legs. I sob in relief, then cringe as I gently peel the spikes away from his legs.

One down.

Now that I know what I'm doing, I send my magic to each lock simultaneously instead of slogging my way up his body. We haven't got long before the guards get brave enough and storm in here.

Finally, the locks on the evil silver cuffs pop open, and they tear away from his blackened skin with a squelch. At the sound, I cough and heave. Oh, God. My chest painfully tightens as

John's blood rains down on the floor around us, but he is stoic and doesn't make a sound. *Be just as brave, Emma.*

I kick the cuffs away from him. His entire body sags and his legs wobble underneath him as he struggles to stay upright. I use my body weight to hold him up against the wall so he doesn't fall. "Sit down on the floor and get your breath back." He nods and I help guide his huge, muscly frame down onto the concrete floor.

John flops back against the wall. I cup the back of his head to make sure he doesn't bang it. His breathing is shallow, and where John's skin is not black, it's overly pale. He is still bleeding. "I got you," I whisper. "Remember our conversation in the rain? When the fae assassins almost killed me." John nods. I wipe the black blood from his lips with a trembling hand. "At the time, you told me I had to fight; I had to promise that I would never give up. Don't make a hypocrite out of yourself, John Hesketh," I say with a growl. "You are not dying today, I will not let you."

"You can't fucking forgive me for what I did."

"Too late. I already have."

It's then that I hear the footsteps.

The vampires are coming.

I step in front of John, blocking the door from him. If the vampires want to throw potions at my hellhound, they will have to get through me first.

CHAPTER FORTY-ONE

To say I'm surprised when Luther and my mum appear would be an understatement. Shock radiates through me as they stand in the doorway, surveying us and the remains of the door.

"What is going on here? I thought we agreed for you to come at ten o'clock," my mum says as she toes the wooden splinters of the door with her blue heel. What? My mouth pops open as I stare at her incredulously. Oh, my bad. Sorry, Mother, how rude of me—I didn't come at the appointed time.

"Oh, I thought I'd arrive early as I was so excited to see you, Mum. Good evening, *Luther*. I don't suppose you have anything for silver poisoning, do you? It seems you are trying to kill your hellhound guest." I grit my teeth and grin maniacally.

"No, we have nothing like that here," she replies as she carefully steps around the door and glides further into the room. Luther follows, content to let my mum speak. "There was a report of an enormous demon terrorising everyone. One of our guards who reported in said it was eating another guard's leg." She sniffs and looks again around the room. "An illusion, I am sure."

Eww. "I didn't eat anyone's leg," I mumble for John's benefit.

The pair of them are dressed so smartly, they both look ridiculous. Luther is back to looking like his usual put-together self in a sharp, crisp suit, and my mother is in a beautiful dark-blue dress.

"The pair of you look nice. I do have to say you're both a tad overdressed for our current location." I wrinkle my nose as I glance about the room and raise an enquiring eyebrow.

They should have condemned the entire building. The place is a hovel, although the poor state of the building didn't stop the vampires from having a state-of-the-art security system, so perhaps they wanted it to look like this— a shithole. Not the ideal place to dress in fancy evening wear, that's for sure. The amount of vermin poop I had to negotiate while I was a mouse was so gross. Luckily, most animals are sensitive to magic and run away as soon as I'm scented, so I am glad I didn't get to meet the locals. I sure didn't want a new rodent boyfriend.

They both ignore my remarks. So for the sheer hell of it I try again. "Going somewhere nice?"

My mum gives me a withering look. Her upper lip curls back with a sneer, showing her pointy fangs. I take a jerky step backwards. Oh, wow, that's a bit different from the trembling and crying that I am used to.

"You were always such a horrid child..."

Oh, here we go. I puff my cheeks out with frustration. Okay, mum, hurry up and get the villain speech out of the way. I have a damsel to save.

Now John is free from those archaic manacles, he needs a moment to rest. Given enough time, his body should be able to dispel the silver that's floating around in his bloodstream. We aren't *yet* overrun by vampires, so I will listen to her speech...oh bloody hell, that wasn't me trying to tempt fate. I groan. "...You never did anything that you were told to do. Throwing yourself on the floor, having a tantrum, saying you were hungry. You were always hungry. You were always hungry. Screaming and demanding. You were a horrible child and I see not much has changed."

I roll my eyes. "Yeah, as a baby I was an evil genius. You are right, I so did that on purpose." I tilt my lips up in a semblance of a smile. "Well, Mum, this has been a fun visit, but we need to go, and by *we,* I mean me and the hellhound." I nod toward John, in case they've forgotten about him.

"When Luther suggested sending you away, I knew it was the perfect solution. You'd done enough: ruined my body, ruined my life. There wasn't a day that went by that I didn't wish you didn't exist. I still wish I'd never had you," my mum continues. Her voice is utterly toneless.

I blink at her with slowly dawning comprehension. John was right in warning me about her. My mum has always been a little *off,* but she hid her hate for me well. I never wanted to believe my mum could be a bad person. For twenty-two-years I thought that she'd sold me to a demon to become a vampire, and for another eighteen years, she led me to believe it was Luther's fault. Wow. Tonight the mask has come off and she's baring her real face to me, fangs and all.

I understand that having a child doesn't automatically make that child lovable or endear that child to you. I also understand that having a kid is really hard work, that parents have the most important and hardest job in the world. I'm grateful I'm here, but I didn't ask to be born. I might have been a naughty child, according to my mum, but I hadn't done that on purpose. I was a baby.

I wait for the pain to hit me.

But there isn't even a twinge. I don't know if she is trying to upset me on purpose, to throw me off track and imbalance me, but it looks like that ship sailed long ago.

Huh. I forgave my mum a long time ago, even if she doesn't want, need, or deserve my forgiveness. I did it for me. Sometimes it's okay to let the dream of someone go, to see them as they really are and be okay with that. After all, she has to be the one to look at herself in the mirror.

I need to wrap this conversation up and get John the hell out of here.

My mum continues, "Yes, it was Luther's idea, but I made the arrangement for you to go to your father."

My mouth pops open and my thoughts grind to a halt with my shock.

What. The. Hell.

"My father?" I choke out.

"Yes, Arlo, your father. It was his fault I got knocked up. At least he could deal with the consequences. Not all women want to be mothers, Emma. What would I want with a hybrid child? I thought he was in love with me and that a child would bring us closer together. But he left, as most men do. Not every man can be as powerful and loyal as Luther." She smiles at him and then sneers back at me. "Arlo took you off my hands with my promise that I'd never contact you. If you made the move to contact me...well, I promised to spare your feelings—" She keeps talking, but my head is spinning. My legs feel oddly weak. I keep on repeating her words back to myself.

Arlo was my father.

My dad.

I wasn't his human *pet*, I was his bloody daughter.

Wow. The entire time that I lived with him now makes some weird sense. Why he called me his favourite but didn't touch me...he made everyone believe he did. It was something I never disputed as he was my demon master, and I learned to be grateful. I was safe and had so many nice things. He had many, many lovers...I was relieved that he never picked me.

What was all that about, then...Arlo asking me to strip in front of his friends? In the end did he know the hellhounds were coming for him?

By human standards, what he said and what he did was seriously messed up. I mentally shrug. Even after all of my reading, I still don't understand demons as a race, not really. If I think about everything too closely, I will freak out. I rub my temple. Perhaps he said stuff to punish me? Protect me? I guess that being his pet, I was invisible; being his daughter, I would have been a target.

Bloody hell. That's why he left me so much money, why he gave me the pocket dimension. I guess in his own way he was trying to protect me.

I thought there was nothing left to shock me. I never really thought about who my father could be as I was so focused on my mother selling me. Apart from the total mystery of what type of creature he was, I classified him as a sperm donor and didn't think any more about it.

You're wasting time. I need to get John out of here.

Another thought rattles to the front of my head. John killed my father, who killed his mum.

Wow, that's messed up. Later we will have a lot to talk about.

I compartmentalise my feelings as it doesn't matter...only John matters, and I need to get him out of here.

I turn my head and my eyes fly to him. He's still on the floor. Oh, God, he looks worse. How can he look worse? I swallow. My eyes swing back to my mum. She's still talking... "Let the hellhound die. You are coming with us." Why mum? So you can use me? I believe you've made it quite clear that you don't like me. "Everyone knows he's a loose cannon—he won't be missed."

"He killed fifteen of my vampires, fifteen. He is an animal," Luther says when my mum finally stops to take a breath. "The hellhounds are irrelevant in today's world. Redundant. No one needs them anymore—that's the reason they sent them off-world. No one will miss him. We are doing the shifters a favour, getting rid of a problem." I growl at his words.

Without my thinking about them, my protective instincts kick in. I allow my eyes to bleed black and my shoulder blades tingle as my top magically parts to allow my demon wings to spread. The purple-and-black wings hang heavy at my back. I growl again, which highlights my black lips, and my smoky black magic pours from my hands. My magic snaps out towards Luther and a smoky tendril wraps itself tightly around his neck. His eyes widen and his hands scramble to pull my magic away from his throat, but he ends up scratching his neck as the smoke holds tight yet shifts away from his grabby fingers.

"Look, Luther, I don't want your hellhound-hating hard-on poking at me. This hellhound is not your concern. John has nothing to do with what is between us. You even look at him wrongly and I will rip your pureblood face off. Do purebloods need to breathe?" I snarl as my magic tightens and his face purples. Huh, I guess so. "The problems you currently have are to do with me. Instead of wanting me to join 'the fold,' perhaps you should look around you." I curl my lip with disgust. "Your House is crumbling around your ears. You're a disgrace to the purebloods."

With my mum revealing her true colours, certain things about the pureblood and his House makes sense—for an example off the top of my head, the dirt that I have on him didn't start accumulating until a few years after they'd met. I flick my eyes at my mother's snarling face and shake my head. "My mother whispering poison in your ear has made you weak."

"Emma, let him go," John says gruffly behind me. There is a sound of scuffing and a scrape of his boots on the floor as he attempts and fails to get to his feet.

What John is avoiding saying is, I can't kill Luther—if I did so, I would be dead in a week. The vampires would come after me, and I can't fight all the vampires.

I flick my wrist and throw Luther across the room. He hits the wall with a crunch. "Come near John again and I'll kill your whole House. Oh, and you're wrong: hellhounds are the pride of the shifters, and the guilds won't take kindly to you holding one of their elite prisoner."

I growl. "You." I glare at my mother. "The vampire council's enforcers are coming. I wouldn't stick around if I was you." She rushes to Luther's side and helps him to his feet. I shake my head again with revulsion. "We are leaving. Believe it or not, I haven't had to kill anyone yet—please don't make me." I turn my back and dismiss them.

My full attention is on John. My magic grows heavier behind me, screening us from the two vampires. I drop to my knees and slap my wings on either side of John, hardly feeling the sting. The light changes to purple as my wings cocoon us. I drop my forehead to his and my thumb rasps across his stubbled cheek. "Shift," I tell him. He needs to heal.

"I can't. Too much silver in my system."

Like a naughty puppy pulling on a leash, my magic pulls towards him. I allow more of it out and it eagerly rushes to John; it dances across his skin and then sinks into his chest.

Oh, that's a bit freaky...I've never seen it do that before.

Within moments the wounds on his neck, wrists, and thighs weep tiny droplets of silver. As soon as the silver leaves his body, my magic attacks it, turning it from a liquid into a cloud of dust—that floats harmlessly to the floor. Wow.

My wings dissipate.

John lifts his chin and takes a deep breath in as his whole body straightens. Using the wall to help, he rises.

In my peripheral vision, I see the horrific, torturous manacles and chains that nonchalantly rest on the floor where I kicked them. I narrow my eyes at them. The nasty spikes still drip with John's blood and skin. I wonder if I can also deal with that...my magic eagerly accepts the challenge, and it creeps across the floor, surrounding the silver restraints until they too disappear in a puff of dust.

"You're full of surprises today, pretty girl." I shrug and help him undo the laces of his boots. I know I don't need to help him undress, what with the whole dissipating shifter magic, but I want to. He needs to shift. My magic got rid of the silver but John still needs to heal. He shucks off his trousers, and suddenly I am intimately close to a naked John.

I look because why the hell not. He is mine.

Wow...urm, yeah...the man is perfectly proportioned. I cough. "Shift," I whimper. John takes me in, on my knees, and his once-tired and pain-filled eyes shine with poorly veiled interest. With a sexy grin and a nod of his head, he shifts.

His massive, bleeding form is replaced by my hellhound. My heart squeezes as my hand reaches out and soft red fur threads through my fingers.

CHAPTER FORTY-TWO

I sit in a comfortable chair positioned so my back is against the wall. The café is unusual and one of my favourite places to visit. They sell the most amazing selection of cakes. I tilt my head to study the ceiling, where a pink-blossomed tree branch spans the space with dangling fairy lights. The clatter of dishes and clink of spoons is a gentle background hum.

I've shifted into Christine, a human with some fae DNA. Christine is in her early sixties. With a blonde bob, bright-blue eyes, and curvy, she is the quintessential elegant English lady. Pretty, but forgettable. Safe.

I pour more tea into my cup and take a sip. When I set my cup back down with a *clink* on the matching saucer, my hand drifts across the table to trace the upside-down indentation of a name...*Liz* has been gouged into the table. I shake my head at the vandalism. I curl my hands back around my cup, enjoying the warmth of the porcelain, and I lean forward so the steam that rises from my tea warms my face.

At first I feel him. His energy drifts into my consciousness and tickles against my senses. Instantly it warms me and makes me feel safe.

I lift my head and watch out the window as he approaches. He steps lightly, his strides sure and unhurried, an apex predator on the prowl. Predatory yet irresistible.

He is hunting me.

People on the street shy away from him. Wow, he'd be great at a concert or out shopping. He parts the hordes of people faster than...well, people can't get away from him fast enough. He screams *danger.*

His dark suit fits him like a glove, from broad shoulders and powerful chest to flat stomach and long legs.

Breathtaking. I have to force myself to breathe.

Huh, a visit from the hellhound—a suited and booted hellhound, no less. I sit up as I watch him, happy and kind of smug with the knowledge that, like everyone else, he won't recognise me. He opens the door to the café and the bell above it jingles.

I blink when his green gaze immediately locks onto me.

Me. Elegant, Christine-lady me.

John's gaze flicks up to my eyes, down again, then back up. Not good. He grins, and my heart stops for a beat.

He is almost embarrassingly handsome. Beautiful. I greet him with a low groan when he prowls to my table. "No matter what face you wear, I will always know it's you," he says. My heart misses another beat. "You can change everything about yourself but you can't change your soul, and mine will always recognise yours in an instant." There is a hint of sweetness in his eyes.

Wow. I wiggle in my chair.

"May I sit?" I nod and he pulls out the chair opposite me and folds his bulk into it, dwarfing the table.

The people around us have gone quiet—they know that there is a predator in the room. I flick my eyes to the closest table, and a red-haired witch has a cup halfway to her mouth. Her cheeks go pink and she looks away when she realises I've noticed her watching. I can't help but grin as she fans her face.

I look back at John. "How are you feeling? Back to normal, I hope?" I rescued him, healed him, made sure he was safe, and then I ran.

I mean, bloody hell; they had pinned the guy to a wall with silver. I figured he needed to get his head around his near-death experience, and he didn't need me throwing myself at him and declaring my undying love. I have to be honest with myself: I've not been the easiest woman to deal with.

My eyes take in every inch of skin that I can see. Shifters' wounds made from silver never fully heal, even after they shift. Silver scars shifters...it scars them horribly. But I'm happy to see there are no visible marks on John's skin. My magic must have destroyed the silver down to its very molecules. I can't help my smug grin, and I give my magic a mental pat on the head.

"I am fine, thanks to you. That was my first experience of being rescued." John runs his hand through his short hair and gives me a rueful grin.

I can't help but grin back at him. I lean across the table and pat his big hand. "You did so good, you didn't cry once. You were very brave." I nod my head condescendingly.

I feel safe in John's company, and silly keeping my Christine persona, so I shift back into myself with a bright smile.

John's rueful grin fades as he fixates on my mouth and eyes. I guess I don't smile at him often. In fact, I'm not sure I've smiled at the hellhound very much at all.

He looks shell-shocked.

I duck my head and look at my hand, which is still resting on top of his.

"I had you in my arms and I lost you. I was so angry, for years. I've blamed myself, blamed you. I never took the time to go deeper," he says. I lift my head and he shrugs his massive shoulders and regards me with solemn green eyes.

"I'm just a man...I know war. Every day is a battle, and any softness I possessed was beaten out of me a long time ago. I came from a time when men didn't show their feelings, and that's something that I've never attempted to change, until now. The mistakes I've made...I can't change them. Shit, how I want to go back and change them.

"From the moment we first met, I should have taken you and my sister and run. I should have done my job as a brother...and as a mate." He swallows and his beautiful eyes shine with pain. "I can't take back those moments, and the decisions I made haunt me. But I can try my best to never let you down, to never frighten you. I can do better. I know what you've been doing: helping others, saving people from evil bastards like me. I don't want to be the monster under your bed, Emma. My soul is lost without you. You are everything good and right and beautiful in my world. I don't exist without you. I'm half a man without you. Emma, give me a chance— one chance is all I'm asking. You help others; save me...save me from myself, I'm begging you. Bring the softness back into my life. I'm asking for *one* chance to let me prove myself to you. I love you."

Fire flares in his eyes and they burn, lighting up our corner of the room. Chairs scrape on the floor and utensils and cups clatter around us as the surrounding tables' occupants suddenly find that they have somewhere else to be.

I barely notice—I'm sure I will be mortified later. But at the moment, I can't take my eyes away from his. The fire in his eyes, it isn't rage or lust. It is more than lust, more than need. Nobody has ever looked at me like that.

Love.

He loves me.

I rise from my chair, step around the table, and reach over. My hand hits his chest. His skin underneath his suit is burning hot; his muscles tense underneath my fingertips. I grab his tie and pull him towards me.

I slam *my* lips against his.

I gasp as his mouth seals mine, stealing my breath. John stands and pulls me towards him, my breasts mashing against his sculptured chest. The heat of his powerful body burns me. He moves both of my hands into one of his and wraps my hair around his fist and claims my mouth. The taste of him floods me and my senses go haywire—it's almost overwhelming. I want to run my hands across his skin, but he holds them tight, trapped behind my back.

When some brave soul whistles, we slowly pull apart.

I lick my swollen lips and drown in his now-beautiful green eyes.

"I love you too," I tell him.

Gosh, I have so much to tell him. We have so much to sort out, so much to make up for. But I know, I know deep inside, soul-deep, that we are going to be okay. Together.

I grab hold of John's hand and lead him towards the nearest doorway. I'm taking my hellhound home.

DINNER

I twist my hands and John's big, warm hand engulfs both of mine to stop me from fiddling. He gives me a reassuring squeeze as we wait for the door to open. I'm the one that should be holding his hand, supporting him...but God, I'm so bloody nervous.

I haven't seen John's sister for a while—not as myself anyway and meeting his pack, his only pack, as his *mate* is scary. She's been avoiding John like the plague, but after asking Ava to make a few telephone calls, I scored the dinner that I promised him.

Inside the house there is a shout: *"I'll get it."* My lips twitch at the sound of running feet, socked feet scampering across what I presume is a wooden floor. There's a small squeak, a thump, and the door in front of us shudders. A muffled, *"Shit."*

I glance at John, and he shakes his head and smirks. I snigger. Whoever is hurrying to answer must have skidded into the door.

With a click, the door is flung open and my heart jumps. It misses a beat and I swallow and squeeze John's hand for reassurance as her energy batters against me. I lock my knees to stop myself from almost taking a step back as her shifter energy crashes aggressively against my senses. It has an innocent, playful quality, but beyond that innocence is sheer *power.* Her energy is violent, twisted.

Forrest.

A tiny woman peeks up at us through a curtain of pale-pink hair that is covering almost her entire face. She puffs and blows rapidly to get the thick, long strands out of her eyes. When that doesn't work, she bats the hair away into some semblance of order with delicate hands. I toothily grin as I take in her now-uncovered, pretty face.

Beautiful but strangely coloured eyes regard us. Her eyes are disconcerting, mismatched—they are not quite gold, and the right eye has a touch of green that the other doesn't. It's a small sliver of green at the bottom of her iris. The impact of her eyes makes it difficult to look at her directly.

But I force myself to.

Even with her mountain of pale-pink hair, the cute unicorn jumper, leggings, fluffy wolf socks, and a growing sweet smile, my demon senses tingle and my instincts scream at me to run back to the portal and go home. She's not what she seems...she is *dangerous*. The pretty facade of the cutesy pink-haired shifter is a ruse to trick the unwary.

Oh, and she is way more powerful than John.

With twinkling eyes she smiles brightly. She tilts her head to the side and looks me up and down, her complete attention laser-focused on me. On purpose, she deliberately ignores her brother.

"I remember you...you're the angel that saved me." Her voice is a shock, so rough and guttural for such a small woman. You would think it would match the pink hair, soft, girly. But instead, it matches her energy and the flashes of hardness that I catch every so often in her eyes. "I remember being frightened, broken. I was so lost in my head, in my pain, and then you appeared, with that beautiful blonde hair." Forrest blinks her big gold eyes and points at my hair. "The light from the corridor behind you made it look like you had a halo...you smelled of horses. You brought me back into the world. Pulled me out of that prison and out of my head. For years I used to dream about you. I thought I'd made you up." She says all this with a nod of her head. Tears fill her eyes and I blink my own away. "I'm sorry…I'm sorry I forgot about you," she whispers.

Like all those years ago, my heart drops and my stomach clenches and before I've realised that I've moved…I rush forward, open my arms, and wrap them around her. Forrest throws her arms around my waist and hugs me back with a strength that takes my breath away.

"It's okay, pup." The words from long ago stick in my tight throat and my voice cracks with emotion. I stroke back the mass of pink hair and gently kiss the top of her head.

Moments pass in comfortable silence. Forrest then stands on her toes and moves my hair away from my ear, and she whispers, "Ava told me it was you…Mr Brown? Thank you, Emma."

"You're welcome. I'm sorry I didn't do more," I say with another hug and a sniffle.

Forrest steps away, and more loudly she says, "You're so badass, you need a theme tune." She nods her head as if her comment is completely understandable. I frown down at her, wipe away my tears, and scratch the back of my head. My lips tug themselves into a small, confused smile. *I need a theme tune?* Uh-huh. I look at John for clarification; he shrugs and gives me a small smile. He is equally confused.

Finally, Forrest follows my gaze, and she takes in her brother, who is waiting patiently at my side.

With a curl of her lip, she growls out, "Arsehole."

It's then that a man calls from deeper inside the house, "Forrest, let our guests inside, you're being rude." His voice rumbles and the hairs on the back of my neck rise.

Oh bloody hell, this will not be a normal dinner.

Forrest's mouth forms a perfect O and with a roll of her eyes, she grabs John's and my hands and pulls us inside.

THE END

Dear Reader,

First of all, I'd like to *thank you* for taking a chance on my book. Wow, I did it again! This is my second-ever book. Gosh, I'm an author—it's nuts. When I first wrote *Cursed Wolf*—Forrest's story—I thought no one would read it. I hoped, but there was no guarantee.

But you guys, wow, you guys read, and more importantly, enjoyed my book. More than that, you *reviewed* my book. I wanted to tell you *every* review is special, and every time I read one it makes my heart sing, it makes me want to try harder, to write better, for you.

Your reviews inspire, help, and humble me, so if I could ask again...if you enjoyed Cursed Demon, and if you have time, please would you consider writing a review so other readers can find my book? Every review makes a huge difference to an author—especially me as a brand-new shiny one—and your review might help other readers discover my book. I would appreciate it so much, and it might help me keep writing.

Thanks a million!

Oh, and there is a chance that I might even choose your review to feature in my marketing campaign. Could you imagine? So exciting!

I dedicated this book to my husband, as that's what you do for the man you love, who brings you endless cups of tea and snacks. But I wrote this book for you.

Love,
Brogan x

P.S. DON'T FORGET! Sign up on my VIP email list! You will get early access to all sorts of goodies, including signed copies, private giveaways, and advance notice of future projects and free stuff at: w w w . b r o g a n t h o m a s . c o m
Your email will be kept 100% private, and you can unsubscribe at any time, zero spam.

P.P.S. I would love to hear from you, I try to respond to all messages, so don't hesitate to drop me a line at: brogan@ broganthomas.com.

ABOUT THE AUTHOR

Brogan lives in Ireland with her husband and their eleven furry children: five furry minions of darkness (aka the cats), four hellhounds (the dogs), and two traditional unicorns (fat, hairy Irish cobs).

In 2019 she decided to embrace her craziness by writing about the imaginary people that live in her head. Her first love is her ~~husband~~ number-one favourite furry child Bob the cob, then reading. When not reading or writing, she can be found knee-deep in horse poo and fur while blissfully ignoring all adult responsibilities.

Brogan Thomas
BOOKS

Printed in Great Britain
by Amazon

59060713R00244